HEATHER PARRY was born in Rotherham and lives in Glasgow. She has won the Bridge Award for an Emerging Writer, Cove Park's Emerging Writer Residency and the Laxfield Literary Launch Prize. In 2021 she was a Hawthornden Fellow. This is her first novel.

Praise for *Orpheus Builds A Girl*

'A compelling, creepy tale – and one that raises relevant questions about who "owns" a woman's body' **The Independent**

'A chilling exploration of power, love and grief, written with incredible precision and an almost uncanny ear for voice. Heather Parry is a major talent' **Julia Armfield, author of *Our Wives Under the Sea***

'Heather Parry is a literary star of the future. I've been a fan of her writing for years, and this novel is all I hoped for and more. Bold, sinister and debate-provoking' **Kirsty Logan, author of *Now She Is Witch***

'Heather Parry is terrifyingly brilliant, one of the most interesting and talented British writers to emerge in recent memory. Orpheus Builds a Girl is a sinister dark flower of a book, both intoxicating and beautiful' **Camilla Grudova, author of *Children of Paradise***

'I am in awe of this wonderful book. Truly, gorgeous, generous and tender and brutal' **Edward Carey, author of *Little***

'A wild, creepy, compelling read' **Jan Carson, author of *The Raptures***

'A deliciously macabre voyage through one man's grotesque

lunacy and the destruction he leaves in his wake. Parry skilfully evokes the horror at the heart of the tale, painting a series of hallucinatory images as the narrative reaches an extraordinary finale, where the organic is pushed into monstrous proportions' **Martin MacInnes, author of *In Ascension***

'The most eerily fascinating Gothic novel I've read in ages, filled with gorgeous, grotesque prose – as if Carlos Ruiz Zafon had written *Lolita*' **P. J. Ellis, author of *Love & Other Scams***

'Superbly creepy from the start… It's a modern take on classic Gothic fiction, and while it certainly owes a debt to the likes of Mary Shelley's Frankenstein, it breaks new ground of its own and will chill readers to the bone. Disturbing and compelling in equal measure' *Big Issue*

'A chilling story of deranged infatuation, medical abuse, coercion and power' *The Skinny*

'Heather Parry explores how even in death women can lose agency of their bodies to the absolute extreme. She's crafted a novel that is mesmerising, grotesque, sympathetic and gripping in equal measure' *Books From Scotland*

'Sinister, grotesque and strangely beautiful – this is an intensely gripping debut, the playground for vividly unforgettable characters and a twisting, seething story, all set on a background of mustily creeping dread. I loved every horrible moment' **Alice Ash, author of *Paradise Block***

ORPHEUS BUILDS A GIRL

Heather Parry

ORPHEUS BUILDS A GIRL

A GIRL

Heather Parry

Gallic Books
London

A Gallic Original

© Heather Parry 2022
Heather Parry has asserted her moral right to be identified
as the author of the work.

First published in Great Britain in 2023 by
Gallic Books, 12 Eccleston Street, London, SW1W 9LT

A CIP record for this book is available from the British Library

ISBN 978-1-913547-66-0

Typeset in Minion Pro by Gallic Books
Printed in the UK by CPI (CR0 4YY)

2 4 6 8 10 9 7 5 3 1

for Kay and Andrew

with apologies

'So do boys and men announce their intentions. They cover you like a sarcophagus lid. And call it love.'

— Jeffrey Eugenides, *Middlesex*

Foreword

I am here to tell you that devils exist. You'll have heard about them in church, about hellfire and horns and pigs' feet, but that is not how they are. They are not so uncommon. They look like us, but with white skin instead of red, and they have no need of shadows; we act as their protection. They control by words and actions, not black magic, and worst of all, they get away with it. Some of us are plagued by one devil for much of our lives. My sister was, and by loving her, I was plagued by him too.

You have likely heard my sister's story already. She has been everywhere these six months past, in the papers and in gossip, her life broken apart and put back together in a way that suits him best. She has been rebuilt, rebroken, mutilated all over again. It has been this way for decades now; it began when we were just young women, and now I am old. You have heard his version from a dozen mouths or more. It is my job to show you the truth as we lived it. The truth as it was.

What I present to you here is the tale he has told. It is unchanged, so you may see how such creatures exist in broad daylight, wrapping themselves in the language of science and love. Between his pages, I have added my voice, to show how things really were, but the rest—it is the story as he wrote it, as he left it for you to read. For he thought of you, dear stranger, before you even knew he existed. He thought of you, and the things you like to believe, and he tailored his story towards your tastes. You will see him, if you care to, sitting by candlelight, writing in his strained hand in the last weeks of his life, thinking of you and me, thinking of the things he had done, spinning his web all over the page. As you read this book, you will come to know him as I knew him, by his own words, his lies, his strange and awful fantasies. You will enter into a world he created. But now, my world is there too.

When you first see a devil, you turn your face away. It's too much, to see the darkness in this world, to see the way it reflects back at you. Some keep their faces turned for all their lives; some work hard to pretend they saw nothing at all. I present this story to ask you to finally look closely—not just at him, but also yourself. And, finally, at my sister.

I had hoped all of this was over in nineteen seventy-three, when we first lost Luciana. I had hoped it was over in nineteen eighty-two, when we realised she was not at rest. Now, I am in my sixties, becoming an old woman, and I am again here, trying to rescue my sister, the truth of my sister, one final time.

Gabriela Maria Herrera Madrigal de Giro
Key West
Florida

Life Beyond Death

The memoirs and findings of Dr Wilhelm von Tore

Preface

While this is primarily a medical text, intended to leave behind the findings I have made over almost eight decades of incessant experimentation and research, I find it necessary to include within it a certain amount of autobiographical information, namely that relating to my relationship with Luciana Madrigal and my introduction to the world of post-death medicine. I make no apologies for this. The reader will find that I have also written a small amount about my upbringing and experiences in Germany; this is included to facilitate comprehension of my greater goal and indeed my position on mortality. I ask the reader to trust that I am only setting forth information necessary to my final project; all other details have been discarded.

I understand that what I am writing here will be subject to the greatest speculation and criticism, and indeed many individuals, including those who call themselves scientists, will dismiss my claims out of hand. Perhaps had my life not transpired in this exact way, I would be amongst them; after all, the scientific method is one necessarily rooted in scepticism. However, I hope that by showing the reader how I came to embrace these admittedly unconventional ideas, despite years of medical training and experience which taught me such things were impossible, I will succeed in opening the reader's mind to the possibility, indeed the proven existence, of life after death.

In my early life as a medical practitioner, I was given almost limitless resources. Money, equipment, time, bodies; I had as much as I needed, and my research during this time was of a quality unmatched since. My necessary emigration brought with it a demotion in role and an enormous loss of resources, and this slowed down my ability to continue my work—as did several personal matters unrelated to this text. It was only my introduction to Luciana that spurred me to transcend the position I'd been given and indeed to surpass my previous experiments in intensity if not in scope. I was forced to build my own equipment, spend my own money and devote almost all of my waking life to my goal, as well as working full-time at the hospital to fund my ongoing research. An enforced hiatus of two years undoubtedly retarded the development of my treatments, and perhaps my project never recovered from this defeat. Regardless, I continued with my experiments, and the results—which, with all humility, may change the very nature of human existence—can be found within these pages.

Where my notes depart from normal medical or scientific method, consider that I was working with restricted means, in my own home, far from a laboratory or surgical theatre where I should have been allowed to work. Putting limits on medical research means that we as a species are held back from the potential of science. Human squeamishness condemns us to perish. Where I have quoted conversations directly, I trust that my reader will allow me some degree of artistic licence. Without recordings of these conversations, I can only quote from recollection, but have attempted to preserve the accuracy of sentiment according to the best of my memory.

On a personal note, I would simply like to say that as I approach my final months and look back on the full century of my life, I cannot say that I would have done a single thing differently. Given the power to change the actions of those around me I would, of course, alter the timeline to mean that my Luciana would never have been taken from me, and would never have been committed to her second fate. However, with regard to my own actions, I rest easy; I could not have done a thing more for my beloved, nor could I have shown my love in any greater way. My conscience remains clear, and I can only hope that as I pass into the next realm to meet Luciana once again, the text I leave behind will save many in the future from losing their lovers.

Dr Wilhelm von Tore

1.

Wilhelm

I was born in Dresden in nineteen nineteen. The end of conflict is an aphrodisiac like no other, and to it I owe my existence. My father was twenty-four at the time of my birth, my mother eighteen. They were married quickly upon confirmation of my mother's condition, but their relationship lasted barely longer than my gestation. Finding the responsibility of a young family at odds with his natural virility and longing for experience, my father left my mother when I was only a few months old, and my mother returned to the familial home. Her own father had died in the war, but her mother, my grandmother, remained. It was in this house that I was raised.

As my mother was but a child herself, my grandmother took on the responsibility of raising the young boy in her home. The house in Striesen was of two floors, and my mother was generously given the bottom level, with a kitchen, bathroom and bedroom of her own. My grandmother and I resided on the top floor, where we had our own living quarters; everything that my mother had below, but with a study, a playroom and a balcony in addition. The washing facilities were on the ground floor, and, in exchange for our room and board in the home, my mother was given the task of taking on this part of the household upkeep.

Now, perhaps, is a good time to give an overview of my grandmother's character and personality. She was fifty-one when I was born; a practical woman, she had waited until her early thirties to marry, and she considered my mother a frivolous fool for bringing a son into the world when she had neither the means nor the maturity to raise him well. She felt it her duty to pour her energies into my development, to account for what she saw as my mother's maternal deficiencies. I can only say that I loved Oma completely and without restraint. I slept in a cot by her bed until I outgrew it, then I slept in her bed itself until I reached puberty. The playroom was, at that point, converted into a room of my own. Yet there were many nights on which I stole through to my grandmother's bed, once she had fallen asleep, and tucked myself into the covers alongside her, comforted by her light snoring and the smell of her hair wrap, which she rarely washed. There is an air about the elderly, a sensory fullness of the rooms in which they reside, and to a child this is an embrace. On restless nights I would watch her sleep, thinking of the years scored into her face, the experiences that she'd had; that I might have. In the mornings she would go through the charade of chastising me, but never without a smile; she slept more soundly with me at her side. Oma was a tiny individual, previously strong, then withering and thinning, very aware of the ways of the world and the darkness and light within it, but she was also a sickly woman, bedridden for much of my life and often confined to her own rooms with the stench of illness around her. When she reached her sixties, an unkind eye might have guessed that she was twenty years older. She was frail in body but in mind she was resolute; she was a learned woman and possessed a singular dedication to knowledge. Despite not being physically well travelled, she had a broad and all-encompassing interest in the beliefs of other cultures, and practised what I now recognise as a somewhat bastardised form of Zen Buddhism, where she engaged in focused breathing and hours-long meditation, lying perfectly still and ruminating on the things she felt and knew. I should make it clear here that she did not find the Asian cultures particularly insightful; she merely enjoyed the way the practice made her feel, and taught me the same, pressing her warm palm to my sternum and teaching me to control what entered my body. She did not believe in the frivolity of an excess of food, having lived through trauma and hardship and being cognisant of the needs of others, and in her later years she preferred to survive on nuts and berries, things that I could collect for her on my daily walks, or that could be bought cheaply, with no need for preparation. Oma always said she had better things to do than cook.

Through my childhood and into my teenage years, Oma read to me daily—European classics mixing with the medical textbooks that my grandfather, a physician himself, had left behind. In this way, I was predominantly home-schooled. I did not often mix with children my own age, apart from the rare occasion where my mother, home from long hours at her factory employment, could wrench me from my grandmother's grasp and put me out to play, or into a club, or at a meeting for young boys. I never took to sports, and my physical activity was focused on inspiring growth. It could be posited that my early exposure to my grandmother's infirmity served as a vaccination against sickness, as I rarely fell ill, and when I did so, recovered quickly. My mother claimed that this was due to my father's robust military constitution, but this is nothing more than supposition. My studies, conversely, consumed me. From a young age I was allowed to remain in the room when the doctor visited Oma (despite the doctor's initial reticence) and as I grew more dextrous and capable, I was taught how to administer her medications, how to move her body to avoid bedsores, how to examine her to check that her pulse was strong, her blood pressure manageable and her temperature consistent. My grandmother did not enjoy being hauled about by the doctor. Her thin frame was light enough for me to handle, and I was more careful with her, seeing her as more than a bag of bones. In my arms she was free from the shame of growing decrepit; she was teaching me, I would remind her, and I could have no better patient to learn on. In my free hours, I threw myself into the romantic and gothic classics. Goethe, Schiller, von Kleist, Novalis; from these I gained my understanding of matters of the heart as well as matters of the flesh, and as I grew older, I read these to my increasingly ailing Oma, watching her blossom once again in the realm of love.

It must have been a strange tableau: a young boy and his grandmother in the same bed, sharing joy in the dark romantic classics; and indeed we shared a deep and powerful relationship. Affection blinds one to the other's faults and to me, Oma was perfect—stoic, capable, wise. I had my father's looks (I deduced as much from a photograph found in my mother's purse) and my grandmother's muscular intelligence; with my mother, I had little that I could find in common.

Of course, part of this lack of connection was a combination of natural childhood rebelliousness and sheer immature egoism. My mother was a harried woman, unprepared for parenthood and forced to work long hours. Oma, on the other hand, had nothing but me to give her attentions to, and she taught me that the world was mine; that I was destined for eminence, that great things were owed to me. She instilled in me a pride in my mind and my heritage, cemented in me a love for the great European cities of old. Her love for Dresden was as infectious as any disease. As she grew unable to take me out to the city herself (which, she said, was a blessing, for she could not bear the presence of the Poles who had begun to plague the city on their way to seek work), I was sent away for afternoons to sketch the sites she used to love, coming back to report which type of people lingered around the Frauenkirche, which performers were coming to the Semperoper, whether foreigners gathered in numbers that should cause concern. I was never a natural artist but worked hard to develop some skill in still life drawing, and with pride I can say that this skill remains in some form to this day. Oma covered the walls of our room in my artworks and said that I was her eyes. I was her everything.

It was on one of my artistic excursions into the old city that an accident befell me. I was thirteen years of age and had spent the morning drawing scenes in my sketchbook, using charcoal to show shadow, pencil to show lines. I was building an entire skyline of the city and was making some progress when I grew hungry and headed for home. Strolling across the road with my papers under my arm and pencils in hand, I was hit by a wagon driven by a young woman. I was not a large boy, and the impact threw me across the street where my head hit the pavement, knocking me unconscious. I woke up five days later in hospital, with my mother at my bedside, playing the dutiful parent. My distress at not seeing Oma was great, but my doctors stated that only my mother should be allowed to visit me in my condition—and Oma, without assistance to leave the home, was effectively confined to her bed. As I awoke, the nurses and doctors came to my aid, and the doctors proceeded to tell me what had happened—and were stunned when I interrupted them in the middle of their explanation, able to tell them exactly when I had arrived at the hospital, how long I had been there, and who had visited me. Trapped in my brief coma, I had nonetheless been fully aware of the things around me; the movements of soft bodies around the room, the sharp introduction of medical equipment into my person. I recognised the doctor who had taken the most time with me and was able to say hello and express my gratitude while the colour rapidly drained from his face. Conversation then turned to my confusion, and all present agreed that I was playing some sort of trick on them, until I, in a proud voice, told the doctor that he had been humming Strauss's *Radetzky March* while he treated me—one of my grandmother's favourites, in fact.

The reaction to this information by the medical establishment sowed the first seeds of distrust in my mind. Here I was, a fit, intelligent young boy, reporting to the medical gatekeepers an accurate recollection of events that had occurred while I was in a supposedly non-conscious state. This should have excited at least a small curiosity in these men. Hearing facts that challenge our perception of the world is at the root of every great discovery, and here I was presenting doctors with proof that I had been fully cognisant for the duration of my apparent coma. Yet these individuals, after brief consideration, simply dismissed my claims. They mumbled words about the unlikeliness of such a scenario and said that I must have deduced the doctor's love of Strauss from something about his person, or something in the ward (where there was nothing). It was a blow to a young boy who deified the medical establishment, the grandson of a physician. How would humanity ever go beyond its narrow understanding of the world if we turned away from clear evidence when put before our faces? I said nothing more about my experiences in my short coma. They did not care to hear, and neither did my mother, who lambasted me for lying to the authorities, for attention-seeking, for arrogance. And yet this experience did teach me one positive thing; that our understanding of the machinations of life and death are highly archaic and obsolete, and our ability to embrace science is hindered entirely by men who would deny the possibility of impossible things.

I recovered quickly from my accident, with only a broken leg and a sore head which hampered me vaguely for several weeks. However, my absence had had a profoundly negative effect on my grandmother. My mother had not returned to the house for the entirety of my confinement, meaning that my poor, proud

Oma had been left near starving, alone and scared, and had been forced to withstand the indignity of defecating in her own bed.

When my mother and I finally reached home, with crutches supporting me, I almost fainted upon seeing the state that my beloved matriarch had been left in, and in a fit of pique I pushed my mother down the stairs to her own quarters. Gathering herself in the small hallway, with pathetic tears running down her face, she shouted back up at me—but I, equally angered and with the strength of righteous indignation, swore that if she ever climbed the stairs again, I would beat her with my crutches and leave the house, never to return.

I went to my grandmother, the magnificent figure under whose care I had grown, now small and terrified in the humiliation of her situation. She gently wept and I held her, caring not for the various odours and stains of dampness that covered her garments and bedclothes. I placed my arms around her and she cried into my chest, saying no words but expressing her gratitude with her grasp. She held me like her protector. At that moment, she was the vulnerable child, and I the adult. The world moved around us and I closed my eyes against the vertigo. My position on the bed brought pain to my leg, but I would not move until she did.

Limping on my crutches, I fetched bowl after bowl of hot water, brought sponges and clothes, and, softly humming, began to rescue my grandmother from her predicament. I pulled back the sheets under which she had lain, gently tugging on the parts where fluids had made the fabric stick to her skin. I patted these areas with the warm water of the cloth, soaking off the dried material so it could be removed without tearing her delicate skin. I held her in my arms and drew her to one side of the bed, then the next, so I could take off the sheets without forcing her to stand, then I rested her head in my lap while I took the pillows, discarded the stained cases, and covered them in fresh ones. I told my grandmother of the intoxicating things I had seen on the morning of my accident, of the city as it was then, of the people out there telling us things we should listen to. I recalled everything I had learned in the hospital as I pressed the sponge to her body, starting at the soles of her feet and her ankles, squeezing the sponge out into the bowl and bringing clean water every few minutes. She was quiet and passive, intently listening to my story as I sponged her calves and knees, smiling against the stench of urine and faeces that permeated the room. Combined with the comforting, maternal smell of Oma, it became sweet, almost delicious. I cleaned her arms and neck while I spoke, then dabbed at her chest. Staring up at the ceiling to hide her shame, she lifted her hips and allowed me to pull down the soiled underwear she was wearing, and all the while I kept talking. Though she would not look at me, I whispered as I gently cleaned around her soiled areas, discarding one cloth and reaching for another, making her pristine before moving on, her nightdress covering my forearms to preserve her modesty. She remained silent as I worked, and when I was satisfied that she was restored to her dignity, I brought from her chest of drawers a clean pair of bloomers, threadbare as that style had been out of fashion for decades, and slid the yellowed material up her legs. She wiped away the wetness from her face and rolled over, ashamed that she should find herself at the mercy of the young boy that loved her, that her agency had been so cruelly removed. I held her as I would have held a younger sister in distress and remained until she slept. In fresh sheets, cleaned and loved, she radiated a strange sort of beauty, one that had gone beyond time. I watched her until nightfall, whereupon I removed the stained sheets to my mother's wash basket, creeping quietly so she would not see me. I retired to my bed that night knowing that I had become a man, and that the world expected much of me.

*

A week later my grandmother passed away. A more romantic mind might suggest that she never recovered from such harsh treatment, that heartbreak can drive a person to death— however, she was old and in poor health, and while I was ready to blame everyone around me, as the grieving young will, I understood even then that the universe is entropic, and death (at least, the first death) cannot be kept at bay forever.

It was a Tuesday evening and there was snow on the ground. The cold had descended quickly and without warning, so I took a blanket from my own bed and entered Oma's room, for I knew that she preferred to sleep with fewer coverings when she could, and being a stubborn woman, would not have prepared adequately for the weather. I knocked softly on the door and pushed it open, finding Oma illuminated in a shaft of streetlight breaking through the curtains. She was pale, having so rarely left her room in the previous years, and still had a sallow look about her, but her lips were full of colour and she looked calm. Again I was struck by her beauty, and wondered, for the first time, about her courtship with my grandfather. How had they met? Where had they married? What was he like as a man, as a suitor? We had spoken so little about him outside of his achievements, yet I was curious, and felt for a brief moment indignation at having been robbed of his influence. I made a note in my mind to enquire about this with Oma later in the day. She looked to be sleeping, so I gently stepped over to her bed and spread the blanket out on top of her sheets; as I had suspected, she had too few layers about her. As I adjusted the covers around her body, tucking them into and under her girth, her hand caught on the sleeve of my nightshirt and fell to the bed—too easily. I stared at the hand and understood immediately that she was gone—but there was no blood running cold, no descending of grief, no floor giving way underneath my feet. I pressed my warm fingers to the soft folds of her neck and waited for the pulse, knowing that it was not there, and in none of these moments did I feel horror. Her body was still warm. I leaned over and pulled on her eyelids; the whites of her eyes were milky, but the iris had turned to black and the eyeballs had dropped into her head, leaving the sockets even darker still. Some say that looking into the eyes of the dead is like looking into an abyss of sorts, but rather, I felt myself drawn into the blackness that existed where my grandmother once was—enticed, even. It was a comforting, protective darkness. Eventually I drew her lids closed and allowed my body to press against hers, to feel the residual heat draining out of her, the slowing of the life systems working in her body. I climbed onto the bed and positioned myself so Oma's back was resting against the front of my torso, and I placed my arms around her neck and chest. Her head lolled against me and I let her mouth fall against my arm; her jaw had dropped and a small line of drool dripped onto my skin. How tender, this moment. There was total peace as she moved between planes, and yet even then I felt that she had not departed completely. Her presence was undeniable, and the body felt as a body should. Oma and I stayed on the bed together until nightfall; I quite naturally fell asleep in her embrace.

It was several days before we were discovered. The separation in the house meant it was common for my mother and grandmother to go without speaking for as long as a week, but in those days after Oma's death I was in something of a reverie, and finally, hearing little movement from the upper floors of the house, my mother sneaked up to see what had occurred. It was late morning, and I had permitted myself to sleep late with my grandmother. My mother screamed, hysterical, upon finding us, and I couldn't find the words to say that the reason I hadn't called her was that Oma was not gone. Perhaps I didn't know that this was the reason—now, with the benefit of a lifetime of knowledge, I can say that what I was feeling was real. I knew that Oma would be taken away from me then, that they would cart her body from our room, from our home, and into a cold place, then into the ground, and it was then that I experienced the true terror of death; not the horror of the loss of life, because I knew the life had not gone, but the fear that the body should be thrown away, and with it any hope of keeping your loved one in the world with you. Had my mother been an astute woman, she might have noticed that Oma had not begun to decay as she should have, that her body was so incredibly well preserved that it had forgone the many 'normal' processes of the end of life, the spills and smells and staining of fresh death. She had not bloated, as I now know that bodies do. She had no rectal or nasal leakage. My mother realised none of this. Had she taken more time with the body, she might have thought about how Oma's way of living had affected the way she moved from one state to the other, might have looked at Oma's stomach, felt her skin, seen the dryness of her, the desiccation of her skin. She might have seen a different type of death, and wondered how her mother's life choices had caused this. But she did none of these things; she saw merely a corpse. We throw away the dead; we cast them into the ground as a means to forget them, to rid ourselves of the responsibility for them. I knew my mother would take Oma from me so I clung on to her body until my mother called the authorities, until five large men came to take her, until they wrenched my hands from around her chest, needing all their energy to fight off this young boy, hysterical in grief, and when she was gone from the room, from our home, I collapsed into childish tears and wailed until nightfall. That night, and from then on, I slept in my grandmother's bed.

2

Gabriela

On the day of her birth, Luciana del Carmen came out of our mother as wet as the sea. She slipped through our grandmother's waiting hands, landed on the floor, and from her very first breath, she screamed as if dying. My father picked her up from my mother's mess and, wiping her wailing face, called her *mi sirenita*, like she had come straight out of the ocean and into his life.

Luciana was born in our family's house in Havana in nineteen fifty-one, just as I had been two years before. After us there came two boys, Andrés Ignacio and Juan Antonio, then another girl, Ximena Maria. Each child was born in the wet season; the screams of my mother would build as the clouds gathered, as the blanket of warmth wrapped around us, and then with the first cry of the baby the rains would come, and so too the breeze, the clear air, the new breath. Each time it happened like this, as if Mamá controlled the skies with her pain. Our grandmother, Tita, said this was the case. Over the years of my life, I have come to believe she was right.

Our parents were Juan Pablo Herrera and Elenita Providencia Madrigal, and according to my grandmother they were very much in love. Papá was a businessman, and he dressed to show it; bright shirts, beige trousers, the kind of smile that drew in strangers. If you lived in our part of Havana you would see him in the mornings, walking around town smoking cigarettes, buying fruta bomba and shaking hands with acquaintances. He was a man who liked to be seen. Mamá was a quieter person; she was studying, in classes for pharmacy most days of the week, but in the warm Havana nights she enjoyed being seen on my father's arm. They took off in his car on the weekends, telling no one where they were going, taking next to nothing with them, and arriving back on Sunday nights, faces flushed with sun and sin. These are the stories that Tita told us of their life before we were born. They got married at her insistence, on a summer break from my mother's studies, because my father was a good man and Tita did not want her daughter to lose him. By the time my mother went back to school I was already forming myself in her belly, and I arrived in the heart of a storm the week of her final exams, three weeks early and hardly breathing. Mamá would not let me out of her sight until my lungs were strong and my eyes clear and active, and by the time I was fully awake in this world, her exams had come and gone. She could have taken them later, picking up a dropped thread of possibility, but by then she lived a different life. My father bought us a house and the two of them quickly filled it; Mamá had three more babies in six years. And then she had Ximena.

Ximena Maria came out of my mother all skin and bones, and didn't ever grow fat like the other babies did. When you held her she felt like an armful of cutlery, like parts of her might drop out of your grip. She never learned to look our mother in the eye, and Lord, that girl cried. For months after Ximena was born, Mamá would go every day to the local church to pray for the baby to be shaken from whatever reverie she had been born into. Tita told us that the church was looked over by St Mary, from Egypt, the patron saint of those who repent; she said that Mamá was repenting for every bad thing she had ever done, for every bad thing we had ever done, for every bad thing her youngest child would ever do if God let her live. Our father told us that we had to be good and quiet, be the best children there had ever been, because mother was talking directly to God, and

God would hear us complaining that we couldn't sleep at night because of the baby's cries. We had to be quiet so that Mamá might be properly heard. But all my mother's conversations with the Lord could not convince him to leave her youngest child on earth. Ximena died before her first birthday. Our mother fell into a sadness that she would never truly emerge from, and I felt a great shame; because we had complained and God had heard us, He had taken the crying Ximena from our home. I prayed to St Mary to forgive my sins, but the baby girl could not be brought back. Mamá would learn to wear a mask of contentment sometimes, for the sake of the rest of us, but she was never the same woman she had been before Ximena.

The house we lived in was big enough for us all to have a single room, and by the time Ximena died my grandmother also lived with us, in a large room on the ground floor, so that she could help with childcare and so that she wouldn't be alone. My mother was her only surviving child and my grandfather had long since died. Our mother's father had been an American soldier who married Tita after the first war, and even though they stayed together until his death, there were many other children in Havana that counted him as their father. Mamá had a dozen half brothers and sisters but she would never admit it, and even though they knew each other's faces they would not speak when they passed in the aisles of the grocery store. Tita became bitter about this as she got older, and she often stroked my skin with a sadness, running her fingers over my face and staring at me as if she wasn't sure how I was part of her family. In the evenings Tita sat Luci and I at her feet and brushed our hair, fretting for our futures. She said because our grandfather was a yuma we were all born in water, this family, neither one thing nor the other, and that if we were not careful we would be seen as strange and disregarded. As girls we must be attractive enough to catch a man, but chaste enough to keep ourselves for marriage; only then would we be looked after; only then would we earn respect. St Mary would help us, so there was no need to worry. But it was Tita, not St Mary, who showed us how to redden our lips and curl our hair, even when Luci was so small that she fell asleep with her lips still painted and smudged the colour on her face the next day by getting her breakfast all around her mouth.

Being the older sister, I thought myself very mature. I understood the grown-ups more than Luci, and I did every chore I could. I loved to help Mamá crush the tostones and mash the masa, thinking if I worked hard like her, she would come back as she was before Ximena; if I showed her I was good, she would become the glue at the centre of the family once more. Every day held so many risks for family catastrophe; if there was an argument too long or too loud, we might crack in half and never come back together again. Luci had no such fear of conflict. She refused Mamá's chores, running around in the yard (and outside of the yard, when Mamá's back was turned) with the local boys instead, eventually coming home to the smell of cooking, and eating two tamales pulled from the pot before they were ready. Everyone thought her very charming, and she was spoiled because of it—at home, at school and in the local fondas too. To my mind, Luci was annoying, childish and greedy, but I couldn't be more than a few steps away from her. I needed to watch her closely.

How do I describe Cuba, as I remember it? It's difficult to try and summon a piece of that place and show it to you here. To explain the essence of one place or another. America is very quiet, to me. Everyone closes their doors, keeping their lives to their own boxes and yards. In Havana you are all amongst each other, even when your houses are apart. Music in the morning comes from one apartment and into another. You keep your doors open against the heat. The casino cheers of the gamblers are screamed from sunrise to sunset. You fall asleep to the songs of the music in the street, the boy who drags his double bass from place to place, the maracas of the thin old man, the woman who sings with no microphone and yet her voice carries to the next barrio and beyond. You wake up because a girl is yelling up three flights to the babysitter who drinks, who is supposed to take her baby before eight so she can go to work. You take a fruta bomba from the stand on the corner on your way to school. After class you get a cup of shaved ice with condensed milk on top and it makes you run all the way home. When the rain breaks in the afternoon you jump through someone else's front door to escape it, then you change your mind and run out into it anyway. The cars go by slowly and the drivers hang out of the windows. There is always talking, day and night. It is hot and it is close and your feet are always dirty. It is loud and everything is bright colours, and every day is alive.

In our house was a piano, a grand piano, big and imposing and demanding attention. No one could play it, apart from a few notes to make a simple tune, but even that felt wrong, because the piano had never sounded right—at least since we children had been around. It had been our father's first gift to our mother when they were dating. The house they lived in as a family had been small and cramped, and when the truck showed up with such an extravagant gift after only their second date, Abuelo was so angry he made them put it in the yard. It was rainy season and my father couldn't explain where he had got it from, and wouldn't take it away, so in the yard it stayed, getting so wet it bent out of shape, ruining the strings inside so the sound was ghostly and off-key. But soon Mamá and Papá were married and had a house of their own, and Papá made sure it was big enough that the twisted piano could sit right in the middle. Mamá had to dust it every day or the keys got gritty and stuck together, and years later the sound of us children bashing the keys made the neighbours crazy. Still, the piano stayed, because she loved it, ghosts and all.

One wet day when Luci was five years old, she ran in from

the yard where she'd been playing castles with the neighbour's boys; they had rushed home to their mother when the clouds opened, so Luci had no one to play with. I was in my room and Mamá was at the store, and Tita was upstairs asleep, taking one of the afternoon naps she had more frequently as she aged. Even speaking seemed to tire her out. I heard the sound of a few scattered notes and came down to see who was home: there was Luci, standing on the piano stool, holding the wooden sword high with both hands and bringing it down violently in front of her. I could see the chips of ivory flying off the keys and into the air, each one hanging suspended for a moment in front of my eyes, Mamá's poor piano spitting its broken teeth onto the floor. I stared at my slippery little sister. If I moved, it might make it all real; if I stayed still, Luci might not really be breaking the keys, and Mamá's piano might be okay after all. I stood and watched until I heard Mamá drop her shopping on the floor. Mamá shrieked and Luci fell to the ground, her cries lost in the widening ocean of my mother's wailing. Luci was all big eyes and shaking lips, like she'd been in a dream and someone had woken her up. Mamá began to scrabble on the floor for the tiny pieces of white that were scattered all around, and when Tita flew down the stairs, pushing me aside, she found her daughter with crushed tomatoes all over her knees, picking pieces of piano out of her spilled shopping. Luci ran out into the rain and hid at the neighbour's house until night-time.

Papá had a man come and look at the piano, promising my mother he could make it good as new again. The man spoke quietly and when he was gone, Papá closed the door of the kitchen and said to Mamá that it was too much. 'Especially now, Elena, with things how they are. And in a year, or two years, who knows? We'll buy a better one, after all this.' We ran to bed before we could eavesdrop more, but the next day, scared that it would be ruined forever, I took my glue and my paints to it. I dipped wooden splinters in the white and tried to stick them into the gaps in the ivory, but they wouldn't go. The glue leaked in between the keys and the paint spilled. I tried to clean it up but it just pushed everything deeper into the spaces. I tried and tried to fish it all out, but then some of the keys wouldn't come up again. I pulled and one came off entirely; I yelped then, in panic, looking around to see if anyone had heard me and come running. But Mamá was already there, just watching. I had done the wrong thing, I had made it worse, I knew it all in a second, and Mamá held me while I shook and panted and went to the toilet in my clothes. All the while she just held me, shushing, not angry in the least. Her eyes were full of pity; she knew I would always be this way.

Even with its broken keys and the bad memories of Luci's bruises, with its bits of splinter that now nicked your fingers when you tried to play and the C that would never come up, the piano remained, a small reminder of how things used to be before the children came. At night when it was hot and we were supposed to be in bed, Luci and I would sneak to the stairs and look down and see Mamá sat at the piano with a daiquiri in her hand, running her hand over the keys but not pressing any down. Mamá smiled sometimes at the piano on her own, even as she stroked her fingers over the badly glued ivory. It was good to see her this way.

Luci had been running towards trouble ever since the day she first walked. In the wet season you couldn't stop Papá's little sirenita from dashing out naked into the breaking rain to play in the puddles and soak up the water. If Mamá turned her back for a second she would be gone, off down the street and over the big road, darting along the Malecón to feel the spray of the waves as they hit the barriers. She would never come back at the time she was told to, and if she was ten minutes late I would cry, so scared that the fragile frame holding our family together would break. That girl seemed to have no fear—not of death, not of our parents, not of God. If she fell, as she did often, she would pick herself back up and carry on, no mention of the scratches on her knees or the dirt in her hair. She came home with dried blood and bruises and could not tell Mamá how she came by them. One time when Luci was seven, our neighbour—who had three young boys that Luci liked—brought her home with her face all covered in blood and her nose out of place. The neighbour was frantic, saying her son had kicked the ball and she was so sorry, so sorry, but Luci did not cry a single tear—not until she was at the hospital and the doctor had to break her nose again to put it back into place. It was never really fixed, Luci's nose, and Tita would stroke it and curse it and say it was the one thing that stopped her from being beautiful—and her own fault at that.

But we were happy when we were small. Papá was doing well, and he liked to buy new things—toys for us, furniture for Mamá, things he could show off with. We were the first in Havana to get a television, a fact we all rode high on for months before it finally arrived. When the delivery came in, the neighbours crowded into our front yard. People followed the delivery men into our house and soon Tita was shuffling back and forth with iced lemonade, and when there was no more lemonade, with rum, and even though it was hot and the air was wet and heavy, more people stuffed into our living room, sitting on the couch, the chairs, the floor and even on each other to see this miracle that Papá had preached about. Papá made a grand fuss of turning it on; he made the neighbour's sons move from the armchair so he could sit in it as if it was a throne. He pushed the button and people gasped so dramatically you would have thought the Holy Father himself had come down. Luci climbed onto Papá's knee to watch, but Papá was not looking at the moving pictures on the screen. No; he was watching the faces of all the neighbours and friends and strangers as they stared at the tiny TV, laughing at the yumas on it. Now when I think of Papá, this is how I see him: playing the machismo game, yes, but also content, making others around him happy. The neighbours stayed until it turned into a party and the men were sent out for more ice, more rum, more candies for the kids. It got louder and louder and when Mamá started to fret, Papá made her favourite drink, bringing one daiquiri after another until she was dancing with a schoolteacher and had given up trying to stop the party. Tita carried us to bed long after midnight and when Luci elbowed me in the back and I woke to the first light of the day, the music was still coming from downstairs. It was the first time I had seen Mamá dance since she lost Ximena.

But things were happening under our feet. Havana was changing and our parents knew it. As we grew, father seemed to shrink. Company at the house became less regular, and when Papá's friends did come over he would send Juan Antonio to the store; when Juan Antonio came back with no ice because the store freezer was empty, Papá would hit him on the legs, and once even smashed his glass on the table. Sometimes there were strange men we didn't know in the house at night, and on those nights the radio was turned off and Mamá sat on the step outside until they were gone. Papá's mood was strange after these visits, and he often went out and stayed away the whole night, which he had never done before. When he was out of the house, Mamá tuned the radio to a station we didn't know. It was all static and talking, the sort of thing that hurts your ears. These were the hot-wet nights, and we went out to play in the street, but Mamá sat close and listened, with one hand on the windowsill, as if the neighbours might hear the sounds coming from our living room and come to take her away. One of these evenings I ran inside from the street to get a glass of lemonade and there was Tita, leaning against the doorway, watching Mamá as she listened to the radio, holding it like it was little lost Ximenita. Tita looked neither happy nor sad; she looked drained and afraid, as if she was seeing time move by, watching things change faster than the rest of us could. Mamá said it was because she was so old each moment moved more quickly for her, because it was just one of a million moments she had already experienced. When Tita saw me running in, she placed a finger to her lips and turned silently to go back up the stairs. Mamá never knew she was there, and she listened to that radio until she fell asleep where she sat. The more our father stayed out, the more we would come downstairs late, hungry for torticas de morón, to find Mamá in the kitchen with her radio. On these nights the four of us slept in bed with Mamá and she held us all night, until Tita broke the new morning with coffee and got in bed with us too.

Looking back now, I can see what was happening. But we only knew that there were cracks in our family where there had been none before.

It was this that started everything. As the changes started I clung to routine, thinking that I could keep everything the same if I only tried hard enough. Luci, on the other hand, was aching for change. She tired of Tita's ramblings and took the scissors to her hair so that our grandmother could not sit and comb it. But Tita still did so, each night before bed, cursing Luciana for making herself ugly. Luci grew sick of having make-up smeared on her face while our grandmother told her she would have to try twice as hard to make the boys come; she would find herself claimed by a bad man with nothing to give, she would end up a mere shadow of her former self. One evening Luci ignored all the calls to come in and I was sent to talk to her out in the yard. I found her sitting on the ground with her arms crossed, facing the house and scowling.

'Luci, just come in.'

She spat in the dirt and drew saliva crosses.

'I'm not having that stuff on my face.'

'You know Tita likes it. You can put up with it. She's an old lady, you can just sit and be quiet.'

'She's wrong about everything.'

She uncrossed her arms and pushed her fingers into the soil.

'She just wants to tell us stories, Luci. She just wants to help.'

She dug her hands in deeper.

'I'm not being painted. Tell Tita to choke.'

She would not come in, no matter how much I begged, so instead I sat twice as long for Tita, letting her paint my eyes as well as my lips, learning how to pull the hairs from between my eyebrows so that boys might want me one day.

It was a few weeks later that Papá, looking sad and old, took us all out in the car to Varadero for a day trip. Papá said Varadero was what the whole of Cuba could be if we all got some sense, if only people had some imagination. We had been many times and we all loved it, with its skyscraper hotels and its impossible pools and its parasols that made us feel like movie stars. But Tita stayed behind, saying she felt ill. When we arrived home at night, full of sugar and sand and stories to tell, we found Tita dead in her bed. We had done it again; we had said something bad and God had listened. I took Luci to the church the next morning and forced her to pray, to say sorry in front of St Mary, but she would not, so I prayed twice as hard, hoping that I would be given so much forgiveness that I could share it with my wayward sister.

3

Wilhelm

I turned fourteen soon after Oma's death. Though I spent my nights in my grandmother's bed and my evenings in the study, reading and educating myself, eating the nuts and berries that I still brought back from my trips even though my grandmother was gone, my mother took it upon herself to try and establish a relationship between us. She was desperate to have my love, for she had nothing else, but I could not give it. I had dedicated myself to my grandmother and felt her absence as something that emanated from me, rejecting attempts to replace her. Towards my mother I felt none of the respect or adoration I had felt for Oma; I did not believe there was anything she could teach me, and though I could tolerate her affections, I could not return them. Despite her entreaties, I had no interest in abandoning my studies to find a job. Instead, I removed myself from the home in the daylight hours, waking before she did and taking food for the day while I found ways to employ my body and my mind. That year I joined a youth organisation that gave me the structure and challenge I needed; it was clear to see that I had been lacking a father, despite my grandmother's best efforts to be everything and everyone to me.

For the first time, I was able to spend time alongside young men my own age, and the effect on me was startling. I was introduced to the simple pleasures of hiking and camping, absorbing oneself in one's surroundings in a more peaceful, satisfying manner than that offered by the bustle of the city. I learned how to pitch tents and build dams, which appealed to my practical mind. The physical training aspect of the group started showing effects just as my growth spurt began, and I found I had shoulders, calves and strong hands—parts of a man. When boys reached full membership, they were gifted a knife, to aid in outdoor activities such as those outlined above, and it was then that we began to hunt, tracking down small creatures of the woodlands and slitting their throats quickly. The intention for these animals was that they would serve as our meals for the evening (overnight trips had quickly become the norm; none of the other boys seemed to mind being away from home, and for me it was a true pleasure) but the scientist in me embraced the chance to dissect real bodies for the first time. I had pored over the literature around surgery and the human body for most of my life and was able to recite the names of bones, ligaments and organs, but never before had I had the opportunity to perform a surgery for myself. One cool night in September the other boys and I caught a fat marmot trying to hide in its den, and before they pierced it and threw it on the fire I convinced them to indulge in a little medical inquiry. I was not the fittest in the group, nor the quickest, nor did I have the highest aptitude with regards to chopping wood or catching fish, but that evening by the sparking fire I folded my legs underneath me, held the blade of my knife quickly over the flames and stuck it into the animal at the throat, opening him up all the way to the tail. I found that, far from being unsettled by the feel of the knife piercing flesh, the process came quite naturally to me; my hands knew the pressure to apply, and soon enough there was a Y-shaped opening, coming down from both sides of the creature's neck and then straight down its stomach. The boys around me were rapt in quiet admiration as I revealed the animal's innards, still warm. I picked every organ out of that creature and laid them all next to the carcass in the dust, showing the boys where each one lived in the body, and stating its function for their education. I then scraped away the fat from the animal and let it melt off my knife over the fire, before showing them the animal's skeleton, the spine and the small bones of the foot. When each boy had handled the organs, touched them and smelled them, I placed each one back inside the creature and, taking a sewing kit from my pack, stitched him back up from tail to head. The others wanted to eat the marmot but I convinced them that the poor soul had been through enough. They told me to bury him, but my juvenile heart cracked at the thought of my grandmother's body, buried in the ground, slowly rotting, and I clung to the creature somewhat hysterically, and instead kept its corpse near me all night. I left it outside my tent and when I woke in the morning to find it had been carried away by some fox or other nocturnal hunter, I had to hide the upset in my stomach for fear of being mocked. We went home that afternoon and for once I was glad of it. After this, however, the other children called me Doc, and I bloomed with a powerful pride, knowing that I had gained the respect of my peers. In truth, academic training was not a particular focus of the organisation and many of the members were intellectually my inferiors. Nevertheless, the acceptance I felt was strong and heartening.

In this manner, within the group, I was turned into an adult. The responsibility to press and clean my uniform was my own, and I did so when my mother was out at her factory job, when I could be sure that the run of the lower floors was mine, for the guilt I felt in her presence was suffocating. As her attempts to reach me increased, I found it intolerable to even be in the same building as her. In nineteen thirty-five, a month after my sixteenth birthday, I left that home, taking with me all the books I could fit into boxes and the blanket from Oma's bed. I left one morning just after my mother had departed for work and was aided by several adults from my youth organisation's administration team. They had arranged for me to move into a young men's assisted housing facility run by the group, and there

I would be able to lodge with my peers, youths I knew from the group already. The home was on the edge of Old Dresden and I left no forwarding address for my mother. I did not need her money; employment had been arranged for me, and, thanks to a mentor, I was to begin my medical training immediately—at no cost. Of course, I experienced true heartbreak upon leaving my grandmother's room; yet I had been shown, before I left, that she was with me.

That final night was uncommonly still, so still one could hear the movements of the rats on the streets outside. I drifted off into a woeful sleep, experiencing grave doubts about leaving the only home I had ever known. I was awoken by a gentle movement around four o'clock. Standing over the bed, her hand on my forehead, was Oma. On my skin I felt a cold dampness, as if touched by a drying flannel, but the warmth of familiarity overcame my trepidation. Tears fell from my eyes and though I remained silent, Oma hushed me, stroking my face as she did so.

'Now now, dear Willi, don't be afraid. I know that you are leaving here tomorrow. Don't be ashamed; you are not leaving me. My soul will follow you, dearest boy. You are not departing me. You cannot.'

I tried to grasp on to her hand but felt only my own flesh. There was another apparition behind my grandmother, a smaller figure: a girl.

'Now, Willi, you must listen to me. In your future there will be great hardship—difficult times for which you will need to be strong. You must remain resolute through these periods and remember that you are doing the right thing. But to give you the spirit to endure, my boy, I am going to show you what is promised you.'

She reached backwards and a small hand took hers. She pulled into sight the young girl, and—how do I describe her? I could echo the romantic poets and tell you that she was all the stars, all the beauty, all the goodness in the universe, but to even attempt to describe her would do her a disservice. Suffice it to say that her delicate, feminine features were framed in an abundance of thick black curls that cascaded almost to her waist, the hair falling over her face and preserving her modesty in the spotlight of my gaze. She looked up from beneath her veil, and her eyes, teak brown, met mine. A coquettish smile played at the corner of her mouth and I may have smiled back; I certainly did not speak, for my rational faculties had left me entirely and I clung to the sheets in fear that I might faint. Oma wrapped her arm around the girl's shoulders and said:

'This girl, my darling, is destined to be yours.'

With that, Oma bent forward to kiss me on my forehead and both figures disappeared. I collapsed immediately into dreams of the girl, of her crimson lips and quivering hands, and when I woke with the dawn, I was ready to leave. To endure what might come for the sake of my promised bride.

So began my intimacy with the paranormal—with the evidence of life beyond death. I could find no rational explanation for my experience, and I knew better than to mention to my superiors at the youth organisation that I had direct knowledge of the possibility of post-mortem existence. As previously mentioned, non-practical education was not particularly encouraged within its ranks, and something that reached so far beyond the plains of accepted medical discourse would not have been welcomed. Instead I threw myself back into my books, reading everything I could find with regards to the existence of the soul, the death of the body—anything that might indicate to me a rational reason for the appearance of the apparition. On this point, medical education failed me. My own understanding of the experience was, of course, wholly scientific; having evidence of my own, I searched for explanation. To this end I widened my reading to the philosophy of the continent, and yet still found nothing to satisfy my rational mind—though I found that I could take the works of Immanuel Kant into my hands, turn them and inspect them, and use them to my own ends. Yet even this was of limited use.

It became clear that I would have to hold my new know-ledge as a quiet secret, conducting my own experiments and research as I went along—whenever the chance was offered to me, alongside my strict training and the many activities that I was required to undertake in return for my lodgings and medical education. My spare time, truth be told, was sparse, and without the facilities for self-directed research, I knew my curiosity would be thus frustrated. Like all scientifically minded beings faced with an irrational experience, my confidence in the event faded as time swept me ever further from it, and within a few months I had buried the memory to an extent where my need for knowledge on the subject was, at the very least, subdued.

Yet even as my daily activities overwhelmed my ability for quiet reflection on the matter, there was one thing that I could not rid myself of: my recollection of the young girl's face. She appeared to me in dreams, in my waking moments, in solitary periods when I closed my eyes. I knew that even if Oma's prediction proved to be unsound, and I never saw the girl again in my life, I would never be free from her haunting image; the radiance, the vibrance, the beauty. She was like a child in so many ways, so delicate and afraid, but the very thought of her roused hitherto unexplored parts of my physical being as well as my romantic heart. I had never fallen prey to such a deep sensuality before. It was as if my grandmother had presented to me the means of my own ruin—and, worse, had told me I could have it. In such ways I thought of the exotic girl: a being to be taken and yet one which possessed so much power. I knew the very thought of her would be the death of me eventually. The taboo of it caused many a sleepless night.

*

In the months following my departure from my grandmother's house, I slowly settled into my new lodgings. Of course, such a shift will always cause apprehension and unease in a boy so young, and while it would be a lie to say my transfer to the adult world was without issue, I soon found myself thriving in my environment, amongst others who shared my goal of education. Over several years, I received a military-style pedagogy which expanded on the skills I had already learned through the organisation. At the same time, I was engaged in the medical training that was necessary for me to pass my examinations, but very little was new to me, thanks to my years of training with my grandmother's body and my grandfather's books. Though I was endlessly frustrated at having to sit through classes I could well have taught, repeating things I knew—and several of which I had learned were untrue—I conducted myself with absolute obedience and simply buried myself in my own studies while the other boys were catching up. However, it must have been obvious to my tutors that I was gifted, and this led to me being picked for a special apprenticeship with a doctor with ties to the organisation. It was under this doctor that I received my first real education. By the time I was nineteen I had been accepted into the permanent team under Dr Karin Magnussen, a brilliant biologist of whom I had heard many impressive stories. In Dr Magnussen's laboratory I was finally offered the resources necessary for real and practical research, and though I was hampered somewhat by the borders of her own scientific interests and my position, first as an apprentice and latterly as an assistant, I was able to undertake experimentation of my own by working long hours into the evenings when Dr Magnussen had left to fulfil her social obligations. It is perhaps difficult to explain to the unscientific reader just how much satisfaction can be gained by the curious mind when it is afforded the means to go beyond what it has been taught, to push the boundaries of what is known. It is not just a case of personal betterment; one proceeds with the knowledge that one is in fact expanding the very limits of human understanding. It is with this inspiration that I pushed forth with my research, upholding my extensive responsibilities and duties in Dr Magnussen's care and then taking my evenings for my own experiments. At first these centred mostly on mice, which are a poor replacement for humans but a necessary place to start. It was on them that I began my first studies in reanimation, for want of a better word. This is not the term I would choose if the reader were more familiar with the intricacies of post-mortem science, but it is the term we must use for the time being.

As I proceeded in my own research, the duties of my daytime work became more and more tiresome. Though our projects were always broad-based biological experiments, we found ourselves increasingly focused on more niche elements, of which I found the scientific basis to be lacking at best. However, in the second year of my appointment, more and more time was given over to this work. Dr Magnussen had her own passions of which I shared few, in honesty. Her great interest was in the eye, both human and animal, and though I admit I did learn much about macular degeneration that later assisted me, I found the excessive focus on this part of the body to be exhausting to the point of frustration. On the subject of twins I had no interest at all; for me, the only coupling worth investigation was that of the human body and the human soul.

Dr Magnussen, for all her scientific brilliance, was also hampered by many of the traits that women share; she was emotional and would erupt into explosions of anger if she believed that our work had been substandard. She also would not countenance any criticism of her research and was vain to the point of arrogance about both her reputation and her professional standing. Though her assistants did much of the labour, she consistently presented our findings as if they were her own, and spent an increasing number of hours socialising with her political affiliates rather than undertaking research in the lab. Of course, if challenged on how she chose to spend her time, she would argue that it was these political friends who funded our laboratory, and it is true that our resources were greatly expanded as the years went on, with more money and subjects being given over to our research. But I found her both unprofessional and patronising, which led me to throw myself more passionately into my own work—when the time was offered.

I found during this period that our definition of medical death is severely lacking. There are compulsions of the body post-mortem that have never been adequately explained, and the process of physical decay is not retarded by but in fact is accelerated by the methods of embalming that are currently favoured by the death industry. I had the opportunity to study, in various types of animals, the rate of decay in bodies treated in different ways—some left in vacuums, some left in open air, others encased in a solution of various nourishing liquids, and still others frozen or buried in the ground. During the course of this inquiry I recalled my experience of Oma's death. While the bodies we experimented with on a daily basis all exhibited similar post-mortem activity (algor mortis, rigor mortis, autolysis, bloat and so on), it struck me that Oma, in the days following her death, exhibited none of these usual signs of decomposition. In fact, Oma's body had barely changed; it neither shrank nor swelled in any particularly noticeable way, and while there was a small amount of post-death leakage, she did not appear to be undergoing the same process as the others I came into contact with—or, it occurred to me, she perhaps was not undergoing these processes at the same speed. Since I had lived amongst my peers and had been exposed to the lives and rituals of others outside my close family, I had seen that my own relatives' reluctance towards an excessively heavy diet was not common, and began to wonder if Oma's ascetic habits may have in some way delayed the onslaught of decay. Of course, she was removed from me only a matter of days after death, so I had nothing in the way of evidence as to the longevity of this condition.

It was in pursuit of this evidence that I engaged in brief employment two large and unwieldy youths in the depths of an autumn night. Being at this time in a position of some regard in the medical field, I found it necessary to keep myself at a clear distance as the youths worked at the grave of my grandmother, to avoid being associated in any way with their actions in the event of passers-by. However, I kept a close eye on their movements and, when the coffin was finally unearthed, managed the transportation of the casket to a nearby vehicle and on to my laboratory, which was empty, given the time of night and the propensity of my co-workers towards socialisation. I paid the men to remain outside, and with a crowbar wrenched open my grandmother's casket.

There she was, the woman I loved, so similar to how she was in life. For a moment, I forgot that she had passed away, and reached out for her hand as if she could reach out and take mine in turn. Her skin, dry but rubbery while she lived, had remained as such, and while desiccation had occurred, there was no visible evidence of putrefaction or excessive rot. She had dried rather than decayed. It was only then that I recalled the pictures in my grandmother's books, the monks who claimed to have transcended the very concept of death, who were rendered as artworks, as things to be worshipped for millennia. I touched her body, felt her achievement beneath me. She was glorious.

It is of course now accepted that the surrounding environment has an enormous impact on a corpse, as does the pre-death diet and lifestyle of the decedent, yet we have previously failed to understand that by treating a dead body as a spent thing, we have robbed our loved ones of any chance they have of returning to their physical form after death, for we have not just discarded it but have in fact placed it in the worst possible conditions to delay its decomposition. Indeed, by throwing bodies into the pyre we remove their existence on this plane entirely—and how could a soul begin to return to such a vessel? Ash cannot support life, and so these souls are destined to expire on whichever plane they exist post-death. Increasingly it became clear to me that we are engaged, as a race, in a type of genocide—a grand theft, in that we steal from the recently dead any chance they might have of returning to us. We kill our dead for a second time. In this, we are all guilty.

4.

Gabriela

In the months after Tita passed, it was as if the whole house had been shaken from its foundations, and I lived in fear that it might fall down around us. The surest thing in my life was gone. I had always known that people died, and that afterwards God takes you and that you exist somewhere else, for at church they loved to speak of this, as both a threat and a promise. When Tita died, I was forced to see that to everyone else living, the dead were forever lost. There was a space in our home, in the whole of Havana where my grandmother had been, just as there was a hole in my mother's soul where Ximena had been, and nothing would ever come along to fill that gap. It burned; a betrayal. Why had no one told me how much life could hurt?

My mother was seized by a new wave of melancholy, a new valley found in the depths of her sadness. She was lonely, I could see it, for the anchor of her world was gone too; who would watch over her and tell her she was unhappy, who would see her doing things she should not, and shift the world around to protect her from her own actions? Papá stayed out longer and longer, coming home angry and full of arguments, as if he'd found them out on the streets and brought them home to show us all. In the evenings they sat in the kitchen, speaking in low voices. After a while Papá would boil over, just a single sentence that tore through the quiet, then Mamá would rise without a word and take herself to bed. On these nights Luci would creep from her room and sneak down the stairs, because she hated nothing more than ignorance; she needed always to know what was going on. Luci would rather know something even if it hurt. More than once I had to drag her from the kitchen door, one hand over my ear so I did not accidentally catch a piece of information that might upset the balance of my life. Sometimes in the morning we would find Papá bent over the piano, his sleeping head resting on his arm, but worse were the mornings when he was not there at all.

In this way, our house became porous. Before we had been a unit, a collective of seven. But there had been cracks, and then they were fault lines. The edges of our family began to blur. The door to our home was never fully closed, people spilling in and spilling out—a stray animal to dispose of, a child gone to play, a parent out taking something to the neighbours. We brought home so many school friends the house looked like a community centre. The dust came in, the rains came in, the winds blew through. It wasn't unusual for my father to put the boys to bed only to find there was another child who had wandered in and been there all day. Sometimes I came downstairs and could find neither parent; sometimes I came in and there were five strangers around Papá, my brothers and sister nowhere to be found. The line that had been drawn through the island had been drawn through my family too. It made me nervous, this blurring, changing shape of us. I needed firm lines, clear boundaries. I needed to be able to close the door.

The turbulence of the island began to seep in. Outside in the streets there were raised voices, scuffles between former friends, whispered conversations; all of this came inside our home too. One day, in the year after our grandmother died, our neighbours came back from visiting family on the east coast and said there was a hurricane coming; that on another part of the island, cows were swimming in deep water, that a lady had drowned on her way home from church. I ran around to fetch the boys from the playground and screamed at Mamá and Papá to get inside, to close all the shutters, to get candles and matches and to bolt the doors both front and back. I imagined those far-off streets flooded with gigantic land waves that were headed towards us to wash us away. But it was more than that; it was a reason to make my parents sit together in a room, to keep my brothers where I could see them, to make Luci sit still, to hold all of us together. Normally I was the quiet one, the one who didn't want to rock the boat, but if my father tried to open the shutters, I screeched so hard I could barely breathe; he was yanked from the window by my mother and told to sit down. We sat together in our living room all night, every one of us dripping with sweat, bored as all hell and desperate to be alone. But I would not have it. By nightfall it had gone beyond anything I could control; I needed to close us up against change, against whatever was coming. So we stayed, two and four on sofas and floorboards, right through to the morning. The hurricane had been nothing but a regular storm. Luci pinched me and said I was a terrible coward. But Mamá had fallen asleep in my father's arms, and the boys had told each other stories by torchlight, and Luci had stayed close to me for the longest time in months. It was the happiest I had been in a year.

Andrés and Juan Antonio, who before were just babies, all of a sudden stood tall on their feet and took their place as boys. Still four and five, they began to hold their shoulders back and walk with their hips forward just like Papá, one first then the other copying, until Mamá smacked them on the legs with a Bible and told them that Jesus watched little boys in particular, just waiting for them to fall face first into sin. But for all their posturing they were softer than their growing bodies suggested. Tonio went from baking with our mother to dismantling anything he could find. He liked putting things together so much that if you looked away for too long he would take all of your things apart, just to give himself something to do. Andrés was the opposite, a finder of things, an appreciator of nature. He would bring home flowers stolen from the garden of the neighbours, sometimes with pollen-tired bumblebees, sometimes covered in ants, always as a gift for Mamá. The things that Andrés tried to keep as pets got worse every year; first it was stray cats and dogs, then it was scorpions, one time a snake, and the last straw was when he gave Mamá a glass jar with a huge spider in—our neighbour told us it was a viuda negra and very dangerous to have in the house. That was the last of the pets, but still if you went to the beach with Andrés you would turn around and he'd be holding a jellyfish and grinning—somehow, by the grace of God, not getting stung.

Luci didn't have such a skill. If there was trouble to be found, Luci would catch it. One afternoon she wasn't outside the school where we usually met, and I could not see her in the classroom either. I found myself at home but could not remember how I got there. Mamá called from the kitchen but instead of speaking, instead of telling her that Luci was not where she should be, I stood at the open door and waited for something to happen, so scared that if I moved at all I would do the wrong thing and cause everything to crash down around me.

'Gabriela Maria, what is it? Use your words, child, you're not a statue.'

Behind me Mamá spoke but I did not turn, for I could see her coming, Luciana, being dragged by her teacher along the narrow street. I watched, perfectly frozen, until the woman reached the door and demanded my mother.

'I'm she,' said Mamá in her church voice, 'so you can let go of her arm, please.'

Her voice was deep and she sounded like Papá. The angry lady let Luci go, and she darted behind Mamá's legs.

'We will not have it, behaviour like hers. This girl is bound for sin, no question, and if you were any kind of mother you would teach her what's normal. What does it say about a woman to have a daughter like this?'

Mamá, you understand, had grown slower, quieter, and less like herself as the years wore on. When Ximena left, she took a lot of Mamá with her. When Tita left, still more of Mamá went. Each time our father went away for the night, he took part of our mother and did not bring it home. But in front of this teacher, she breathed into her whole self again, so beautifully that I hoped her rage might last forever, that she would stay angry and puffed up and once again Mamá.

'What is it exactly that my demon child has done, Señora Contreras? This little girl here, what evil has she made?'

The teacher stepped into the house, and around me I felt it shudder.

'Your daughter is full of the most carnal knowledge. And where did she learn it? It is a shame on your home, that such a creature might live here.'

Mamá's face tightened.

'Go upstairs, girls.'

Luci grabbed me by the hand and took me to her room, where she sat silently by the door so she might hear the conversation. But I stomped around and sang and chatted nonsense, so Luci strained to hear until a long time later, when Mamá pushed open the door and bellowed at her:

'Come here, Luciana del Carmen. We are going to church.'

What had happened was this: in the final class of the day Luciana had asked to go to the toilet, and away she stayed until the class was over. Señora Contreras had gone looking for Luci, to find the toilets empty and no girl to be seen. She looked in all the hallways, all the classrooms, and then the store cupboard, and it was only when she looked into the school's tiny chapel that she found Luciana—on her knees, with a boy, both of them with their clothes pushed down at their ankles, the boy's hand on Luci and Luci's hand on that new and interesting part of the boy. Señora Contreras had grabbed Luciana and marched her straight home, cursing her all the way for her behaviour. The boy, who knows? He was not dragged from that room. He was left to be.

For a week afterwards, Luci did not go to school; she stayed at home with Mamá, helping with the household and going to church. She was made to repent, to repeat lessons, to pray to St Mary; the saint of those who feel sexual temptation, who know things that they should not know, who need to be helped from falling into sinful behaviour. At school the rumours started, that Luciana del Carmen had been found with a boy, that Luciana del Carmen had put her mouth on a boy, and the boy, he heard these rumours, and said yes, it did happen, that little temptress made him do it, for the boys would call him 'hombre' after, and the girls would make him an object of forbidden lust, a person with whom they might find some trouble. But Luci, she said she just wanted to see, and the boy did too; she knew about boy parts from Andrés and Juan Antonio and knew very well about her own, but wanted to see if all boys had the same. It was far from kissing and touching and all those sorts of things. I asked Mamá to go to school and put a stop to the rumours, to put Luci's story forward too. But she said we just had to ignore it all; that silly boys told stories and that they would go away. So Luciana del Carmen was called a whore, those weeks and every week after in school, because some lies might sink into the gutter and drown, but others, they get accepted as truth.

My poor sister, so desperate to know, convinced that the world had secrets and was leaving her out on purpose. The little bat of curiosity beat inside Luci, and it made her stand silently at doors to overhear an argument, it made her look inside of boys' clothes, and it made her, one day, steal a small radio from the house of our neighbour so she might listen that night to the secret something that Mamá listened to. I begged her not to, but she listened on the stairway to the secret station, then tuned the small radio until it played the same thing. With that radio the doors of our house were torn off; with its cracked voices and heavy words the whole of Havana came into our home. She brought it to me and I sat there, not wanting to run away, not able to snatch the radio out of her hands, and as she turned the dial and listened close, she finally forced me to hear those words: rebelde, guerrilla, revolución.

5.

Wilhelm

In nineteen thirty-eight I married a stout and unattractive woman for whom I had built up some mild regard. In those times, convenience and a fair pairing were most important, and the creation of children was culturally paramount. As a nationalist, I felt it my duty to do what I could to this end, and I was introduced to my wife by other members of my organisation; she was a friend of their wives, and I was told she would suit me. I had built up a comradeship with the men around me, men with whom I might speak about science over a glass of beer in the evenings, and the promise of a greater companionship with them was attractive, for I had had so few peers in my life. The wedding was an austere affair, and we quickly took ourselves to the task of producing offspring. However, to my dismay, I found that my new wife was a failure in this arena, being barren and of insufficient emotional fortitude to face the facts of her situation. As the impossibility of conception became clear, the act of coupling grew increasingly distasteful, to the point of revulsion. Her personality became hysterical. Only a year after our marriage, I left, becoming somewhat estranged from my married colleagues as a result, and settled in a small but adequate home where I could throw myself back into my work.

One point of note. During the process of our wedding day, I felt a presence near to me. Of course, such occasions require the attendance of close family and friends, and in this particular situation almost all of these attendees were of my wife's blood or acquaintance, so this sense of claustrophobia could be explained by the very matter of the wedding. And yet I could not shake the perception that I was being watched, closely, by someone whose opinion of the proceedings was not high. It wasn't until we came to exchange vows that I saw who this person was: the girl who Oma had promised to me some years before. As the clergyman instructed me to place the ring on my fiancée's finger, I saw the girl over the man's shoulder, her body in the shadows of the church, and though she was far from me and the distinct features of her glorious face were not easy to ascertain, I saw her wipe a tear from her pert cheek. She seemed physical in that moment; a real manifestation of the figure that had been shown to me by my grandmother. I was so affected by this that I dropped my new wife's hands and jolted to the side to see, but as I did so the apparition vanished. I looked again for her but it was clear she had gone; I made my excuses, the clergyman laughed, making a proclamation about the hand of God being always nearby, and the ceremony went on. Yet I could never remove from my mind the pain on the girl's face, nor the knowledge that the woman I had married was in someone else's place.

The following year, war was declared against us. For those of us resident in my country, this meant both everything and nothing. My work continued as it had, for medical research is always for the good of the general populace, and especially so in wartime, where casualties are often and many, and medical treatment is scarce. Of course, it cannot be denied that hardship came upon us, especially as the conflict went on, and in such times there can be no stability, no complacency. As doctors, we were protected to a large degree, but some non-essential research was put aside to be replaced by that which might benefit the wartime needs. My own experimentation was once again de-prioritised, and those of us under Dr Magnussen's small dictatorship were pressed to focus solely on the projects she and her political friends deemed the most worthy. We were subjected to both the whims of those in power and the shifting needs of the wartime effort; we were moved around often, reassigned to new areas and required to mobilise with mere hours' notice. It was not unusual to find oneself in a makeshift laboratory, expected to work swiftly and successfully. While equipment would quickly be pulled together, commonly from nearby universities, it was necessary that my colleagues and I learned to work with whatever we had to hand. One positive outcome of this was that our resources were expanded greatly in certain areas, and even though my work was not my own, it still offered me an unprecedented opportunity to augment my knowledge in fields of medicine that would later prove themselves to be wholly worthwhile.

It was during this period that I was also offered my first chance to experiment with the effects of radiation on the human body. To today's reader it will seem ludicrous that the medical community was so enrapt by the potential effects of radiation, but at the time, the entire world was under its spell and fascinated by its possible uses; later, of course, certain forces in the war would harness its power in the most destructive and heinous ways. As doctors, however, we were able to see its huge potential for good, and we were also advanced enough to realise that it held negative consequences when not employed correctly. This knowledge saved me from the loss of an arm or the growth of a tumour in my later years—or, most likely, severe radiation burns. I, personally, was fascinated by radiation, the presence of a barely physical force that could yet have incredible and measurable effects on the human body. The discovery of radiation as a method of sterilisation was a significant one, and opened doors that had previously remained closed. Studying the effects on the body's internal organs in response to radiation therapy was one of the most fulfilling projects I worked on under Dr Magnussen and, to her credit, she allowed me to take the lead—though I suspect this was due to her increasing laziness, and to the demands of her personal relationships with the political elite, with whom she could often be seen carousing.

Certain factors also forced my hand in terms of the work I undertook, and though I did not appreciate it at the time, I was also introduced to an area of medicine that I had never had an interest in before: the effects of freezing upon the body. In hindsight, the effects of a rapid temperature decrease on the processes of the body should have piqued my interest from the very moment I realised that medical death, as we currently term it, may not be what it seems. Yet so often these things only come to us in a roundabout manner, and so in this way I was introduced to experiments in freezing.

The trauma research project was perhaps the one most directly linked to the war effort, as pilots would often be required to eject from their aircraft over large expanses of water, and after dropping into the sea would experience enormous drops in body temperature from which they would then need to recover. Our task was to study the effects of five hours of submergence in near-freezing water (temperatures between five and nine degrees Celsius) on a clothed body, or of two hours of exposure to freezing and below freezing temperatures on an unclothed body. In addition to observing and recording the body's internal responses to these conditions, including heart rate, temperature and muscle movement, we experimented extensively with the most effective means of bringing the body to an adequate temperature quickly, then observed what permanent damage had been done. For instance, an unclothed body left out in freezing temperatures for two hours may lose several appendages to frostbite even when recovered fairly rapidly after the period of exposure. One of the more fascinating phenomena we observed during this time was that bodies that were allowed to drop to twenty-eight degrees Celsius could be brought up several degrees by the act of copulation with another person of normal body temperature, even if the cold body remained inert throughout.

During these experiments it became clear that the effects of cold upon the body could potentially be harnessed to retard the process of decay, or to even place the body into a state somewhere between life and death. In cooling the body, the heart rate also decreases significantly, which places less stress on all systems of the body and puts the patient into a semi-suspended animation, as we would perhaps term it now. Indeed, in nature we see this phenomenon occur with no help from humanity; the wood frog (*rana sylvatica*) self-freezes in ice during the cold months, and when temperatures thaw, it recovers and goes about its life with no ill effects the following spring. I conducted a series of experiments on creatures of increasing size and of various different families to see what consequences this freezing would have on animals other than the wood frog. It became immediately clear that the process of freezing and thawing caused significant damage on a cellular level if done too rapidly or without sufficient care—most obviously, the creation of ice crystals could rupture tissue and cause permanent damage to cells. One way in which to avoid this was, I found, to race a body to a stage of vitrification rather than freezing. This process inhibits ice formation as it transforms liquid substances into a non-crystalline amorphous solid, meaning that the damage to cells and tissue can be managed and avoided.

To put the findings of this work into laymen's terms: the natural degeneration of the body can be arrested by extensive cooling. It can be effectively halted if the body is carefully taken to a state of cooling and allowed to remain there with proper medical oversight. This, of course, has incredible consequences for humanity. If cooled properly, the physical decay of the body could be stopped from occurring entirely—including if a body dies a non-violent initial death and is kept from the embalmer's table before the cooling can take place (my many unpublished papers detailing my specific work in this area can be found in the locked drawers of my home laboratory). This leaves open the possibility of reanimation of the body when medical science has advanced to the point where the effects of a disease on cells can be reversed. I am heartened to see that this very theory, cast aside as mere fiction at the time of my research, is now gaining some prominence in the fields of technology, though it is most unlikely that my efforts in this area will be cited at any level. This is, sadly, the fate to which many German doctors of the time have been subjected; our work, though appropriated by many others after us, has been largely erased from history.

Perhaps the most personally pertinent period of my research, however, was in the field of tuberculosis. This was unfortunately a brief focus, and it necessarily gave way to projects that were more pressing given the political situation of the time. However, hindsight allows me to see that this period of work was to change the course of my life immeasurably. Despite having no previous experience in this area, I was chosen to undertake research 'in the field', as it were. I was taken away from my laboratory to perform this research, into conditions that were not favourable, but of course complaints were not well received. My task was, broadly, to find out whether a natural immunity to the disease of tuberculosis existed, and if so, to ascertain the manner in which it worked, so that a vaccine could be manufactured. I considered this one of the most potentially ground-breaking tasks I had been given, as tuberculosis was a scourge at the time and remains so in certain areas of the world. I was driven by an almost godly sense that I could be saving the future lives of millions of men, and although the work was difficult, often indescribably so, I endured. I worked with live *tubercle bacilli* (the active bacteria that are largely the cause of the disease) and was able to study how they gripped the body, how the body responded and how the condition developed from infection to fatal illness throughout each stage. I had, until this point, only a rudimentary understanding of this disease and had no particular interest in it. However, the potential positive impact of my work awakened in me a great and persistent fascination with the condition, which would remain for the rest of my life. Unfortunately, a natural immunity to the disease was not apparent, and eventually I was sent back to the laboratory to continue other research.

I have stated previously that the fact of the war had little effect on me and my colleagues, but for a shift in the focus of our work and the expansion of resources and funding given to us. My memories of that time evoke a strong sense of togetherness, of working for a common cause. Having set up my own home, I was free to use my spare time as I saw fit, and I established a number of friendships with others who shared my values and education. I partook in regular visits to the theatre, and to concerts of classical music, and trips to the countryside with others my age—though many were married and brought their wives with them. It seemed as if the world was made for us to enjoy it, and the outbreak of the war does not feature in my mind as a restriction on that freedom. Perhaps it is a natural effect of the distancing of time that I cannot remember any particularly negative consequences of the war on my personal life during the first years of the conflict.

Yet it would be false to state that this was the case by the mid- nineteen forties. The act of defending ourselves against our enemies began to take its toll, and as conflict stretched ever onwards, the integrity of our country began to disintegrate. The single most catastrophic and affecting event of my life occurred in the first two months of nineteen forty-five.

My home city, as I have intimated in this text so far, had always been a source of great joy for me as a younger man, and this continued into my adulthood. After the devastating loss of my grandmother, I took particular comfort in my daily wanderings through the majestic buildings and streets that we had loved together. One could not walk through the city of Dresden without observing the pinnacle of human talent; the architecture, the art, the very substance of the city was a testament to human innovation. Dresden was the foundation of my romanticism, my understanding of love, my appreciation of the sublime.

The war effort had taken me from my home city, but it was to Dresden I returned early in nineteen forty-five for a short period of rest and recuperation. Dr Magnussen had, with maniacal rapidity, disbanded our latest research project and fled to Berlin. Thus abandoned, an anxiety spread through my colleagues; with no project or occupation for the first time in a number of years, we decided to escape to quieter parts of the country until we received further instruction. I returned to Dresden with a colleague, Gerhard, whose own home town was, at that time, unsafe for him to return to. I took a hotel room, not wishing to engage with either my mother or my childhood acquaintances, and my colleague took another nearby. We spent several weeks recuperating from what had been, in retrospect, an incredibly taxing undertaking. The residents of the city had been largely isolated from the effects of the conflict, on account of the fact that Dresden was not a port, nor a significant transport hub, and it had no factories; as a location it had no strategic importance, and the vast majority of the city's inhabitants were intellectuals embarking on a life of study, spending time in quiet contemplation of the higher sciences and arts. Two previous attacks on railway sites outside of the city had caused little concern to Dresden's residents, so firmly did we believe that there was nothing to be gained from an attack on the city itself; so ardently were we committed to the idea that our enemies were men of humanity and mercy.

It took eight minutes for enemy forces to release five hundred tons of high explosives and two hundred thousand incendiaries on the city of Dresden. She was, simply put, annihilated. Three hours later a second attack dropped one thousand, eight hundred tons of bombs on the already devastated body of the city, as desperate survivors strained to pull the remains of their families from the wreckage. From this second death, we would never recover.

I can barely stand to describe the events of that night. I feel my chest tighten at the very movement of my hand writing these words. Yet so many things have been written about that night, and so few capture the agony.

The night was quiet, and then it was not. The cacophony of the attack was great and unexpected. Everywhere, the dead. The burned and the injured. Flaming bodies staggering from ruin to ruin, the remains of half-people screaming out from piles of matter, reaching for the appendages that had been torn from them and thrown just beyond their grasp. The living trampled over them, screeching, screaming, looking for an escape. Babies covered by wet cloths, their parents clutching them as they ran through the black ash, an impenetrable fog of destruction. The streets burned, the buildings burned, the city burned. Ash in the lungs with every breath, as if the rage of the enemy was inside you, burning you from your heart. You looked up to see an absence where places should have been. Your beloved buildings burst into an explosion of bricks and matter and then were gone. In a moment everyone you knew was lost; you were alone. My memories are indistinct, indeed are just fragments of it all, but one image has returned to me time and time again, in my waking hours and in my sleep, and it is this: I turned my head to call for Gerhard, my colleague, who had fallen behind, and there I saw him, a human adult so quickly and completely consumed by fire that the remaining figure was that of a child. Around him, there was chaos, but both he and I stood still, trapped in that moment, and as I looked at him I could feel the sensation of being burned while living. I stayed there and watched Gerhard until I could be sure that there was no life left in his body. The ruin of it; the indignity. He fell, finally, and I wept as I ran away. I wept and I did not stop.

Twenty-five thousand died that night, and my beloved city, my grandmother's beloved city, was razed to the ground. To see such beauty removed from the earth changed me; the damage never left.

I fled, aided by the organisation's contacts and a fake identity conferred on me half by luck and half by a large portion of my savings. Leaving Dresden behind, I descended into the blackest depression. I knew my heart could never stand to see something so beautiful destroyed; not again.

After being made an exile from my own country, I made my way south. By manner of train I landed in India, in despair. Leaving one of civilisation's greatest cities, full of brilliance and romance and reason and art, and being forced to take residence in a country swollen with heat, marred by poverty and bereft of real culture, was the cruellest blow. Yet as the dust settled on the global political struggles, international travel became something of a suicide wish for those of us with German names. So in India I stayed, and though I confess that I hated that place from the minute I entered it, against my own wishes, I did my utmost to buoy my mood.

I have little to say about that country and the time I spent there, apart from to say that it gave me time to take stock of my situation, which was highly distressing. I had lost my career and my colleagues. My home, my adored city, had been cruelly and pointlessly destroyed. I have read since that the attack was one of the worst atrocities of the war, and I conclude the same. Money can be repaid, justice can be served, but destruction cannot be undone. Recall too that I was still a young man upon my exile; just twenty-six at the time of the bombing. Having emerged from the shadow of my grandmother's loss and found a social place in which I might flourish, I found that it was all taken from me in an instant. This threw me into a pit of despair from which I could not rouse myself. Bombay has many ways for the distressed to further damage themselves and I made use of all these methods. I scratched a living as best I could, tending to those with next to nothing, and I did so in a state of disembodied grief. It was only when I was chased out of my residence in that city, yet again a victim of bigotry and scientific misunderstanding, and forced to turn south once more, that I managed to put one foot in front of the other and begin walking forward again.

For all the disdain I have for that country and the deficiency of its populace, one thing did come of my years within. While looking for a place of solitude and security, I found myself in an institution for the study of one of the major religions of India, and it is here that I was able to gain a greater understanding of the precepts of Hinduism. At first, I must confess, the subject held no particular interest for me. The place was simply a fortress for a short period, one that offered sparse but regular meals, quiet reflection and, most of all, privacy. Yet out of respect for my hosts I began to pore over the many texts in the compound and found within them ideas that spoke not only to my own experiences but indeed to the revelations that I had come to through my research.

The dominant belief in the Indian subcontinent is that of the indestructibility of the soul. In the Hindu faith it is believed that the life force of an individual outlasts their physical, bodily expiration; atman, as they term the soul, is permanent, and is not party to the changing forces of the physical universe. This, of course, spoke greatly to my own beliefs on soul/body bifurcation. Being ignorant of the medical advances in the civilised world, the Hindus were as yet unfamiliar with the idea that the physical body itself could be rescued from the penalty of decay; rather their beliefs tended towards the concept of the removal of the soul into another body, a new body; they called this reincarnation. I knew that, had I my research in totality, I would have been able to prove to my hosts, kind and generous with information as they were, and curious as they were they for new learning (though, as I found to my own detriment, they were not so forgiving as their holy books would suggest them to be), that reincarnation does not necessarily have to include the introduction of a new body. Rather, if the human body could be saved from the degradation of burial and even modern embalming techniques, it was theoretically possible that a displaced soul could be returned to its home, its original body, with little to no negative effects—and could there continue on its life after the first death. It would be a reanimation, a welcoming back, rather than a reincarnation.

I will not waste any more pages of this text with further mention of that place. It would please me to be able to say that my time in India was instructive and informative, and I suppose in a certain way it was. However, I also felt the absolute degradation of my self-worth occurring at an alarming rate, and harboured a loneliness which I would never have assumed to be within my own emotional range. Looking back, I can see that from birth to my exile, I had always been amongst others. I had been pressed to my grandmother's breast, held within the comforting embrace of my young organisation, and then had become a firm and respected part of the medical community, a role for which I was well compensated and within which I thrived. On my departure from Europe, I had none of these things, not even a sympathetic ear; of my travails I could speak little, so strong was the prejudice against my own at that time. I took on several identities to protect myself, always shielding my true nationality and pretending instead to be Polish, and this caused a fragmentation of the sense of self that cannot be explained to those who have not felt it. I began to do more formal medical work for those in India who had the money to pay doctors, and given my Western heritage I was afforded a level of trust. In this way I was able to make a small income—though always speaking English. I spent hours reading aloud in my sparse room so as to lose any hint of an accent that might give away my nationality. I was a traitor to myself. And yet through these means I was eventually able to buy my way out of that godless place with a stated destination of the south of the United States. I pulled myself together, discarded any unnecessary accoutrements that the superstitious and largely irrational Hindus had gifted to me, and set my sights on America.

6.

Gabriela

My birthday is at the beginning of May, and I had my tenth birthday in nineteen fifty-nine, with a party that Papá insisted on throwing for me. Parties had always made me nervous; I would lose sleep in the anticipation of them for the week in advance, and when they happened, the excitement of having friends nearby and being spoiled quickly gave way to anxiety. Was everyone else having a good time? Had I talked to everyone equally? What if I became overwhelmed with giddiness and knocked over something valuable? Every party ended in my silent tears in the bathroom, and my mother would always know afterwards, though I put on my best smile, which in photographs is shown as a grimace. But gifts are often a gesture of what someone needs to give, rather than what the other person wants to receive. So we had a party. Papá invited all the children in my class, but half of them would not come, and their parents kept them inside the house in case my father went looking and asked why they hadn't shown up. But it was Papá they stayed away from, not us, because the children still talked to us every day at school, and we walked home together and stopped for ice cream, but that day there were only the children who lived on our street, whose houses were the same size as ours, and throughout the party Papá looked sad, and drank a lot, and had to be put to bed before the cake was cut. It was soon after that birthday that Luci and I, wet from running in the waves over the Malecón, heard the noise of crowds pushing through the thin streets of Havana Vieja. Papá said we should never follow big crowds, that nothing good ever came of that, but Luci took my hand and pulled me through the knees of the many people who then swept us along with them. It felt like carnavales, everyone smiling and excited and waving the flag. A young woman picked Luci up and took my hand, speaking to us quickly, like something was about to change our lives. It was so hot that day and the stink of sweat made me feel sick to my stomach, but the woman lifted Luci up onto her shoulders so she could breathe the clear afternoon air. I tugged at her leg and soon a young man picked me up and put me on his shoulders too so I could see. There were more Cubans there than I had ever seen before, more people even than I thought could ever fit in Havana. Where had they come from? It was as if they had all walked in from the sea to watch the man at the podium. He had a thick brown beard and wore the greens of the military, but the people around us shouted and cheered at everything he said. My fingers dug into the head of the man who had lifted me up, because he was dancing on his feet and I was afraid of falling off. I was becoming scared, but I looked at Luci and she was transfixed by the events, her face in a wide grin. I began to cry and pummelled on the man's head. He let me down and I pulled at the woman's waist until she dropped Luci down too. I dragged Luci out of the crowd and ran home, feeling in my blood that something was happening and that it was not good for us. For our family, at least.

We returned home to see my father crying into his glass. Mamá was in the living room but Papá was in the kitchen alone, and when he saw us he told us to get out, to leave him, to go and enjoy the city while we could. But Luci and I were too afraid to leave the house again, as even Luci could feel something shifting underneath us, could feel that the life we knew was at risk of crumbling down. There is something that happens to children when they see their parents cry. We had seen Mamá grieve for baby Ximena, but Papá was always solid, always keeping himself together. But now something had shattered him and we could not understand it. Luci and I went upstairs to try to distract Juan Antonio and Andrés, but we four simply sat on the floor, underneath the open window, listening to the euphoric cries from the crowds outside.

The next few years were confusing to us. The city was like a party at times, and when it was not, there was a hope in the air that everyone seemed to feel. But not us. The things that were simple before were now difficult; the store had no ice, our fridge was less full, the company we enjoyed was threadbare and shallow. These things meant little to us, but they seemed to chip away at who my father thought he was. The other children in our classes were happier, more grounded. Some got new shoes where they had bare feet before. They grew bold where they had been quiet. Everyone seemed to be getting bigger, but Papá, the largest flower in the yard for so long, was withering.

Our parents had always argued, but quickly and with passion, early in the mornings or late at night, or when Papá took us in his arms and promised us things we were not supposed to have. But for two whole years—and two years, for children, is a lifetime—the arguments never seemed to end. They once had their fights in whispers, but now they came out in sharp words at the kitchen table. They made us four children feel nervous at home, like anything we had to say should be kept quiet, and we should not tell our parents about the joy that all the other families seemed to feel, because we could not feel it in our house. Papá started to be careful with his money. He would turn away from people when he opened his wallet, and spent a lot of his time on the telephone speaking quickly and quietly. At night we told each other that Mamá and Papá were going to live in different houses, and that we would be split down the middle, with one girl and one boy going with our father and one girl and one boy going with Mamá. We spoke of these things as if they were the Sack Man coming to get us, and after the lights were turned off we could hear the boys cry.

Eighteen months after we heard the man with the beard telling his stories on the Plaza, we returned home from school to find Mamá packing all our belongings into boxes. Papá was on the phone shouting things and talking about money. In the early evening a truck came with several men and between them they dragged out the grand piano, scratching it on the doorways. Papá yelled because they were not careful; they stumbled and a leg smashed against the wall, almost coming off completely. The piano was pushed into the back of the truck and driven away without even some plastic thrown over to preserve the top. Papá watched it go. He lit a cigarette and mumbled, almost too low to hear, 'Even the dead are given the dignity of a sheet.' Two weeks after the piano was taken, it was us children being packed up, as if we were belongings too. Papá was babbling about Florida, how Florida was just like Havana, how Florida was full of Latinos.

Key West: he said the name in English. 'It's just Cayo Hueso. Where the bones fell. Spanish, see, Spanish underneath it all. It is built on Latinos. It will be even more home than this dying place.'

Unlike the poor piano, we did not go on a truck. We left Havana on a boat for America. The piano, sword-chipped and water-swollen, stayed on the island.

On the day we left, Luciana was the first one awake. She washed, dressed and fed herself ready for her coming ordeal, then took her place on the kitchen floor and waited for us all to find her. There was nothing else in the room, just a few bowls and the crumbs of our store cupboards. She was the only piece of furniture left. I woke soon after and went straight to Luci's room, sure that she would be making a fuss in some way, and when I found her bed empty I ran straight down the stairs. She said nothing when she saw me; she did not have to. The cold in my veins struck and I sat down on the bottom stair, unable to take my eyes off her but unable to make anything else happen. In my head, they might leave her; if God listened to us once again he might make Mamá and Papá go, leave the house and leave silly Luci sitting there all alone, just like she wanted. I prayed silently: please, please, no. Close your ears and turn away this time.

Papá was up before Mamá. He padded downstairs looking as if he had barely slept, clutching the only coffee cup that hadn't been packed; it was still stained from the day before. He looked at Luciana only once then ignored her completely, pulling the coffee from the empty cupboard and looking out into the garden instead. When Mamá came down, she only looked exhausted by what she saw, and then joined my father at the window. We ate, we washed, we packed the last of our belongings into boxes and bags while Luci sat in the middle of the floor. When the car arrived, we rushed to fill it, the boys with their lips wobbling though they tried to keep them still, and me telling stories so that I might not think about what was happening. Papá yelled for Luci. She did not come. He said to come immediately or he would leave her in Cuba. She did not come. He yelled and we could all hear the cigar smoke in his voice, but still she did not come. In that moment, I saw what Papá was growing into: an old and worn-down man, his lungs damaged, his anger tired and his power almost gone. He took the suitcases out to the car and demanded we all go ahead. We got into the car and sat in silence for fifteen minutes. None of us dared to breathe in case we missed a noise. Andrés began to softly cry, but no sound came from the house. There was no shouting or screaming or crying or crashing. It was the longest fifteen minutes of my whole life.

Papá came out of the house and slammed the door behind him. He had Luciana over his shoulder, as if he were a young man again and she was a baby, and her face was angry and red. He did not put her into the back of the car with the rest of us but instead put her on his knee in the front passenger seat like she might try to jump out, like she might roll right out of the back of the car and stay in the street in Havana. I prayed for Papá to hold on to her tight, for the fabric of my family to hold tight. We did not speak again until we were on the ferry, and still all the way to Florida Papá did not let Luci out of his sight.

It was seven hours across to America. Just seven hours to change who we were entirely. As we neared that new country Luci slept, still red and with her face all covered in rage. I slipped under Papá's arm while he looked out at the dying afternoon and asked him why we had to go to America. He said we were leaving Cuba because Mamá needed ice for her daiquiris; no woman could live in so hot a city without her ice.

7.

Wilhelm

It came to pass that the only way to reach the United States would involve my return to Europe, a fact that filled me with a most intense and crippling type of fear. For this reason, even after my intention was set, my journey to America stalled by several months. I practised my English accent daily, listening to the more highly educated Indians to try and ape the Cambridge inflections which they had picked up when they were at university in England. It also gave me time to ensure that I had purchased the best alternative passport that I could afford—a Polish forgery with a different name and all the necessary papers to guarantee I would be allowed to reside in America.

When the day came to begin my travels, in the spring of nineteen forty-nine, I was beset by panic attacks of such severity that I had to take to drink and other self-administered medications to force myself onto the trains. The closer we came to Europe, the worse my paroxysms became, and I cannot bring myself to speak of the terror I felt upon making my way to Holland, from where the ship was to set sail. Indeed, my memories of this time are mostly lost, and for that, at least, I am thankful.

I arrived in Rotterdam within hours of the ship's departure, which allowed me to board without delay. I shut myself in my cabin and opened the door only for the inspection of papers until the ship had left the harbour, and for the first few days of the crossing I was excruciatingly ill, which I can only attribute to the stress of the journey thus far (although the culinary options coming through the Middle East, of which I consumed mercifully little, could also have had some bearing on my situation). The liner on which I was able to cross the Atlantic was scheduled to stop in Cuba, a country in which I had no interest at all. From there, however, I knew that I would be able to take a ferry to Miami, my chosen destination. I had grown accustomed to the warm climate of the Indian subcontinent and felt that the humid nature of Florida would aid in my emotional recovery. The scheduled stop did mean that there were many passengers from the Mediterranean, and though I mostly kept to my own business during the long journey, terrified of finding passengers who harboured an aggressive bias against me due to the fact of my birthland, I allowed myself short breaks from my cabin, during which, from beneath the brim of my hat, I could steal glances at the women around me, teasing myself that I might recognise the one from my dreams.

Upon arriving in Havana, we found that the entire city was in the grip of some sort of festival. Again, due to my own paralysing fear of being discovered a German and therefore subjected to the worst type of prejudice, I remained away from prying eyes for the few hours before I could board my ferry onwards. However, I felt a magnetism towards the people of Cuba which at the time I could not account for, but which now makes perfect sense. The city itself was an explosion of life. On every wooden balcony—there were several storeys on each building—were young children, mothers, grandmothers straining to see the goings-on below. Music, which was at once brash, irritating and enlivening, poured out of every slum, every corner store, every bar and restaurant—all of which, in turn, spilled out onto the streets. The colours of the place were hypnotic; far from the stoic and respectable greys of Western

83

Europe, brightness spilled from every available window and hand, and draped around every body. The women in that carnival were like nymphs, impossible to look away from, and they exuded a kind of magnetism that forced the physical body to move close to them; for several too-brief hours I was unable to tear myself away from their presence, and only left when it became clear that I would miss my onward journey otherwise. Closer to the seafront, there were large bands playing music, huge American-style cars which seemed at once to be a frivolous masculine pretence and yet at the same time impressive, and an endless array of feminine creatures decked in intricate outfits in which they swayed and waved and sashayed and coquettishly motioned to the men in the crowds. When the time came to start my onward journey, it was an effort to tear my eyes away from them. They possessed magic.

In the nineteen fifties America was a fascinating place to land. The country was experiencing a post-war economic boom, and it appeared to me that I had settled in the land of plenty—a feeling that was only sharpened by my recent tribulations in the destitution of India. On the advice of fellow passengers, I made my way without delay to Key West and quickly found lodgings in a house just out of town. Florida was very unlike I had imagined it would be; the presence of palm trees astounded my expectations, and as I had never before resided so close to the sea, I began to take long walks in the early morning along the beach, before the sun-seekers and families descended on the sand and brought it to life with radios, picnics and their incessant squawking. Americans in general seemed unconcerned with the fate of their brothers and sisters across the Atlantic; if Europe, when I left it, was a cadaver being consumed by flies, America was a baby, coddled and washed and full of bright-eyed promise. The sea air did much to banish the dust of Dresden's demise from my lungs and my soul, but more than that, the half-day in Havana had imbued me with a new energy. The infectious quality of the Americans truly affected me; I too felt as if I could begin anew and achieve great things.

Within weeks of settling in Key West I came to the realisation that there was a mask on my person that was restricting my comfort. There is a rare condition known as *calcific constrictive pericarditis*, in which the lining of the heart hardens and becomes almost solid; this prevents the heart from being able to beat, and turns the sufferer slowly grey and exhausted. My new identity, taken on to protect me, was now solidifying around me, and I was greying. To all in my new home, I was not Wilhelm von Tore; I was a Polish dentist with a name befitting that personality, and this was reflected in my papers. It came to feel like a constricting presence about me, a calcified lining constricting my ability to live in any real, blood-flushed sense. Truly, I realised, there is nothing more important to a man than his own name; to remove it from a person is to erase him, to state that he has no enduring identity in the world, to reduce him to a thing. I made efforts to contact some of my remaining acquaintances in my mother country, mostly former colleagues, and after a difficult period of administrative struggling, I was able to arrange the sale of some of the more valuable items still in my legal possession, in storage in Germany, and set up a system to have the resulting currency transferred to my new American bank account monthly, though this process was far from straightforward. In letters from colleagues in Dresden I heard tales of the city's depression and their own rejection from society, and though a longing for home had been present in my chest since the ship set sail across the Atlantic, I knew then that I had made the correct choice. No doubt many of my friends wished they had done the same.

With money reaching me from Germany, I was able to settle my situation, retaining my false identity as a Polish national but soon purchasing a new, higher quality Polish passport with my own name. I could again be Wilhelm von Tore, but I would never again be a German. The final action I undertook with my former name was to purchase for myself a small amount of scientific equipment. I was even able to have some specialist pieces shipped directly from Europe, though this was at huge expense, and constituted a tiny fraction of what I had once had to work with. Events shortly afterwards kept me from setting up a home laboratory, but having such items in my possession allowed for the possibility of engaging in my own science at some future time, and for this I was very grateful.

Of course, a foreigner is never truly a full citizen in his adopted country, no matter how much liberal voices like to claim otherwise. For my part I was happy to prove my worth, as an outsider must. To this end I took up a menial medical job at the local hospital, despite the effect this had on my sense of self, and over the next few years I took any available opportunity to exhibit my capabilities and gain a professional standing. I took on thankless tasks in order to suggest, at the right time, a potential solution to a challenge that had arisen. I could not speak of my pre-war and wartime work, nor the findings that had arisen, but in this way I was able to show that I had a preternatural ability for someone of my position, and was promoted, eventually, to the role of radiologic technologist. This, of course, was still far, far below my abilities and was unchallenging to say the least, meaning that my days were often unsatisfactory and long; I felt it necessary to impress upon my superiors that I had a work ethic outstretching that of my native peers. Yet I was grateful to be in a medical environment again, and I had faith that after a period of time, I would be given the means to continue my former experimentation. In addition, owing to the peculiarities in the healthcare system of that country, it was a lucrative career, and I was quickly able to attain an enviable wage. As I was not willing to risk my settled life through excessive socialisation—and, truth be told, because my opinion of others remained low—I kept largely to myself outside of work hours, maintaining the necessary civility with my landlady and my neighbours, who would make veiled comments about the fate of Europe and America's inflated role in it whenever they could.

The one event that marred an otherwise peaceful and happy period of my life was one precipitated by a grudge held against me by my landlady. She claimed to be in possession of incriminating documents that had been mailed to me. However, by American law it was illegal for her to be in possession of anything sent to me via the US Mail. And yet it was true that these documents would show that my papers were not legitimate, and this could therefore threaten my continued presence in America.

To this end, I met and married a local woman, Felicia Morgan, after a short courtship. As my personal income was more than adequate at this time, I was able to establish us as man and wife in a small house in the centre of Key West. All of this I did against my natural wish to stay away from the inhabitants of the area, because I am acutely aware that a young wife needs the society of others, or she will become lonely. As previously mentioned, the organisations I belonged to in my teenage years put a great value on family and the duty one has to one's spouse, so to claim that I did not consider these things would be erroneous and untrue. Upon the fact of our marriage, I began to file the necessary paperwork to gain permanent residency and the right to work; again, I used my own name, clinging to it as if it were my very existence, but used my Polish passport rather than my own, which I had burned some months before, feeling like a traitor to my country and weeping with the shame of it. To her credit, my wife signed all the papers I asked her to, and sponsored my application when it was needed. Against my wishes, however, Felicia quickly became pregnant with first one daughter, Cecilia, and then, not a year after her birth, again with the second, Amy (here I should clarify: these were names bestowed on the infants by my wife. I was not consulted in this decision-making process, and in her post-natal neuroses Felicia became quite incensed at the suggestion that these names, which she claimed to have chosen years before, may not be suitable. While my wife remained in the hospital following the births, both of which were relatively traumatic, I registered the girls instead with German given names, allowing my wife's choices to be their second names—hence, their legal names are Irma Cecilia and Herta Amy). Despite my reticence towards the pregnancies, I found parenthood to be acceptable; I returned from work to find my daughters fed and bathed, and often spent a considerably satisfying hour or so with them in the warm Florida evenings, walking in the garden with a child on my shoulder. That part of my German identity should be so inarguably set within America was a secret pleasure, buried deep within the more acceptable enjoyment I took in my children. Though my tolerance for Felicia soon waned, I continued to provide a secure home life for my wife and her children and was able, through my job at the hospital, to ensure that the best medical care was extended to them, despite the fact that my wife, though she was older than me and towards the end of her natural youth, had never thought to purchase insurance for herself. She demanded I take a greater role in the family, yet did not seem to appreciate that my work was the only thing providing for us all; I of course did not mention the hours I spent in the hospital of my own accord. I quickly grew to find Felicia's company intolerable, and she began to resent my necessary absences for work, my long nights in the laboratory, the way my attention wandered to greater things than the local gossip or the purchasing of new furniture for the home. Of course, when one's mind is consumed with attempts to further one's knowledge, there is little time to spend cooing over messy toddlers and attending to the hysterical accusations of women.

After little more than two years since my youngest daughter's birth, I moved out of the house and away from Felicia and our children. I retained, however, the work permit I had been able to gain after our marriage, and was therefore an American citizen. I could not be removed.

8.

Gabriela

America in the flesh was so different to the America we had seen on our television. As the ferry reached its destination, there was no Statue of Liberty to welcome us; Andrés was inconsolable about it. There was, however, a stretch of beach, so long and so familiar that I asked Papá if the boat had turned around and taken us back to Havana Bay. He ignored me. He was still hanging on to Luciana's hand and watching her every move. But we steered right by the beach and kept going, to a place full of cranes and enormous metal boxes. When we drove off the ferry, a strange man met us at the marina and took Mamá, Juan Antonio and me into his car with all of our bags. Papá, Luci and Andrés stayed in my father's car. I started to cry quietly as we drove through the streets of Miami— Papá said it was Miami, a city—for some of the buildings were so big they felt dangerous, and the streets were so straight, like it had been made on squared paper, and it was all wrong and overwhelmingly unfamiliar. Yet I was glad for the heat of the sun through the window, and pressed my forehead to it so I could pretend I was still at home.

We were taken first to a boarding house, where we stayed for two weeks with all of our bags still packed, wearing the same three outfits that Mamá washed at the end of the day, leaving them to dry in the sun. We were all packed into one large room, our parents sleeping on the floor while we slept on the bed. Papá took us out each morning to walk for hours and hours through the streets of our new 'home country'. He was feeling sad and guilty; you could tell because he bought us treats so sweet they burned away the inside of our cheeks, forced so many Cokes down us we all felt sick by the time we got back to the boarding house. Mamá would send us to bed and turn off the lights because she was angry with Papá and wanted to lie angrily in the dark instead of yelling, so we spent the nights holding our stomachs and praying to feel better, while the voices on the street spoke a language we couldn't understand. I asked Luci if the Lord spoke English in America. She said not to be so silly. There were big posters everywhere in Miami, and no music at all. The food was different, it was heavier and more brightly coloured, and for days after we arrived Luci was ill, greedy on the candies that Papá gave her and then holding herself and moaning the rest of the day, unable to eat proper meals. She would not even look at the plates put in front of her.

Papá, though, he thought it was heaven. He felt guilty because of Mamá's feelings, and because we were in such different circumstances to what we'd had at home—but it was temporary. He kept saying this over and over: it is temporary, mis pequeños, and soon we'll have a bigger and better house than we ever had before. When I clung to him and cried and begged him to go home, he took me out into the street and picked me up in his arms for the first time in years, for he always said I had grown too mature.

'Look, my little zunzuncita, don't you see that other Cubanos are here?'

I opened my eyes at that and saw them.

'Look at the cars, straight from the streets of Havana. Palm trees and the same blue up above. The sand, it will be hot underneath your soles, and when the rain comes you'll feel just as wet. See this man?'

Walking by us was a man in an expensive suit and a hat that matched. He had a thick gold watch on his wrist and carried a bag made of leather; you could smell it as he passed by.

'Just watch him.'

I sat on Papá's bent knee and he kept me facing the right way. The man stopped and bought a newspaper, then went to his car, which was shiny and large with no top and looked like it had come from space. It was new, that was obvious, and Papá kept watch until the car turned around the corner and out of sight. He remembered he was talking to me.

'One day, querida, your Papá will be this man. Or you will marry this man. Here, there is opportunity. This is just like home—but better. You will see it soon enough.'

Papá, in fact, could not help but say all the ways that it was better. Buying groceries, he picked up every version of every food, saying: what choice, what choice! If we complained about wanting empanadas he took us for sandwiches, told us we could pick anything to go in it—but we always ordered the Cuban, and were disappointed when it came.

In truth, Luciana never liked America. All the children of our family were at difficult ages to move to another country, and none of us spoke English when we arrived. Why would we have needed to learn, before? Papá did not want to think that his future was as an immigrant, but, being practical for once in his life, had been secretly learning the basics. My mother didn't have the language, not really, and never would. Beyond what she needed to get by in this new alien world when she was forced to interact with it, she spoke as she always had. With Mamá it was always Spanish.

That first Sunday, Papá told us to put on our best clothes and clean shoes—forgetting, I think, that none of Luci's shoes were shiny, because she wore even her Sunday pair to run around in the yard, and found the kind of stains that will never come clean. He took us to a mixed church near our temporary lodgings, where there were some other Cuban people, but not that many. We did as Papá requested and smiled at everyone, talked with the older ladies and other children who stared at us. But after the service and a limited amount of socialising, everyone went to their own homes and closed their front doors. My father had shaken hands with many people and had put his business card into the pockets and palms of other Cubanos, but still they went away and closed their doors and we were left smiling in the street like billboards. We walked back to our strange new house in silence, my mother and father behind us.

'They will get used to us,' said Papá in a low voice. 'They will open up. We are new.'

'Perhaps the gusanos aren't as friendly as you think, my—'

I spun around on hearing the smack. Mamá was already holding her face, my father red and dropping to his knees. He evoked all the saints in his desperation for forgiveness and she, without shedding a tear, simply remained half bent over and holding her cheek, the cheek that was red and angry, looking at her husband with big wide eyes, refusing to move from the picture of his guilt. She made him look as he begged. He held her calves, he clutched at her waist, he held his own stomach like he was going to faint in a puddle on the ground. Luci, Andrés, Juan Antonio—none of us moved. This family was not ours; we were not who we used to be, in this new place with these new things happening. Eventually Mamá left my father on his knees, took Luci's hand and then mine, and told Andrés and Juan Antonio to come along because we were going back to our cursed new house. We turned around and went with her and did not look back. Tentatively, Luci asked if she was okay.

'Your father has hurt himself.' It was all she would say on the subject.

Soon we were allowed to move into a house that had been purchased for us, Papá said, with his money before we had arrived. We packed our bags into Papá's old car and drove for a long time, on a road that skimmed over the top of the ocean—

like Jesus, Luci said, and got a slap from the front seat. I pressed my face against the window (safely closed) and tried to look for creatures underneath, but the water was so blue my eyes started to show nothing but a strange black mass. The further we drove, the happier I felt; we went through islands that looked more and more like Cuba, and I crossed my fingers that we would drive all the way home and forget we ever left. But we didn't go that far; we only made it to Key West.

Papá was trying so hard to make America an improved version of Cuba, in our eyes at least, so this house was a big one, much larger than the one we had in Havana. Each of us had a more spacious room than the one we'd had back home. The backyard was very big and very, very green, and there was a fence around the outside of it to make sure no one could come in. He even bought a new grand piano for Mamá, and it came on a big truck, but it was so badly scratched it was more brown than black, like a badly kept relic. Mamá told them to take it away, but my father slammed his hand on the door frame and said the piano had to come inside. They put it down in one of the empty rooms. No one played it, no one touched it, no one even pressed a key. The house was in a Cuban neighbourhood, which gave Mamá hope, but music did not play from the windows, and the buildings were not painted, and although Papá would do his best to start the parties that he'd always enjoyed, the Cubanos kept their heads down, as immigrants do. As Tita used to say: you can put rum, sugar, soda, lime and mint into a glass, but still it will not be a mojito.

You would think that Mamá had found a whole new God on the way to America. She had hardly put her bags in the house before she was out looking for the nearest church—perhaps to rid herself of the bad experience in the last one, where no one wanted us. She was damp with sweat and she needed to eat but out she went, leaving all of us in our new home, surrounded by unpacked luggage and a lot of dirt and dust. When she found the church, a basilica of medium size, she was glad to see a few Cubans there even in the daytime, good Catholics who would be there every Sunday like her. She stayed a while and prayed for her new life, for her baby Ximena, for the people she had left behind. After her prayers she discovered something about the church that made her so excited she ran home to tell us, and in that moment you might have believed she was almost happy to be in America.

The following Sunday we were all dressed up in our very best clothes, our hair brushed and our shoes tight on our feet, which seemed to have grown a size or two on the ferry from the island. Mamá, having noticed that all the American ladies wore hats in church, had taken money from Papá's wallet and bought herself a white hat with a wide brim, and that morning she spent an hour gathering up all her thick, Cuban hair into a bun and making sure no strands would escape. As much as she tried, the hat would not stay on the back of that mass of tamed curls, so she gave me a quarter and had me run to one of the neighbour's houses to borrow a hat pin. She knelt on the floor and held the hat in place while I, with shaking fingers, stabbed it though the white material and in through her hair. She didn't flinch once; she kissed my hands afterwards and told me I'd done a good job. The hat stayed in place, her shameful, wild hair hidden, the yellowed fake pearl of the pin sitting against the white material and making Mamá look older than she was. Luci had bows in her hair and a white dress that she pulled at, as if trying to make the outfit unravel from the knees upwards. Mamá slapped Luci's hands away and wiped dust from the hem of her skirt. Next to Luci I was pristine, and even the boys were walking straight and upright, because all they ever wanted was to make Mamá happy.

Everyone in the church watched us throughout the ceremony, noticing that we did not know the English words to their songs. But they smiled, at least. Mamá was radiant, though I saw a small trail of dried blood behind her ear, where I must have stabbed her with the pin enough to pierce her scalp. She kept us there kneeling and praying until most others had gone (Andrés and Juan Antonio were playing a secret punching game, each with one eye open), then grabbed me and Luci by the wrists and took us to the front. We kneeled beside her and she pointed, barely lifting her hand, to a box on top of a plinth at the very back of the church.

'In there, mis cariños, is a holy relic. It is a bone from St Nicholas himself, a bone from his smallest finger. It is blessed by God.'

She looked to me and I smiled my most impressed smile, my eyes watering with the intensity of it. She looked to Luci, who was picking at her dress.

'Luciana, we're blessed to have been brought here. Do you know what this means?'

'No, Mamá.'

'He is the saint of children. It means our life here will be watched over. He sits beside Ximena in heaven, I'm sure of it. This is a holy place. You must act as if God is watching always, and Ximena too. Be your best here, mis cariños, and he will always hear your prayers.'

We all knew that Mamá's true prayers were for us to go back to Cuba. But bone or no bone, there was no going home.

*

It was on the streets of Key West that Luci, Andrés, Juan Antonio and I became young adults. From the moment we stepped on American ground we were no longer children. We had responsibilities; we had to work hard to be as good as the American kids, that's what Papá kept saying. 'America loves people who work hard. So work hard.' The four of us spent months in English class with an angry woman called Mrs Williams who did not speak a word of Spanish and hated if we spoke it in her home, which was decorated in white that had turned grey-yellow because she smoked cigarettes every second of the day. She spoke sentences and we repeated them, making the sounds more or less correctly but having no idea what they meant.

'My name is Juan.'

'My mother takes in sewing.'

'My father is a doorman.'

'My sister is a camel.'

Luci leaned over to slap the back of Juan Antonio's head, only to find herself hit on the knuckles by Mrs Williams. One for each, no matter who did the name-calling. If she heard you whispering, it was the knuckles. If you got it wrong, it was the knuckles. We learned in her class to be quiet unless we were told to speak and then only to say what words had been given to us—nothing more.

Our hatred of Mrs Williams was the only thing that made us try hard with English, and though we learned little in her horrible home we practised together every day, watching cartoons and reading comics and listening to the radio. When Papá had a good month, he took us to see films, sitting in cinemas with fathers in their neat hats, the children loudly chewing candies, every seat full around us, just another family in the dark, and we re-enacted the scenes for days afterwards, being the animated little dogs or the monkey or sometimes the adults, swaggering along with our hips forward and sending our eyebrows so high in feigned surprise they might have fallen off our faces. The easiest way to speak English, to get the right inflections and sounds, was to do it in the voices of the people we'd seen on screen, so for a month Luci and I would only speak our new language in the voice of Hayley Mills from *The Parent Trap*, two Cuban girls running around Florida speaking in cut-glass English accents. Soon enough we could pass basic English tests and were sent to the American school. No more Mrs Williams. Luci spoke so well; in honesty I was jealous of her. We had missed almost a year of schooling, but we did not have to be kept back at all, as our general standard of education was high; at least this is what was written on the reports we took home to our parents, who were pleased.

After our first day of class, Luci came home and cut her hair again, just as she had to spite Tita—but this time, it was so short it barely covered her ears. She looked beautiful, refreshed, and finally freed from the weight of expectation. Mamá was horrified, but Luci calmed her rage by saying that it was what all the American girls were doing, and she just had to fit in. While they argued I threw the scissors in the garbage bin outside.

My father had not calculated that doing business in America would be more difficult than back home. Perhaps he forgot that in Havana he was a man everybody knew, but to Florida he was a stranger. He spent so much money trying to make us happy that soon there was not much left. The house was full and the piano was new and we all had clothes and furniture and even some pictures up on the walls, but suddenly there was worry everywhere. When he finally 'made some friends', Papá bought an even bigger TV than the one we'd had in Havana and watched it in the evenings when he came back from work. He made cigars in the daytime; he rolled the Cubanos. He said it was a good way to make money quickly. Life in America was expensive, with four growing children to clothe and dress and feed and educate. Mamá began to shop at the discount grocery stores, and after a while stopped bringing home the yuca and chicharrón that she had been buying from the special stores nearby. Home was just that little further away.

In school, we became more like Americans. We stopped listening to music from the island, except that which Mamá played quietly in her room, and instead we got used to the radio, saying all the things they were saying just for the practice, and forcing ourselves to like the songs they played. Juan Antonio grew big in the shoulders and became Anthony outside of the house, though he would always be called by his full Sunday name at home. They put him into sports, because he would push people around but not hurt them, and Andrés spent so much time at the beach he eventually picked up a surfboard, though he was always skinny in the hips and looked more like a swimmer. On the pitch and in the water the boys were around the gringos, made bonds with the gringos, and so they were invited to parties with the gringos, to the big houses and in the brand-new cars. This made life easier for them in a way it was not for Luci and me, but we weren't angry at them. They were accepted, and Mamá was happy to see it. But even though they fit in at school, they both hated to study; it was not unusual either to find Luci skipping class to go to the beach with Andrés. Me, I stayed close to Mamá, my hands in dough, my hips next to hers. English soon was a secret language for us kids, because we knew if we spoke it fast and under our breath Mamá would never understand, so we used it more and more, and Mamá spoke less and less. Still, she dragged us to church every Sunday, trying to make friends with the other Cuban ladies, but never actually talking to anyone but us.

With Juan Antonio playing his games and Andrés in the water, it was often just Luci and me walking the streets and going to movies. There was no choice but to be like the others; we could see that the other children from different countries were not allowed in unless they worked hard to be the same as the American kids. We walked like those girls and styled our hair like those girls and soon we were going for milkshakes and being invited to parties, and every time we lost a Cuban word and learned a new American one Mamá walked to church and prayed to that old dead finger and Papá patted us on the head and told us we were doing well. All their children spending time with Yankees; soon we would stop being Cuban at all.

One day Mamá came back from church bothered, as if she had heard something that she didn't like. She called Luci over to her; Luci, who was growing like sugar cane, tall and stringy, with none of Tita's hips or the hair that had hung thinly from her temples.

'Luciana del Carmen, what is happening to you? You are becoming more boy than girl every day. This hair, all salt from the ocean and your knees always bleeding from the rocks. Why can't you be more like Gabi?'

Luci looked at me and we both laughed. Mamá did not. She took a comb out of a drawer and began to tug through the short, knotted strands of Luci's sea-tangled hair.

'No boy will want to marry you if you look like an animal, Luciana del Carmen. God sends husbands for good girls who look after themselves. Remember all the things Tita used to tell you. We'll pray to St Nicholas for a man who does not mind a salty girl.'

But Luci had learned she did not need to argue. She was no longer a small child; we were teenagers now and had the freedom of the streets with a new language to speak. She could nod and say *yes, Mamá, of course I will*, but she would do exactly what she wished. She hid a smile despite the comb on her scalp, because the boys had already come by for both of us, and we were ready to hold hands with young men whose palms were sweating, and to see what girls got up to in the back of their cars.

But as we became like the yumas, Luciana became sick in the soul. She said that the dryness of the climate was too much; she said that it was too quiet; she said that the air was tight and full of smoke, that the cigarettes caught in her throat, that the food could not feed her body. Mamá was right about one thing; even though we had all the food in the world, and even though she ate more than Andrés, Juan Antonio and me put together, Luciana stopped growing, and when she turned fourteen, fifteen, sixteen, she still could have passed for years younger. Her beauty matured but her body remained small, all arms and legs and eyes too big for her head. Luci, my little tree frog.

9.

Wilhelm

Upon my departure from the house I shared with Felicia, I took a room in a small boarding house, dismayed to be yet again in a place where I could not properly unpack all of my research equipment (on the event of my proposal to Felicia I had taken all the laboratory materials I had managed to procure and placed them into secure storage). The urge to science is often described as an itch, but I think of it more as a will towards greatness, the drive to continue the forward motion of discovery, and without it one can feel bereft. Yet to consider setting up a laboratory in the cramped conditions of my post-marriage room would be folly at best, and the landlord, a corpulent man with a drinking problem, could simply not be trusted.

With my salary from the hospital and the steady pension from overseas, I had soon saved enough money to purchase a small piece of land on the east of Key West, a little way from prying neighbours. My living costs were low, as I had never taken to expensive dining and subsisted largely on the sparse diet that Oma had favoured before me, and so the vast majority of my income could be put towards establishing a residence in which I could feel comfortable. A number of large salt ponds in the east of the island had recently been filled in and this area, though soon to grow, was relatively sparsely populated. The estate agent who facilitated the purchase (at considerable financial benefit to himself, it must be noted) worked hard to impress upon me the upscale nature of the area, and mentioned several times that amongst Key West's more notable residents were a number of artists, including Ernest Hemingway and Tennessee Williams. I put an end to his boasting by telling him I considered American popular culture to be coarse, and had him deduct a significant amount from the asking price. Thus settled, I erected a fence around all four sides of the land and built a driveway for the wide, American-style vehicle I had procured at a discount rate from another European making his way to South America. By introducing this gentleman to certain individuals who had facilitated my own entry into the country, I was able to enter into a deal that would guarantee me another income stream, this time quarterly from South America. I took precautions to ensure that the deal would be honoured, and it was.

The construction of a modest but entirely satisfactory home was at this point well within my means, and I undertook this work immediately, with the help of local labourers who constantly tried to convince me that I owed them more money than I did. Before the home was completed, I was forced to dismiss the workers and finish the construction myself; unfortunately, an altercation with my landlady and several of my neighbours also occurred around this time and I was forced to move into my home before it was ready, which led to several months of difficulty. Thankfully, the move occurred in late spring, and by the middle of summer my home was completed. Owing to a certain notoriety in some areas of Key West, mostly stoked by the misplaced rage of my former neighbours, I could not place my name above the door. However, inside, it was truly mine.

I set about turning this home, finally, into my own laboratory. I ordered book after book, steadfastly replacing the veritable library that I had abandoned in Germany—though a number of these books were not available in English translation, and I was suffering from a paranoia at the time which kept me from ordering anything in German. To fill this void I purchased a number of titles by the likes of Gorky and Krasin, whose work, preceding mine, also led them to the belief that human death could indeed be transcended through the harnessing of science and technology. The Russians believed, as is their romantic wont, that their work around mortality might point the inhabitants of the planet towards a new truth. Emboldened anew by this consideration, I built a working home. I took my things out of their safe storage areas, working under the cover of night so that the members of my new community were not alerted to the presence of valuable materials and unwieldy equipment, and though this made the moving onerous, I was satisfied that my belongings would remain secure in my home. I also set about building some of my own equipment; I have some skill in the realms of engineering and electrics as well as within medical practice, and I spent day and night putting together machines that might help me continue my research.

I was, at this time, able to arrange for the delivery of some of my notes and papers around my former research. Upon the swift dissolution of Dr Magnussen's laboratory, a huge amount of paperwork had been placed into covert storage, and though it took months of phone calls and a large amount of money, I was able to have my own files sent to America via boat, putting me in direct contact with a number of distinctly undesirable characters. As I unpacked these papers I was relieved to find that they had in fact survived the transatlantic trip with only a little water damage, owing perhaps to the conditions aboard the ship or the humid conditions in Key West. My first task was to make copies of all these notes and findings, a job which I unfortunately could not entrust to a local typist, given the very sensitive nature of the research. However, this did have the agreeable effect of familiarising me with the content of my writings again, and I allowed a very real sense of pride to sweep over me. No matter what had happened in Europe, no one could look at my life's work thus far and tell me it had been wasted. I had done work that enhanced the state of humans in the world and would continue to do so. It was inarguable.

I passed my days without the fear of deportation; I was legally established in the country and now owned my own home. I relaxed into my new lifestyle and took up once again the research that had formed my most fierce interest. As I grew more accustomed to my new locale and the generous perspective of the recent immigrant wore off, however, I began to notice the dark underbelly hidden beneath the sanitised facade of Key West. Increasingly, my trips to buy food and other necessities would bring me into contact with my neighbours. While new buildings and freshly painted business entrances gave the impression of prosperity, many families, including those long-time inhabitants of the island, had little in the way of money and their manners belied their deprived upbringings. Though many of its residents parroted the estate agent's boasts, there was little evidence of either Williams or Hemingway, despite the local beggars' habit of pointing at any building and saying it was 'home to a famous writer' in order to force a donation from your hand. Certain parts of the island held the permanent and pervasive stink of sea creatures from the mooring of the shrimp boats, and worst of all, there came upon the area a strong influx of immigrants from Europe, most notably a large community of Poles, whose determination to speak their dog-Russian meant that language increasingly polluted the streets. Incapable of properly establishing themselves in the country or unwilling to do so, they swarmed together and purchased homes next to each other, forcing out American families and creating ghettos of foreigners into which few Americans would walk. I found myself instinctively avoiding establishments where they might gather, yet my work at the hospital meant that I was known to many in Key West as a Polish immigrant, and the gossiping mouths of the local women led many of the Poles to regard me as one of their own. Where our paths crossed, I could hardly avoid being accosted in a language I did not speak and did not wish to hear. As the ghettos shifted and grew, I marked those neighbourhoods as out of bounds on my excursions, and if a Polish family entered an establishment in which I was eating or purchasing goods, I would leave; it was easy to identify them from their shabby dress, their facial structures, and their excessively loud manner of communicating.

However, there was one place where I could do little to keep myself from these newcomers. As they encroached further into Key West they, of course, began to appear in the hospital, often seeking treatment despite having no way to pay their bills. Yet my instructions were not to investigate finances; I was there to treat, and so I did.

I endured perhaps a dozen of these interactions without major incident, only a growing sense of displeasure and disgust at their very manner of being. Yet on a September Tuesday in nineteen sixty-eight, a young family came into my acquaintance: a mother, father and a small boy who had 'fallen from his bed' and broken his femur. The boy himself was stunned and quiet, as was the timid mother, but the father, dark-eyed and with several teeth missing, impressed himself upon me from the moment he entered, shaking my hand with his hairy paw and slapping me hard on the shoulder as if we were old friends. He kept his hands on me while blabbering in that awful language, fluids flying from his mouth and onto my equipment, diverting my attention from the injured child at hand. I removed myself from his grasp and bade him sit down, in English. Unsure, he sat, and let me take his son; after a moment of silence he started again, elbows at his knees, leaning so far into my workspace that I could smell his unwashed mouth. I ignored him and spoke to the child in English, of which he appeared to have a basic understanding, but despite myself I could feel the colour rising in my cheeks, my body growing hot. The man's questions remained unanswered and I would not meet his gaze; in English I told the son to pass my words on to his father, and he translated. The father again grabbed my shoulder roughly, this time turning me physically towards him and away from his ailing child. His saliva-flecked lips were cracked and red, and his accent so thick that he would always be an immigrant.

'But you are from Poland, no?'

I went back to my work, ignoring the sweat soaking into my collar, the inability of my hands to stay completely still. Like an insect under glass I was caught and could only squirm. The boy was X-rayed and I ignored the hushed conversation between husband and wife. I gave the boy instructions for what to do next and showed the family out, looking at the son so as to avoid the glare of the parents. I locked the door behind them and took an extended period to gather myself and steady my nerves. The immediacy of it had thrown me sideways and destabilised the security that I had begun to feel.

Yet the ordeal wasn't over; the man had spoken. Through his child and his scattershot English he had told other members of staff that I was not Polish, and between whispered asides and blatant questioning, the suspicion about my identity grew over a tense and terrifying week, the culmination of which was being called in for a meeting with the chief administrator early one morning. I took a cup of coffee, which I rarely drank, hoping that it would calm my nerves or at least act as a distraction from them. The administrator, a feeble man who wielded his power as if it could turn on him at any moment, motioned towards a chair and waited until I'd taken it to sit down himself.

'Mr von Tore,' he said, checking my name on his papers. 'I'm sure you've a busy day ahead so I won't keep you long. How long have you been with the hospital now?'

I told him quickly, enunciating more clearly than usual; I called upon the British inflection I had learned from the upper-class Indians. With effort, I drew myself up to a straight sitting position, and heard my grandmother's voice speaking to me, encouraging the young Wilhelm to pull his shoulders back, to lift his chin, to be a man.

'We've had no problems with you in this time, and I hope this will continue. But I am going to have to ask for some documentation from you beyond what is generally necessary. Don't take this as a comment on you personally, Mr von Tore, as an individual or as—'

'As an immigrant?' I asked, boldly, more boldly than I could fathom. He was unsettled by it.

'The thing is that we have a duty to confirm the identities of all employees at the hospital, and if this is called into question, further investigation is necessary.'

'I believe I presented my passport and work permit when I applied for this job, sir. My marriage certificate too, and in fact all documents that were requested of me.'

He pulled a pen from his desk and moved it around his fingers; I noted his distraction, and felt my own nervousness retreat. My indignance at the persecution I faced, not as an immigrant Pole but as a displaced German, finally had an outlet.

'That's entirely correct, Mr von Tore, and while this would usually be sufficient, there are aggravating circumstances in this case—'

'The circumstances being that I am an immigrant?'

He put the pen down.

'Mr von Tore, I hope you're not insinuating—'

Here I took my moment, pushing my chair back and rising up slightly from it.

'I feel, sir, that the insinuation is all yours, and I'm afraid that the accusation is a grievous one. This is not the first time that I have been the subject of scrutiny due to my nationality, though the previous scenario was altogether less polite. I'm sure it has not escaped your attention that my countrymen have been through the worst horrors known to man, in the previous decades. And could it truly have passed you by that it was these conditions that led me to flee my beloved homeland, in search of the America that, I was told, welcomed all with open arms?'

I allowed a moment of silence before I went on.

'I would consider it a failure of hospitality if I were obliged to present to the press an indisputable case of prejudice against a person who was forced to flee his country because of violence, worked hard to establish himself as a useful addition to the society that took him in, and yet still faced the same type of personal attack and snide intrusion that he faced back in Europe. If you must, remove me from my position, but do not, sir, tell me that I am wrong to be a Polish American.'

By this time I was standing, strong on my feet, my hands on the desk between us.

'The hospital is glad of your employment, Mr von Tore—'

'Then I hope we can leave it there, and I will not have to make this a public case.'

I walked out of that room and to my office, leaving the administrator's door open for all to see, striding as strongly as I could until I reached my own office. There, I experienced a fit of anxiety so harsh it shook me to my core. I prayed that my gamble had been worth it, that my bluff was not obvious.

My employment remained, but my confidence in my acceptance at the hospital was forever dented.

10.

Gabriela

Over the course of my life, I've learned that a person should be careful what they pray for, because you can't control when God listens and when He doesn't. Maybe my mother was right that the Lord was looking right down on Key West and listening to everything she said; soon after she implored Him to send us husbands, Luci began to run towards the boys as if they were magnets, and she made of metal. While Luci looked young, she did not act it. As soon as her hormones arrived, she felt the weight of her virginity as if it was made of lead. Finally taking Tita's advice, Luci batted her eyelids at Papá until he gave her paper money which she spent on red lipstick at the local drugstore. Taking Mamá's rollers and pencils from her bedroom drawer, she painted her mouth and eyes and accentuated the curls in her cropped hair. Tita would have been proud. Me, though—I could see it was the dawn of something dangerous. I was not surprised when Luci told me she was going 'dating' with the biggest boy in the school, a boy two years above her with a dark look in his eyes and the body of a grown man. I would tell Mamá, I said.

'Don't worry, Gabi. He's bringing a friend for you.'

'I don't want his friend. They always have grubby hands and lumps in their noses. Let's just go to the movies alone, Luci.'

'What are you so scared of?' She dug her fingers into my ribs. I wriggled away and slapped her hands.

'I just don't want to be drooled over by some overgrown baby.'

For me, boys were still objects of fear. Maybe that was true for Luci, and half the fun.

'You know what Tita used to say, Luci. If you put yourself about, they will think you're cheap. If you want them to value you, you've got to keep them at the end of your arm.'

Luci was looking in the mirror, pressing a dollar between her lips, leaving a mouth stain on the edge. She stopped and rolled her eyes so hard I thought they might spin and turn inwards for good.

'Abuelita was an old fool from a different time and a different place. This is America, Gabi. The "land of freedom."' Her voice was swollen with sarcasm. 'So let's go taste some.'

It was happening. I could go along with her or let her go alone. I let myself be carried along.

You wouldn't have felt it if you were there, but the air around the house was turning sour. Maybe it had been turning ever since we arrived, but around this time it began to thicken, as if we were staining it with our presence, and we breathed it in, that bad air, Luci most of all. I would catch her with her hand at her throat, struggling to swallow, finding it hard to fill her chest with fresh breath, but a second later she would be running again, straight towards the outside world, to find something new and dangerous. So when it was Tonio who got caught in the heat, I was caught by surprise. And so was Mamá.

It was eight o'clock at night and the boys were not home. It wasn't so unusual for them to be late after school, because sometimes they played sports and sometimes they walked through the streets, and sometimes they were not at school at all, and didn't have watches to tell them when to come home from the beach. They had different groups of friends, of course, dictated by their ages, and one would be home before the other. But this time, neither of them appeared. The sun was starting to set, and Mamá did not know where the white boys lived so could not call their mothers to ask.

'Maybe they're dead,' said Luci, taking a shrimp from the now cold plate and biting off its head.

'Luci,' I warned, as Mamá's eyes closed in annoyance.

'Maybe Andrés got carried off by a wave and Tonio died trying to save him.'

I pinched her hard with the ends of my nails; she grabbed the soft flesh just above her elbow in pretend pain.

'It might be that, Gabi.'

'It's not,' I said, glancing at Mamá, who was silent.

'Maybe they both got run over by a bus.'

'I'm going out,' said Mamá quickly, her sandals slapping against the broken tiles on the floor. She yanked open the front door and did not close it behind her. By the time I reached it and tried to run after her, she had already stopped, because she could see them—Tonio, on the sidewalk, his back against a painted wall; Andrés at his side, lamenting, in tears that were made of rage but came out as sadness. Mamá stood still in the warm wind and watched her boys hide in plain sight, wanting to come home but not knowing how, and she stayed watching until Andrés saw her, and ran to her, and clung to her as she went to Juan Antonio. She sat down by his side, not looking at the dried blood running from his forehead to his chin, the blue bruise below his cheekbone, the lip that had been split by the force of a foot. They didn't speak then, but afterwards they told us: Juan Antonio had gone with his friends after practice, and Andrés had tagged along too, wanting to walk home with his brother who had so impressed him on the field. They went to get snacks at the store near the school, the place where everybody stopped with the lunch money they had left over, to buy black taffy and candy cigarettes, so they could roll up their shirt sleeves and put a stick behind their ears and act like they were Marlon Brando. There were a few boys, maybe eight or nine, and they were loud with adrenaline and full of testosterone, so they threw packets of chips and knocked over cartons and ate popsicles they had not paid for. The owner of the store, a white lady Mamá's age, told them all to get out, but one of the gringo boys grabbed a barrel of candies as they went. They all ran, but it was Tonio who felt a strong hand on his arm, felt the pull backwards, was yanked to the floor.

'It was him,' she said, to whoever was there to listen, 'that one, he took it.' And he denied it, and showed his empty hands, the nothing in his pockets, but the woman's husband grabbed him tighter, and when Tonio tried to run the man grabbed his foot, and his head hit the floor, and the man kicked his face and his back, and screamed all kinds of names at him, took the coins from his pocket to cover the cost and told him never to come into the store again. One more kick for good measure and there was Tonio, bleeding in the street, and he could not get up until Andrés came running back, and propped up his brother, and made him walk home, where they might, if they were lucky, be safe.

They didn't speak, this all came out after, but soon Tonio too began to gently cry, and Mamá stood with her arms around her boys, the boys that had flown too close to the sun and had their wings clipped by fire.

Papá went to the police station later that day and was told they were keeping an eye on our family, on our boys with the hulking shoulders and the black looks in their eyes, and when Papá came home he slapped both of his sons and told them to behave themselves, for the police were looking now, and it was all their fault.

From then onwards, Tonio was branded a thief. He had never stolen a thing in his life, and never would, but that didn't matter. The kids at school, the parents, the people who ran the shops— they all had the word in their mouths when my brothers went around; not only Tonio but Andrés too, for why would they concern themselves with the difference? It was a Cuban boy, the brother of the girl who liked to let boys fill her mouth. Mamá wouldn't go and speak to the woman in the shop, because she didn't have the English, and had no one to support her, and had lost her voice in the strange thick air of America. Papá wouldn't go because he feared the police, and would rather have his sons tarred than have officers at our house, seeing what my father had been forced to do for a living. Mamá stopped talking to the other ladies at church, and Papá wouldn't bring people home, and the boys, well, they shifted into the groups of gusanos, still playing with the gringo boys on the field and in the water, but going to their own people afterwards. They thought they'd been Americans, they thought they'd been allowed in. But on dry land, off the pitch, they were still Cubans after all.

I tried my best to pull the family together around me. I invented things I wanted to do, so that the boys might stay home and my parents might join us too. We needed some peace, some time to be together as a family, but Luci wouldn't hear it. She went out in the evenings and I told Mamá lies so she wouldn't worry; when we stayed out too long and came home with torn hems Mamá shouted at me about judgement and reputation. I was floating alone in the middle, trying to make everything okay. Luci, because she was younger, did not get half the shouting but was allowed out regardless. I suppose it is the way of things. But like me, Mamá was pulled from both sides. She was scared, and she was alone, but more than anything she was worried for me and Luci, scared that we would not be wanted. For all the arguments, she showed us how to draw our eyes more naturally, and she showed me how to pin up my hair so it would not get ruffled, and would run oil through it on Sundays so it would be shiny all week.

The excess of choice that Papá loved so much, it was there

for us too. The white boys liked us because we were unusual, because they could compare our skin to food, because they had heard things about girls of our type and Luci did nothing to prove them wrong. They took us out for cloying dinners on sticky seats. It was always a movie or a milkshake or a Coke with ice cream on top; even now I can't look at an ice cream float without wanting to vomit. Luci's boys would see that I was concerned with her, not really interested in my date; my eyes were always open when we kissed, and if Luci's date looked in my direction and saw me watching, all the better. They tasted of tomatoes and sugar syrup and they forced their wide tongues into your mouth while they pulled your hips towards their crotch. For me, it was just tolerable, and sometimes not even that, and when they reached down to the bottom of my skirt I sometimes let them, because I had no reason to say no.

But Luci was never satisfied. There were secrets she didn't know and feelings she hadn't felt and she needed to collect them all like stickers in a book. It wasn't enough to have different boys. I knew something was brewing when Luci laid me down on the bed and told me she was taking the hairs from the top of my nose.

'Gabi, you look like Papá.'

'There's nothing there, idiot.'

'Sit still. This is why the girls at school call you Dog Face.'

Did the girls call me that? I had never heard it, and Luci was often a liar. But the thought of it made me feel hollowed out, so I didn't move. Every hair she pulled out made my eyes water; the tears spilled down the sides of my face and into my hair. When she was finished, she took Papá's razor from the bathroom and started to drag it across her thighs.

'What are you doing?'

'Gabi, keep up. It's what everybody does.'

'For what?'

'For what do you think? No boy wants to touch hair there.'

I watched as she ripped tiny holes in her dry skin. Blood came to the surface in small spots, and some made little trails to her knees. She carried on.

'Luci, it should be wet. I think it should be wet.'

'It's working.'

I took a towel and pressed it on all the blood spots.

'We'll have to wash this. If Mamá sees the mess she'll know what it is. You know what she'll say about St Nicholas and you inviting the boys.' As she brought the razor to the soft parts of her inner thighs, Luciana laughed. Poor Mamá.

'Mamá should read some more about that saint of hers.'

I knew there were stories in church that were kept secret from us, stories about the sinful things that saints had done before they chose the path of the Lord. These were the subject of gossip amongst the young Catholics, as if we knew these people and they lived just nearby. It was always difficult to know which ones were true and which ones were lies, but that was the case for everything. I waited for Luci to speak again.

'In the old days, fathers paid men to marry their daughters. It was like a bribe: take this girl and I'll give you this money. One day when Nicholas was alive he met a man who had three daughters and no money, so he couldn't make the bribe. The daughters would have to go with men for cash. Nicholas gave money to their father so they didn't have to do it, throwing it down the chimney, one bag for each girl.'

Luci spread her knees apart and almost bent double to watch the razor run next to her underwear.

'Always we hear about value, value, value. But they're wrong, Gabi. It's not about grabbing a man for marriage. It's all about sex. Men will pay for it, and men will pay for you not to have it too. The value is all ours.'

I didn't have a date that night, but she did; a boy who could see that I would be a barrier and had made sure I was not invited. Luci told Mamá that she was staying with another girl from class. I should have gone with her. I stayed awake until the morning, ready to run into my parents' room and tell them everything, but I couldn't do it. Luci, younger than me but with bravery enough for us both, had all the curiosity that I did not have.

She came home after breakfast, eyes fiery with new knowledge, with the joy of fresh sin, and she insisted on telling me about it on the warm sand of the beach later, though I squinted at the horizon and tried to lose her words under the noise of the waves.

After that, the boys knew that Luci would so they thought I would too—and I let them. Tita's words rang in my head, about girls like us and what would happen if we did not get them to marry us, and in my head Luci argued with her, but still I could not make myself act one way or another. I never said no, and I never said yes; I just let things happen whichever way they would. Every date was a double date, because I insisted, and so Luci's boys began bringing their most horrible friends, so that I might get bored or go home instead of sitting with their arms around me. But I was so scared of leaving Luci that I let them hold my legs in their clammy hands and sweat into my hair. In the back seats of the cars I always angled my body so I could see out of the window. It was easier to lay still and listen than it was to say no, and the American boys didn't seem to mind. When an especially mean boy pushed a few dollars into my hands after he'd pulled up his pants, I laughed and reminded myself to tell Luci later.

The first of the vomiting came at the movies. Luci had to run from the back row right down to the entrance and out into the foyer. She got to the bathroom just in time. The second time it was after church, and Mamá made her lay in bed for the rest of the day with ice on her temples. It happened at school, at the beach, in the night-time, but still she didn't believe me until she missed her period twice. She woke me in the night, and it was the first time I had seen her scared.

'Gabi, you have to help me.'

'We'll tell Mamá.'

'I will swim all the way back to the island before I tell Mamá.'

There was only one option. I asked some of the girls at school, the ones everyone called 'trampy'; they said it would be three hundred dollars and they would take us to the man themselves. Of course, we didn't have it, not the money nor the guts, and we spent another two weeks trying to steal cash from our parents and sell our clothes to the girls at school. Luci was beginning to panic and we still had nothing. So I went back to the trampy girls, and said it wouldn't be possible for us to go to the man. I told them this, not ever mentioning Luci's name, letting them think it was a friend of mine, letting them think it was me.

The oldest girl, the one with the darkest hair who had a little pity in her eyes, walked home with me and told me everything. Boil the needle, she said, in a pan of water, like potatoes. Put towels underneath if you can wash them in secret, or if not, use something that you don't mind throwing away. Put something between your teeth so you will not scream, and get it all over with before you lose your nerve. She pressed some painkillers into my hand and told me to take as many as I needed.

That very evening Luci and I stayed awake until the darkest time of the night, until everyone else had been asleep for hours, so they wouldn't be awoken by the sound of a girl weeping. I put the biggest pan on the stove and took the neighbour's hat pin I'd stolen from Mamá's drawer, saying thanks to God that Mamá was too scared of the neighbour to go and give it back. Luci, who did not look afraid, held her stomach as if wanting to plunge her fingers through the skin and pull out a small irritation. As I dropped the hat pin into the pan, Luci laid out some papers on top of the piano stool; it was the last place anyone would look if they did wake up and come downstairs to find us. I cried a little over the pan but dried my eyes before I went to my sister. I had to be mother, doctor, husband; I had to be it all.

She was already laying on her back with a rolled-up Sunday dress in her mouth.

'Ready?' It was Luci asking me, through the layers of fabric. I nodded.

I knelt on a pillow as I'd done every week for years, and again I prayed, but for something different this time; for safety and forgiveness. She was all there in front of me, Luci the woman, Luci the breaking wave, Luci the brave sinner. I held the pin and felt the burn of the metal against my palm, but the cold blood came through me again, the terror of doing the wrong thing, of making it worse, and I simply stared at the task and could not go through with it.

'Gabi, come on. Before someone comes down for a glass of water.'

I put my hand on her damp, rough-shaven thigh and swallowed down, trying to shake myself into action, but I was trembling against her and she could feel it.

'Gabi, you have to do it.' There was more urgency now; she was losing her nerve. The moments before pain will do that to your conviction.

'I can't,' I said, because it was true, and I cried pathetically, wishing we could all go back to the time before this was the case, before this knowledge was in our heads and bodies, before we had gone into cars or stepped into America or heard about lipstick from Tita.

Then Luci's hand was around my forearm, and without waiting a second she pulled me inside of her, the stab of the pin catching on her before it was even in, her sharp breaths telling me it was hurting before it even properly started, and only then did I hold the hat pin straight, but still I could not move myself, and it was Luci that had to pull me all the way to where she began to weep and shake, her low moans disappearing into her Sunday dress, the blood coming quickly and drowning my hand, and I held my other palm out to catch it but quickly there was too much to hold. Luci kept stabbing, kept going, until she could no longer grasp me and instead she fainted, and I pulled her from the piano stool and onto the newspapered floor, holding her between my legs with her head on my chest, and reaching down I pushed balls of paper against her crotch, red seeping through the local gossip and advertisements for car loans, and I held her that way until she came back from unconsciousness, put my hand over her mouth to stop her from screaming, and when the bleeding stopped at dawn I gave her all the pills I could fit in my hand and helped her wash them down with water. I threw the newspaper in a bin three streets away.

She was in bed with cramps and a fever for four days, and when it came time for church on Sunday I begged Mamá to let me stay home. My pleas had such ferocity that she tipped her head and looked at me with her mouth a little open, seeing something I did not want her to see, and quietly took Papá and the boys out of the house. Around the time they would be accepting the body of Christ, Luci started to sweat and cry out so I got her into the bathtub. It came out into my hands and stained her legs and she could not look at it, not even once. Instead she clung to the side of the tub and grabbed at me, her eyes wet and her lips pale and her whole face full of fear.

'Gabi, is it bad? Is something wrong?'

I looked down at her, my baby sister, skinny in the legs and arms and covered in blood.

'It's finished,' I told her. 'It's over now.'

I cleaned her up and gave her more pills and hot tea and she cried pained tears until she fell asleep. I quickly washed out the bathroom and threw away the remains.

No. God forgive me, there's no harm now in telling the truth. I told Luci I had put the mess down the toilet, but I lied. It was only a small red knot, no bigger than a curled finger, and it felt like knuckles when you touched it, but it was something, and so, to my shame, I took a small jewellery box from my bedroom, wrapped the something in a white handkerchief and put it inside. I told myself I would give it to Luci when she felt better, or if she needed to grieve, or if she ever felt that she had done the wrong thing. But these things never happened. And still I kept the something.

This should have made us more careful with the boys, but it did not. For Luci, it made her more determined; she would not be held back by her own body. We had made a pact to only go with Cubanos, because if we got into trouble again we would at least be able to blame someone like us. We were becoming women and we did not know how else to show it; isn't this what women do?

After that night at the piano, though, Luci lost weight, more than she had to lose, and I thought it was all from the trauma of the event, but she did not get better. Mamá fussed, and made chicharrón for Luci, pure fried fat so that she might get heavier, and Luci ate it dipped in ketchup, but still she did not put on any weight. I was so scared that it was my fault, and so terrified that Papá would find out what we had done, that I made excuses and explained away Mamá's fears. I ignored Luci's long mornings in bed, and her coughing, and the way she held her chest, and the dampness of her sheets when she finally left her bedroom. A long year and she was not better, but still I kept quiet.

Eventually, desperate to distract, I accepted a proposal from a plain boy named Felipe. His mother was so Catholic she had made him scared to even kiss a girl on the lips, yet like Luci he was a victim of his own hormonal movements, so our dates always consisted of him rubbing his crotch on the outside of my dress and then crying against my chest later. He was sweet enough, and seemingly terrified of me; he was always trying to tread the well-worn path of movie romance, but the actions were two sizes too big. I started to bring Felipe instead of a hand-me-down boy if I went on double dates with Luci. When he calmed down, when he started to be himself, I realised that he was sweet, and interesting; he had many hobbies, and liked to make things, and I felt a swell of emotion one day when I thought: *if I ended up in the same way as Luci, would this boy hold me close, would he treat me right?* I knew he would. We finally had sex that night, me looking right into his eyes, and it was the first time I'd felt something like pleasure. He got down on his knees before our tenth date and presented me with a ring his mother had told him to bring. I laughed at how close he looked to falling over, how obvious our coupling must have been for her to instruct him to marry me, and he laughed along with me. He was okay, that boy. A marriage would give us all something to feel happy about, so we said our vows in front of the holy finger and we had a small party in the street with the other Cubans and Luciana wore a dress that would have fitted a girl three years younger. All through the ceremony and the whole of the party afterwards her chest strained with her breathing and she looked like she might fall over. The swelling in her stomach had gone down and the hot shivers and nightmares had stopped, but she still looked sick, and I prayed at night that I had not poisoned something inside of her. I was twenty-one, and Felipe only twenty-two, but all the men shook his hand and all the women patted my stomach and told me my time was about to come.

At the end of the night, Luci collapsed. There was blood on the front of her dress, blood in her mouth. My father shook as he carried her to the car. I went home with my parents, leaving Felipe on the street with his friends who were toasting him becoming a man.

11

Wilhelm

Despite being able to rely, with some degree of certainty, on my various income sources from abroad, I was aware that my presence in Key West was still that of a foreigner, and to simply hide away in my new home would have brought attention from my new neighbours. So in the interests of furthering my research and staying visible, and thus anonymous, I kept my job. As I worked to prove myself over the years (not out of any career interest, but simply because, as a foreigner, it is always necessary), I was eventually allowed to expand and improve the radiology department. My progress here was painfully slow; if I ever attempted to take initiative or to exhibit my actual skill, I was quickly put in my place. To those around me, I'm sure, I was an arrogant foreigner not versed in their ways, but my ability and my intellect were both restrained during this time. I was not permitted to hire any assistants (and indeed on suggesting this, I was given a severe reprimand, of the sort that further damaged my relationship with my superiors), but with a growing hospital budget I was able to invest in more up-to-date equipment and, over a matter of a decade, was in fact able to furnish my own home laboratory from some of the hospital's overstock. If there was no possibility of a suitable promotion for me outside my home, I would continue my own work on the side.

I could say here that my career at the hospital was rewarding, but truthfully, it was not. For the entire period of my employment, during which I grew into a middle-aged man, I was given nothing more than menial work, and I always felt it necessary to exhibit my worth and my dedication to this unchallenging work again and again. Having to grovel at the feet of one's employers never disposes one particularly well to those people, and I felt a bitterness rising within me as the years of my career passed and I moved into a different phase of my life. The only satisfaction I had was from my own laboratory and my own research. I chose to see my hospital work as simply a means to an end. Then suddenly, the years of drudgery were given meaning.

It was June twenty-second, nineteen seventy, and given my broad medical experience, I had been asked to stand in for the phlebotomist, as he was suffering from a digestive issue and was unable to work that day. Hardly had I arranged the room in a way that suited me when I was informed that an outpatient was on their way to me for testing. As the girl was not a regular patient at the hospital, I would need to file the necessary paperwork for her parents to be charged for their visit. This was a regular occurrence and of course well within my capabilities. I usually undertook such tasks with barely any need to engage my faculties; I worked as if in a daydream, my mind often on the experiments I was to begin that evening at my home laboratory. This is the only reasoning I can give to explain the fact that I did not, at first, recognise the creature who entered the room. I was told that a young woman, in her later teens, was being sent in with her mother, and that I was to take a blood sample from her as well as the routine tests for general health. There was a timid knock at the door; I waved them over to the bed and chair and told them to make themselves comfortable. The girl was wearing a pale dress in a flower pattern, with short sleeves and a hem which sat above the knee. I chatted amiably to the mother, despite her obvious difficulty with English, explaining to her patiently that the tests were routine ones to ensure that we could understand her daughter's situation. I brought up my own chair and took the daughter's left hand, and what descended on me was a certainty that I knew this girl; that she was someone about to change the course of my life. As my heart rate increased, time slowed. In the stretched moments of that interaction, I was almost too scared to look up and find that I was wrong in my presentiments, and that I would look into the face of another unremarkable girl. But as I finally lifted my eyes, the face I looked up into was that of my promised bride—the young woman Oma had presented to me in a dream all those years ago.

Her teak eyes alone would have been enough to confirm it, but there were the high cheekbones, the slightly cleft chin, the coquettish manner of the creature who had appeared to me in my youth. Her hair was shorn short, but was dark and thick. She had the provocative air of the Spanish. It was, undeniably, the face of the woman that I had seen in my dreams.

We looked at each other for a moment. Hers was the look of someone who knows they are finally home, that after years, indeed decades of searching, they have found where they belong. It was the first time I had looked into the face of a woman and felt the urge to throw myself at her feet, to beg her to let me worship her, to build a throne on which to place her, to lose myself in her beauty forever. So much passed between us in those few seconds that I felt faint. It was her mother, her voice tainted with incivility as well as the accent of an unassimilated and uneducated immigrant, who said:

'Doctor, are you okay? You are white.'

I grasped at my professionalism.

'Yes, yes, of course. Excuse me.' Here I took a moment to gather myself and to steady my tone. I turned to the girl. 'What is your name, my dear?'

'Luciana,' she said, and the sound of her voice affected me most profoundly.

'Luciana,' I said, smiling slightly, for this was a game we were playing, pretending that we did not know each other, and as I spoke her lips pursed into a pout, suggesting so much with so small an action. 'I'm sorry, Luciana, but I'll have to take your other hand for this task. This one is too perfect to spoil with a pinprick. It will need to be untouched for your wedding day.'

'She is already married,' said her mother quickly, with a strange fear in her eyes, and for the second time in as many minutes I felt dizzy.

'She's young to be wed.' It came from me unbidden, but there it was.

'I'm nineteen, and unmarried,' said Luciana to me, glaring at her mother with teenage frustration, 'but Mamá greatly wishes I was.'

She took her left hand away from me and replaced it with her right. As I took another implement from my set I closed my eyes for a moment.

'I'm not scared of the needle,' she said, as I turned back to her, ready to take the blood, and I noted then that her voice was birdlike—young and musical. It felt so familiar, and yet exhilaratingly new. She spoke with strength in English, and so I surmised that she must be the most educated of the family.

'Forgive me, regardless,' I said as I pressed the needle into her flesh. She did not flinch. I let her blood drip into the receptacle and then pressed a soft piece of gauze onto the small wound, keeping myself from pressing my lips to her finger, knowing that her mother, who it seemed had barely even blinked since I took her daughter's hand, would have come at me like an animal. Instead I simply held on to my young bride's hand until the bleeding had stopped entirely, then secured a fresh piece of gauze against her skin. She watched me. I felt electrified.

'Come, Luciana.'

She did not move at the words of her mother.

'Luciana del Carmen,' she said again, and then spoke in Spanish, hurried and with a barely concealed anger.

At this, Luciana pushed herself from the side of the medical bed and placed her feet on the floor. Her mother drew her close and, with a fierce arm around her shoulder, ushered her out of the door so quickly that the girl could not even look back. They left the door open behind them and any passers-by who happened to look in would have seen a man on one knee, a vial of his lover's blood in one hand and the fingers of the other pressed to his nose, to take in the scent; against his lips, to feel warmth; and finally inside his mouth, to taste the sweet sensation of fate, of destiny, of his promised bride.

I lay in my bed that night paralysed by the enormity of it. The delicate features, the lifted brow, that look, that sexual yet child-like look in her eyes. I had seen it all before, had felt it, even, and there was no denying that she felt the electricity between us too. *Luciana*—I let her name roll around my mouth, speaking it into the silence of the empty room: *Luci*. Even the process of forming the word turned my face into a smile.

I felt no rush to seek out my bride in the streets of Key West. The universe had already shown me that no matter where I went and no matter what happened, she would be delivered to me. Instead, I spent a few days in gentle repose. Rather than medical textbooks, I allowed myself to swim in the deep waters of the romantic greats. The words of Goethe reverberated from the sparse walls of my house. The home would need furnishings; a woman could not be expected to live without the fripperies they so favour. I resolved to purchase some finer bedsheets, some softer towels and a few flower vases.

Luciana came to me again much sooner than anticipated. A week after her first arrival in my life, she was sent back to me at the hospital, this time dressed in a pale blue churchgoer's dress, frilled at the neck and long in the arms. I wondered at her mother's hand in this outfit, as it seemed much more conservative than on her previous visit. Upon the usual doctor's inspection of her blood sample, my love had been referred to me to receive an X-ray of the chest, and though the doctor's notes gave no indication, it was clear what he feared. Hearing Luciana's cough, the rattle in her chest as she brought her handkerchief to her mouth and gallantly did her best to quiet her paroxysms, I knew that the X-rays would tell both the doctor and me what we already knew. The tests confirmed it: my love was suffering from tuberculosis.

The shadows on the scan of her chest were beyond argument. Luciana's X-rays showed that she was most likely in the latter stages of the illness, and though its development can be halted when detected early, at later stages, it is almost certainly terminal. I knew that the medical establishment had achieved no cure for this disease, and yet not for a second did I feel anything like grief or despair. After all I had seen in my life, I now possessed something like a divine knowledge: I knew I could save her.

Had I not been studying and experimenting for many years in the very subjects that could offer Luciana a reprieve from her grave? Did radiation not do incredible things to shrink unwanted growths in the body? Did freezing not stave off the seemingly inevitable march of disease and decay? I had seen men with frostbite and gangrenous appendages survive with nothing more than limb loss and some small tissue death. I had seen eyes taken from one creature and placed into the next. Had I not met my own deceased relative, felt her presence as strongly as when she was alive? Medicine had shown me that the impossible was possible. Rather than fear, I felt an intoxicating anticipation.

I turned from the X-ray viewer and delivered the news to Luciana and her mother, remembering that they could not be expected to receive the news in the way that I had, and tempering my tone and manner accordingly. While delivering a diagnosis was strictly the purview of her doctor, I felt duty-bound to state the facts myself. After all, it would be I that would care for Luciana when the medical establishment failed her.

Luciana took the news with unexpected grace. Her mother, conversely, immediately paled and began to cry. I passed the woman a tissue and attempted to comfort her, though I could not bear to touch her.

'Please don't panic unduly, madam. There are options of treatment for your daughter and please rest assured that I— that we at the hospital will exhaust each and every avenue of possibility to ensure she receives the best care.'

At this, she collapsed into violent tears. The Latin type of woman often throws herself deeply into the well of emotion, and I had witnessed such reactions before. I remained calm, passing soft smiles to Luciana to ensure she was not too affected.

'But have no money,' stuttered the mother. 'No insurance. How will I pay? How will I pay?'

Luciana placed an arm around her mother. I seized my chance.

'Madam, please. I will personally extend the full breadth of my medical skills to the care of your child. I will do so asking for nothing in return, except the company of your delightful daughter, and the consent to try every possible cure open to us in order to save her life. I will ask for no money; you will keep your home, your valuables, your means to an enjoyable life. You will surely agree to this.'

She took Luciana's hand, then, and looked up into the face of her child. It was clear that the woman had little option. She was right in her assumption that any treatment would be costly. I did not mention that any treatment Luciana would receive through the hospital would be with the aim of prolonging her life rather than rescuing her from death.

With a squeeze of her hand from Luciana, the woman nodded, and once again began to wail.

Stressing the advanced nature of Luciana's illness—which must have been hitherto ignored by her parents, for they could not have failed to see that Luciana was both frail and in pain, so aggressive was the coughing that beset her at regular intervals— and the necessity to begin treatments as soon as possible, I was invited to the family home. Being very aware that I should not seem too keen and therefore undermine their trust in me, I set a date for several days later.

The house was large but unfit for the family. It was clear that the purchase of the place was intended to project a level of wealth that they did not have, or at least no longer had. The walls of the living area were adorned excessively (and tastelessly) with gilt-framed paintings and fabric pieces of art, all of which clearly had some value, and there were large vases everywhere, though none of them contained flowers. On every surface, photographs showed the grinning faces of long-dead people, the pictures worn away inside the frames, and crowding too close to these adornments were dolls and knick-knacks and statues of religious icons. There was a saint at every turn; Catholic relics hung on each available piece of wall and stood on the floor, over the doorways, in every corner. Thick, faded curtains, beginning to mould, hung at the sides of the windows, and most startlingly of all, a battered grand piano stood alone in its own room, which I glanced into as I was shown to the living area. A thick layer of dust was visible even as I walked by, and it struck me that this family were desperately clinging to the former days of their prosperity. It was clear to me that I would have to take Luciana's care into my own hands, for these people could not be trusted to make the correct decision for their children.

The children, too, were many. There were two sons as well as another daughter, the girl older than Luciana, and the boys younger. They were large boys—young men now, I supposed—of the rough, animalistic type that I had seen on my brief trip to their island some years before. They appeared to have some literacy, and indeed there were a few Spanish books scattered around the house, though very few, if any, English ones. I would bring Luciana some stories in English. She would enjoy them.

I had hoped to be received in Luciana's bedroom, for some necessary privacy and so that I could talk to her frankly, but in fact the family met me in the living area, each one of them present, though Luciana's brothers and sister had no business there. I wondered briefly if the sons, large and burly as they were, had been summoned to act as physical intimidation, but put the thought to the back of my mind. Whatever stupidity her parents might engage in, I had to ensure that Luciana received the best of my care.

The father spoke first, when I'd barely had time to sip the cold lemonade her mother had brought.

'So you tell me that my daughter is sick.'

He spoke in heavily accented and laboured English, though his proficiency was far greater than that of Luciana's mother. Still, I knew I would have to speak as plainly as I could.

'Yes. I gave my medical diagnosis to your wife.'

'You tell me that you can treat her.'

'Yes.'

'For no money.'

'Yes.'

'Then what is it you expect?'

Through all this Luciana remained silent, and it struck me as distasteful, a father bartering for the health of his own daughter.

'I ask for nothing more than the opportunity to explore every avenue of possibility, in terms of a potential cure for Luciana.'

He sipped at his rum over ice and sucked in the air upon

swallowing, never taking his eyes off me. He did not speak, but let the disbelief fill the room.

'I have been a medical researcher all my life and I have knowledge gained through years of experimentation. Much of this research lies outside the remit of the accepted medical mainstream in this country, but it falls firmly within the standards of what is accepted as fact in Europe.'

He glanced at his wife, who returned his slightly panicked look and widened her eyes; she had no answer to his entreaty.

'The American medical community is extremely conservative, as you yourself have found, sir,' I said, the word tasting acidic in my mouth, 'and they live in fear of an increasingly litigious population and the huge insurance enterprise that allows the populace to sue. For this reason, they are afraid of attempting lesser-known cures, because, frankly, just a single patient could ruin them.'

I leaned forward at this point, taking my hat in my hands, and adopting a tone more suited to the man in front of me. I resorted to flattery.

'You are clearly a man who holds his family in high regard. Speaking frankly, sir, the hospital cannot help Luciana, and I would not be allowed to treat her with my own methods within the hospital. I am a man who receives great satisfaction from discovery, and I believe I have discovered a way to cure your daughter. At the hospital, they will not listen. If you allow me to treat Luciana, my payment will be the opportunity to prove that I can cure this disease. My remittance will be the respect of the medical community when I prove that I am right.'

He took another sip of his drink, looking this time over to Luciana, who sat with her hands at her knees, a china doll. I knew in that moment that he would give her to me.

'For my own part, I am still bound as a doctor by the medical code, which states that we should do no harm. I will subject

Luciana to nothing that will cause her undue pain or suffering, and any treatment I give her will be intended to rid her of this terrible disease—a disease that will otherwise surely kill her. Let me say that again sir—madam,' and at this, I looked into the face of Luciana's mother, who was already close to tears, 'without treatment Luciana will surely die. Soon.'

I sat back, placing my hat by the side of my feet, and lowered my face in deference to the truth that had just been laid down. I stole a glance at Luciana, who had moved over to her sister and was holding her gently as she cried. The two boys now appeared smaller and paler; the spectre of death makes us all humble.

The father stood, at this point, and slowly walked across to the window, unsettling the dust on the curtains as he did so; the particles of matter were briefly illuminated in the bright light of the outside world. The man turned away from us and looked out of the window—no, he picked up a statue, of a saint I could not name, and ran the pad of his finger over her face. His shoulders rose and fell. He turned around slowly, replacing the statue. He turned back to the room, but not to face Luciana. He spoke in Spanish, quietly, and Luciana responded, a short answer of just a few words. When the man spoke again, he spoke in English.

'Then let him do what he wishes.'

I took my chance and left the room, stating that I would be back the following evening to begin treatment, and resisted every urge to run to my girl and hold her, to kiss her, to tell her that I would be her saviour. Instead, my hat in my hands like some common beggar, I kept my face to the floor and left the family to their arguments. It was enough to know that the following day, Luciana would finally be mine.

12.

Gabriela

After the wedding, it was planned that Felipe would move into my parents' house, into my room, because his mother only had a small apartment and Felipe whispered to me that he would not be able to fulfil his husbandly duties while he knew that she was listening next door. We would save up to rent a room of our own, for Felipe already had a job and we could save quickly enough. I surprised myself by being truly excited about this; in Felipe's arms things were simple, for he loved me and I believed it. There was nothing to hold together, no worries about our stability, because he was smitten with me, and I grew that way in return. We could have a home together, and there things would be easy, and my mind could stop fretting, and I could let someone hold me for a change. But in the following weeks Luci got sicker and sicker, and I put Felipe off, telling him to stay with his mother because our house was full of illness. He moaned and protested but finally said he would wait; it would only be a little while, then we could get a room together somewhere. But Luci did not get better after the wedding day, and another man entered our house instead.

He was a snake from the start. He was wearing all white, a linen suit and a hat made from straw, and he took it off as he came inside. He moved like a small, guilty child; he fidgeted at his cuffs and tried not to make eye contact with anybody. He shook Papa's hand but didn't speak to the rest of us. He sat down and placed his hands carefully on the arm rests. This settled him. He felt the place was his, and to anyone else he would have looked like the master of the house—a small old man with his chin raised and the air of someone who had been responsible for many ills. A taste burned in my throat, like when you eat something bad and your body rejects it.

He told us that Luci was going to die and we could not afford to save her. He said that he was the only one who would be able to treat her and the hospital would not do it because we didn't have enough money. He also said the hospital would not try to save Luci's life, it would just try to keep her from dying so quickly. America, it seemed, would not even try to keep us alive.

The doctor was clever. I could see from the first moment that he wanted to be nearer to Luci. His eyes were never still but moved around the room, like a dog when it does not want to look at a bone in case the bone is taken away. He stared at my father a few times but otherwise he looked at his hands, at the wall, at Nuestra Señora de la Caridad del Cobre, at the photos on the mantel, at the layer of dust that was still there because my mother was not in her right mind when she was cleaning. But every few seconds he looked at Luci; at her ankles, at her wrists, at her hair, which was growing like it, too, wanted to be Cuban again. Like she was a magnet and he was soft metal. My father could see it too, and it explained my mother's twitching, her anxiety of the previous few days. It is not hard to see a man's darkest desires. No matter how cleverly they think they hide it, you can always see it, plain as day.

You know already, but I will say it: the doctor was Wilhelm von Tore. I suppose by telling you all this I am trying to show you that it is not that we were stupid; it is not that we couldn't see that he wanted Luci from the start. Luci, so suddenly small and frail. No, it was not that he was threatening physically. He was already fifty and my brothers were easily twice his size. But when the rest of the world tells you that your loved one will die, the man holding out a bottle of snake oil looks like a priest with holy water.

Several times I wanted to speak. Several times I wanted to open the front door and push him out. But then—who would save Luci? Who would save my mother from losing another child? Who would save Papá from the heartbreak of failing his family?

My father gave Luci unwillingly, but he gave her. They spoke for only thirty minutes, and by the end, she was his, a little creature on which to do his experiments. The man left smiling, though he thought we could not see.

13.

Wilhelm

You're not an American man,' said Luciana, and as I glanced up I realised she had been looking at me quietly, taking me in. Heat flooded through me; terror at being seen, being exposed. It was the first evening that we had spent together, and I was engaged in a repeat of the same tests that I had taken at the hospital, this time with my own equipment.

Her dark eyes were wide and engaged. Her mouth sharpened with a devilish grin, as if amused that she had caught me out.

'You're right, my dear. I—'

I faltered, almost, forgetting the fact of my passport and my papers, close to revealing the truth.

'I come from Poland, though I have been here a long time.'

'I'm not an American either. I'm Cuban. We all are.'

'Yes,' I said, taking her right hand and pricking her slightly with the syringe. The subject of nationality was one I wished to close quickly, having never quite recovered my confidence from the incident with the Polish family.

'I'm sorry for what they did to your country.'

Pulled from my romantic thoughts, a shiver ran through me. I stopped for a moment, cold fear in my chest. Her eyes were full of innocent kindness; I realised she was referring to Poland, and could not help feeling a brief flash of bitterness.

'It was a terrible time,' I said, hoping to end the conversation. I placed my hand on her knee and, leaning over her like a schoolteacher, I said, gently, 'I will listen to your heart now, Luciana. I will press this to your chest; please try not to speak.'

At the beginning of my relationship with my darling, I would describe to her all the ways in which I was going to proceed; I would show her the problems she had in her body and tell her how we were trying to cure her. Partly this exercise was undertaken to prepare her for any painful or invasive processes that would occur. And yet Luciana, for all her lovely nature, immediately refused the treatments I described.

'Thank you—but I don't want any of this. I feel much better now.'

Placing my instruments by the side of the bed, I took Luciana's hands in mine, and ensured that she was listening to me as I spoke.

'I'm afraid that is not true. You may feel that your body is recovering. You may feel a lack of pain, for now. But your body is sick and it will not get better, unless you let me proceed. It is important that we try every method that we can, for many patients with your disease do not live to see many more of their birthdays.' In this, I hoped to bring to her mind the gifts and parties and attention she would miss if she died. But she still smiled.

'Today my chest feels much lighter, my head feels clearer. I have no pain and my strength has returned. Yesterday I walked around town with Gabi and we went to put our ankles in the sea. All the while I felt strong and happy. I think I'm already getting better.'

At this, I am ashamed to say, my temper flared.

'You went walking, yesterday? In the town, alongside cars? Through the streets and by the roads? You did all of this?'

'Yes.' She looked both defiant and a little afraid.

'Luciana, I have told you already. The dirty air of the roads will damage your lungs. The exertion of walking will make you weaker. You simply cannot go wandering around a filthy city in your condition. Do you have no regard at all for your own health?'

She pulled her hands away from mine.

'It was a clear day, and the air was fresh.'

'Luciana, there are many things I could give you that would at first invigorate you, then leave you half destroyed. I'm afraid that you simply do not understand what is happening inside your body. Breathing in the fumes from cars will kill you.'

It pains me to write those words, and to admit how quickly I lost my temper and said those harsh words to my love. But the idea that Luciana's family would force her to engage in activities that would shorten my time with her, with my promised bride for whom I had been waiting for decades, inflamed my passions and stabbed at my heart. It is painful for any physician to see their patient engage in self-destructive behaviours, those that go against medical recommendations or indeed medical orders, but when the doctor is in love with his patient, it is hard for others to even comprehend the strength of the feeling.

Luciana recoiled from me and her gaze dropped into her lap. There, I saw my chance.

'Luciana, if you want to be around to enjoy the beaches with your sister, you must allow me to treat you. You must let me save you.'

Her face that of an admonished child, she continued to stare down at the bed. Like every good parent, my urge was to reach out and hold her, to tell her all would be okay. But like every good parent, I knew that sometimes it was no good to do so.

Eventually she spoke, still refusing to look up.

'I suppose I must be wrong. Try whatever treatments you choose.'

So she allowed me to proceed. I later laid down a new rule to the family: no more excursions.

*

Of course, at this time Luciana was experiencing a condition particular to those with tuberculosis; a euphoria that prevented her from seeing the plain facts of her illness. The sting of certain jellyfish brings a feeling of impending doom to those stung; tuberculosis achieves the opposite. Though it was painful that day to receive confirmation that Luciana was not in her right mind, it at least confirmed to me that I would have to proceed considering myself her best guardian. Her family clearly had not considered her illness serious—and could they be expected to? With a minimal grasp of the language and having failed to notice Luciana's very obvious sickness until she was so ailing she had collapsed, they were not adequately prepared to ensure her well-being. I took on the role of her guardian with pleasure.

We proceeded with the treatments, beginning with significant amounts of radiation therapy. As previously mentioned, I had been part of a research team much earlier in my life and we had noted that the effects of targeted radiation helped to rid the body of offending growths. To achieve the levels I felt necessary, I took hospital equipment and altered it so it was sufficiently powerful. The regularity required in order to see immediate improvement in Luciana's condition meant that I attended to her at her family's house several evenings each week, though I will admit I took great pains not to appear too often, lest they become tired of my presence and push me further away from Luciana. In order to fortify her body against the relative onslaught of these treatments (for the severity of their effect on the body cannot be denied), I took the liberty of arranging for a large delivery of schnapps from my home country, at my own expense. I knew that the spices in schnapps would assist Luciana's immune system, and the fruit sugars would allow her to gain weight and fight off the effects of the radiation on the healthy parts of her body. I brought this to her house at each visit and encouraged her to take it in small doses over the course of the evening. I also made a habit of bringing with me flowers, comic magazines or small gifts of jewellery, to offset the difficulty of undergoing such treatments. She was such a young girl, really, so much less mature than others her age, and as her health deteriorated, so too did her physical body grow more frail. To bring her the brief joy of some pretty present was the least I could do.

It was on one of these occasions that I first proposed to Luciana.

The positive effects of my treatments had begun to show. Luciana had gained some weight around the chest and her hands were more plump and more delightful than ever. She had been sleeping better, giving her complexion the glow it should always have had, and she reported having more energy. Pressing my cheek to her breast, I could hear that the rattle in her breath was lessening, and she even appeared more intelligent, engaging in conversation about the different flowers that I was bringing, and how they were best cared for.

To celebrate the success of the treatment, I bought from the expensive bakery on the other side of town a selection of delicate cakes and pastries of the French variety that I had enjoyed in my childhood; in Dresden there was a boulangerie a short walk from my grandmother's house. For Luciana I purchased crisp croissants, wet with butter through the middle; macarons, lilac as new bruises; and eclairs, still soft to the touch, that would drip cream when she bit into them. I brought also a new type of schnapps for Luciana to enjoy, as well as a book of some romantic poetry, so that I might read to her while she reclined in bed.

> *Ah, where will I find*
> *Flowers, come winter,*
> *And where the sunshine*
> *And shade of the earth?*

Her father, entertaining some of his brutish friends down in the kitchen, had turned up the radio excessively loudly, but this at least meant that we could speak without a family member eavesdropping. I had begun to suspect that her mother listened at the door during my visits.

'Your father should keep that music turned down; it is not good for you to be disturbed.'

'Oh, don't be ridiculous. I could go down there and join in.'

At this, she began to rise; I placed my hand on her shoulder and gently pushed her back onto the bed.

'Let's not risk all the improvements we've had thus far, Luciana. You'll only get better if you rest.'

'I've been behaving myself, haven't I?' She pouted her lips slightly; they were thick and full, and it was very alluring.

'You have, it's true,' I admitted, pouring her another drink. She took the glass between her lips and swallowed the schnapps in one.

'This is very sweet,' she said. 'I can't believe I've never had it before.'

'There are so many more things I'll show you, Luciana, when you're better and I can take you away from here.'

She heard my comment, but befitting her age and delicacy, she looked down and did not reply.

'I believe I've proven to you that I can care for you despite your illness. You can't wish to stay in this house with your parents forever, and to live in the centre of such a town is to commit yourself to a relapse of your illness. Darling, when you're better, I promise I will take you somewhere where the air will revive you. We will go sailing on a boat to wherever you desire.'

'And what if I want to stay here?'

'Then we will stay here together, if you insist.'

She fingered the edges of the poetry book I'd been reading, looking more than a little excited as she chewed her lip.

'I think it best for me to focus on getting better. As you say, I'm still very ill.'

'Yes, indeed. But you are getting better, Luciana, thanks to me.'

Downstairs, a cheer went up; it irked me how little these philistines cared about their own daughter.

'I'll take you somewhere to recuperate, my dear. I won't allow my young bride to be hurt by the actions of those around her.'

'You are too old,' she said suddenly. 'I'm not yet twenty; I am too young for it.'

'You lack the shyness of the young, Luciana, so I think perhaps you have proven yourself old enough.'

This quieted her. I stroked her hand and we listened to the music from downstairs. From my medical bag I slipped a green velvet box and hid it in my hand.

'I have something for you.'

She narrowed her eyes and despite her best efforts, her mouth pulled itself into a near-grin. She was, after all, little more than a child, and every child loves a surprise.

'What is it?'

'Close your eyes.'

She did as she was told, and stretched her hands out in front of her. As I moved to place the box on her palms, I saw her open one eye—oh, my darling, cheeky girl.

She felt the velvet on her fingers and her eyes snapped open.

'If this is a ring—'

'Perhaps you should open it, rather than guessing.'

She held the box in her left hand and, rather tentatively, pulled the lid open with the thumb of her right. Inside were two exquisite earrings, diamonds, that I had been waiting for since Luciana first came into my care, when I had sent for them directly from Germany. She moved the box from side to side and the stones refracted the light of the overhead lamp into her eyes. She squinted for a moment.

'They look so…expensive.'

'They were.'

'Why give these to me, when I can't wear them anywhere?'

'Luciana, these would look their most beautiful even if they just lay on your pillow as you rested. But these, my darling girl, are for our wedding day.'

She had little to say; her breath, no doubt, taken away by the generosity of the gift. I removed the box from her hand and took out one of the earrings; I brushed her hair, which smelled of sea salt and had grown longer as her illness progressed, behind her ear, and brought the pin of the earring to her lobe.

'I don't have—' she said, mumbling, as she stared at the blanket on the bed, stunned a little by the formality of my proposal. On closer inspection, her ears had not been pierced.

'No matter, my darling,' I said, placing the earring onto the bedside cabinet and reaching into my medical bag. I took out an unused and sterilised needle, placed my own thumb behind her earlobe, and quickly and professionally drove the needle through it. Luciana squealed and the pitch of the noise stabbed at my senses—but I kept on. I caught the blood with a small piece of fresh gauze and pushed the pin of the earring through the new hole.

With both my hands, I turned her to face me.

'They suit you, my darling.'

She stared at me, wide-eyed, so long that I grew concerned that she had fallen into some sort of stupor.

'The pain will be worthwhile, so that you might look resplendent at our wedding.'

Her face reddened in a most unattractive way, and the bottom lip pushed out from her face, distorting her looks somewhat. She was a petulant child at moments like these. I did not let her gaze break from mine and she recovered herself slightly, though her voice shook slightly as she spoke.

'You are too old. What if you should die?'

'What if you should die, my dear? What if *you* should die?'

She turned to the window and we spoke no more of it. I could feel her resistance, but knew it was only due to what would be said of us. I would pierce her other ear as she slept. That night, I began to plan our wedding.

14.

Gabriela

He came to see Luciana almost every night of the week, in the evenings after his job at the hospital was finished. Even at the weekends, he came after dark. I suppose seeing Luciana in the daytime might have exposed flaws that he did not want to see.

It was incredible how quickly he turned our house into his own. Not by planting a flag and calling himself its master, but by walking in and taking one inch, and then another, and then ten. He spread like a damp patch on a ceiling, one day just a small stain and then suddenly everywhere, getting into everyone's lungs, making everyone choke. He made a grand fuss about bringing some large medical equipment into the house, making Andrés and Juan Antonio help carry it up to Luci's room— rather, the boys carried it while he did nothing but tell them they were doing it wrong. These pieces of machinery were in boxes, but I looked when he turned away and I could see they were home-made, like he had built them out of parts. Mamá always left Luci's bedroom door ajar when he came, but soon it would be almost closed, and no matter how many times I pushed it open again, no matter how many things I used to wedge it open, by the end of the visit it was firmly shut. He came not only with his medicines, if they really were that, but also with flowers and ugly necklaces and cheap chocolates. At the start, Luci complained about him, hating the way his dry fingers felt against her chest, the way his body loomed over hers when he listened to her breathing, but as the weeks went by, she grew quiet about it, not joining in when the boys mocked his old-fashioned suits or his strange way of speaking. I slept next to her each night when he left, wanting to hold Luci close and see what he had done to her, and while at the start it was his old cologne I could smell on her skin, soon enough it was the sweet breath of alcohol. I asked what he gave her; she just closed her eyes and shook her head. But for all this, Luci said she felt better. She got a little heavier and breathed a little more clearly. She said it was working. So we let it go on.

While Luci was coming back to herself, Papá was moving further away. He was distant from my mother, yes, but now from us as a family as well. He worked too much, because Luci needed it, and lots more yumas came to the house, and Cubanos too, speaking quietly in the kitchen and asking my mother to fetch them rum. We would all be shushed and sent upstairs, even Mamá, but we knew what these meetings were really about, because after half an hour each time the burned-sweet smell of cigars would climb the stairs to meet us. They smoked so many that you could chew the air afterwards. My father was starting his own business, becoming his own boss. It was dangerous, and the presence of the men made the house more anxious. Mamá hated it. But she had no alternative to offer. They needed the money. To make his guests stay, Papá would put on music from home, and get to talking about politics; he was missing Havana, though he would not speak Spanish in the house anymore, and because of this he barely spoke to Mamá, who hated English. When his guests had made their way home, Papá continued to talk about the island. He said they were taking Havana by the neck and strangling it. He drank on his own then, for Mamá would not listen to him drone on in English, and all of his friends left when business was done. He slept longer in the day, waiting out the hangovers, so we saw less and less of him, and when we were home we tried to be quiet, because despite the growing space between them, Mamá said he was working hard. Mamá said he was doing his very best.

Luci started to get better and would ask me to take her out so she could feel the outside world on her skin. He would have kept her buried in that room, the curtains closed against the sun, and would have her lie still and quiet all twenty-four hours of every day. What kind of life is that? When Luci asked, I helped her wash, put her arms into dresses and held her arm as we walked. We took breaks when she was short of breath and we took care to walk as close to the sea as we could, but it was worth the effort when we got to the diner and ordered three-scoop sundaes with melted chocolate sauce and, for Luci, strawberry sauce as well. She was gaining a plumpness that made her look more adult than she ever had; more like the woman she would grow into than the child she had been. I was so happy to see the new roundness of her upper arms as I held the restaurant door open and she stepped in before me.

On one of these trips she spoke of Felipe. We still spoke in Spanish, feeling as if we had a secret language in public and could speak more honestly than we could at home, where we were understood in both languages, for the boys loved to eavesdrop.

'Gabi, where's your husband? You're only just married, you should be shaking the walls down.'

'All of that can wait,' I said, staring at my spoon, wishing that I already had that safe haven I'd wanted, where I could pretend all of this, Luci's illness, wasn't happening. 'We're busy with keeping you alive just now.'

She scraped her spoon on the inside of the glass, enjoying the sound it made.

'You should bring him to the house. He will be mad if he doesn't get what he was promised.'

'He's not buying something from me, Luci. A marriage is not a contract of sale.'

She lifted her eyebrows and pursed her lips, remembering our conversations past. I laughed.

'Besides, the whole house smells of illness thanks to you.'

'Well, God forgive me,' she said, hands together, looking up, miming a prayer.

'He will come to live with us when you're better. He'll just have to keep it caged until then.'

She went back to scraping the inside of her glass.

'And what if I never get better? And your poor husband is so desperate for your love that he's permanently erect and brings shame on the whole family? Will you divorce?'

I winced at the thought, then laughed again.

'And put Mamá in the ground next to Tita's turning corpse? No, we will just have to put you out in the street so you can shame yourself with all the boys and take the attention from us.'

Immediately I wished I hadn't said it, but Luci either hadn't heard or did not care, because she was seized by a fit of coughing so bad that her palm was wet with blood afterwards. She wiped it on a napkin to keep me from seeing, but she wasn't quick enough.

'I'm too sick to think about dating. And what is marriage really? I've got no need for it, even if I get better and find myself running around with stupid boys again one day.'

I dropped my spoon on the sanitised countertop and took her hand, waiting till she returned my gaze.

'Luci, you will get better. Look at you: we're walking, we're eating, we're laughing. You will get better. You are getting better.'

She placed her hand on top of mine and smiled softly.

'I don't think so, Gabi. I don't think I will. But it's okay. I will go sit with Tita on a cloud and judge you all from heaven. At least heaven won't be America.'

At that, she reached her spoon over the table and took the

last mouthful of my sweet black cherry. I laughed, the greedy little Luci never changing, but as I looked at her, black under the eyes, her hair thinning as it grew, her chest heaving for breath, my hope for her recovery died a little too.

15.

Wilhelm

Throughout my treatment of Luciana her family grew more hostile—not just to me, but to the very idea of Luciana's recovery. In addition to the excessively loud music that would play directly beneath Luciana's bedroom, disturbing her rest, the house would often smell of the thick cigars that the immigrants would smoke all hours of the day and night. My concern was not for her father's health; he could smoke himself to death if he so wished. But poor Luciana, laid up in her sickbed, was at the mercy of the man's choices.

I voiced my concerns to Luciana frequently, but she would put her hand on mine, smile that beatific smile, and tell me not to make a fuss on her account.

'Look, I promise it doesn't bother me. Please don't start an argument.'

That was Luciana's way. She thought only of the good of others, disregarding her own health in the process. She never wanted to break the peace, never wanted to take too much for herself, never even wanted to fight for her own benefit lest someone else be made bereft.

For the sake of my beloved bride, I kept the peace—although I did take the liberty of installing a home-made air filter on the dresser by Luciana's bed, to at least cleanse the room of that foul odour, and opened the windows to the fresh sea air.

*

For all Luciana's loveliness, she had certain habits that would grow to irk me as I tried to work. The most significant of these was her incessant questioning. She asked about every single piece of equipment. She asked about every move I made, every piece of metal I pressed to her skin, every note I made in my book. Even routine treatments that I had administered many times before had to be explained again and again, with all these processes taking twice as long as I held my patience and gave Luciana the information she, for some reason, required. The need to hand-hold the less educated is a constant annoyance to the expert. I dealt with this stoically, but could not deny that the situation was impacting on my ability to treat my patient.

She also became somewhat difficult, insisting for instance that the pollen from the flowers I brought her was making it hard to breathe, or that she felt awful the day after drinking some of the schnapps that I had had sent over from Europe especially on her behalf, at great expense. It also seemed to me that she would turn away from the physical parts of her treatment, deliberately making it more difficult for me to place things against her body and examine her properly. In this way, she was growing more and more childlike as the euphoria of her illness gave way to petty anger, a situation one often experiences with terminal patients who begin to see little point in the medical interventions they continue to receive.

Of course, as a professional one can endure this—but only for so long.

One evening, in the stifling hot midsummer, the sweat on Luciana's skin was so thick as to prevent me from listening to her breathing, and she shifted around so aggressively that I abandoned the examination. She then sent herself into a fit of coughing.

'It's these goddamn flowers!' she cried, pointing to the bouquet that I had brought her that very day. 'They get into my throat, into my lungs. Won't you take them out of here?'

I placed my stethoscope down and set my hands calmly on the dresser, facing the wall as I spoke so that Luciana might not see the tightness around my mouth.

'Luciana, please do consider that I am taking on your case at my own cost, with no recompense for my time, energy, or expertise—and no gratitude for the vast expenditure on medicines, tinctures and parts needed to build the equipment to treat you. I know you are graceful by nature, but that grace seems to be unfortunately failing you in this instance.'

At this she began coughing again. I waited until she was struggling for breath.

'Perhaps you'd prefer it if I just left you alone? You seem to be aggravated by my very presence.'

She fumbled for the glass of water by her bed but could not reach it. The coughing continued; I knew there would be blood in her palm when she brought her hand away from her mouth. I picked up my bag and slid my stethoscope into it.

'I shall be on my way, then.'

I stood up and allowed her to see me there, standing, packed up, ready to leave. She reached out again for the water but had barely the strength to lift her arm.

Her eyes widened. I took a step. She held her hands out to me instead, raising her body upwards as if to beg me not to go. I relented in a second, pressing the glass of water into her hands and then gently injecting her in the throat with a mixture of my own creation, one that pacified the muscles therein.

She fell into my arms, her head against my shoulder, and wept quietly in shame at her behaviour.

'It's all right, my darling. I understand that this situation is difficult for you. We cannot always bear such suffering with humility. I forgive you, my darling girl. I forgive you.'

I thought it prudent to forgo treatment for the rest of the evening; the coughing fit had quite taken her energy away, and she fell asleep soon after. I allowed her head to roll into my lap and stroked her shoulder-length hair while she slept, taking from her nightstand one of the books of German poetry I had brought for her, reading while she rested. I left only when I myself was on the verge of sleep, slipping quietly out of the house.

The following week, however, I arrived at Luciana's home only to be told that the girl would not receive me. They had appointed one of the idiot sons to block my entrance and give me this information.

'I am Luciana's doctor. You have no right to stop me from seeing my patient.'

'Luciana is too tired and weak. She does not want to be disturbed,' he said, struggling with each word despite having lived in the country for many years.

'Disturbed? With medical treatment?'

'She does not want it today.'

The boy towered over me, his height aided by the step he was standing on. Behind him I could hear the mutterings of the other brother and sister conspiring against me.

'You have no legal right. Luciana is my patient, and the law necessitates that I be given unrestricted access to her. If her treatment is delayed this will be considered negligence on your part. If she dies, it will be upon your head. Voluntary manslaughter via the rescinding of necessary medical treatment. Do you wish for your life to be ruined because your sister says she is tired?'

He glanced over his shoulder and I heard whispers. I bit at my lip and both of my hands grasped the handle of my medical bag, close to snapping it in half.

'Surely it is her choice,' he said, upon advice from those behind him, but the certainty was gone from his voice and I knew I would be allowed inside. My relief was visceral.

'Your sister is extremely unwell, boy,' I said, reaching for the name but realising I did not know it. 'It is normal for the critically ill to become tired of their treatment. But in pandering to her obstinacy you are hastening her death. I will walk away from this house if that is what you really wish, but your sister may be dead by morning.'

He moved from the door. The sister, behind him, whispered angrily. The voice of the mother could be heard arguing against them, telling them to move out of my way and let me through. As they turned I took my chance and strode into the house and up the stairs before the boy could be entreated to stop me again.

Luciana's door was closed. I entered her room and closed the door behind me, knowing that this small act of privacy would enrage her sister, but caring little.

I regret that in this instance I failed to hold my anger at bay. To be almost denied access to the woman you love most in the world, and to the one whose very life relies on your continued presence and attention—well, it is too much for anyone to bear. I felt her slip from me as I stood on that doorstep, and when I finally saw her, sitting up in bed as well as she ever had been, I was torn between righteous indignation and intense concern. I ran to her and held her, then stepped back from the bed.

'I presume you heard the fuss downstairs?'

She stared at the floor, not even having the will to meet my gaze. She was listless, and had begun to believe in the inevitably of her own demise despite my constant protestations that, if allowed, I could cure her.

'I must tell you that at the hospital today I nursed a girl not much older than you who died of the same disease you are suffering from. Like you, she was curable, though of course the medical establishment would not believe it. Unfortunately, this girl did not have a doctor so attentive that he would care for her in her own home to his own physical and financial detriment. She only had a family who continued to bother her and busy her and take her out of the ward for trips. So today she died in my arms. This will happen to you, Luciana, if you do not come to your senses and allow me to treat you properly.'

At this, still staring at the floor, she began to gently cry, her breast heaving, her face almost immediately covered in quiet tears.

'When I met you, I knew you were an uneducated girl, but I did not for a moment believe that you were so ignorant that you thought that Cuba and Key West were all the things worth seeing in the world. Did we not speak of our plans to sail together in the clear air of the ocean? Did I not promise you that I would travel with you all the way to Europe, to show you the grandeur of its history, the splendour of its spaces? This is not a selfish endeavour, Luciana. I saw in you a spark of something so much better than you are allowed to be in this home. I saw the potential in you to be an intelligent and well-travelled woman, turning heads as you walked on your husband's arm through the streets of Vienna, Paris, Rome. How small-minded you must be to think you have already lived all the life worth living.'

Her weeping grew louder and I heavily closed the bag I had brought.

'I came into this home because I knew I had something to offer you that other doctors could not. I have knowledge that no others do, Luciana—and over all of this, I love you, I love you and I want you to be mine. I can deliver you from death if only you will let me. But yet I think you drive yourself towards death, I think you want to die. I think you want me to walk out of this door right now and call back one of those boys that used you like a rag before I came along. Perhaps this is what I will do. I will bill your family for the hours at your bedside—but not until after the funeral.'

At this, and at my subsequent steps towards the door, Luciana began to move frantically, rolling herself over and descending into a fit of coughing while reaching over to her bedside drawer and ripping it open. Onto the floor she threw everything therein—bits of paper and books and necklaces— until she reached a small blue silken bag.

'Please, just take this!'

I turned to look at her, making sure my demeanour remained cool.

'Abuelita left it to me, it's all I have! Take it!'

She threw the bag to the bottom of the bed, near her feet, and fell back onto her pillows (I had told her family there were too many), coughing so violently that blood vessels broke in her beautiful dark eyes, and she began to spill tears due to the exertion. I gently sat down by her feet and lifted the bag. Inside was a cheap, old, weathered ring; the thinnest gold wedding band I had ever seen. It was an heirloom, something special to her—the 'something borrowed' that all brides must have. I knew that, despite her childish attitude to her condition, this was a symbolic moment; she had come to the realisation that we must be married. She had finally assented to my proposal. I sat quietly for a moment, flushed with excitement; it was true, this glorious creature was giving herself to me. She was mine.

I went to Luciana and let her face, calmed slightly but still wet with tears, fall warmly against my breast. I pulled her to me, her hands at her mouth like a child, and held her as tight as my aged arms would let me.

'Please,' she wept. 'Please. I don't want to die.'

That was enough. She wanted me. She had chosen me, chosen a life with me. It was the first moment of pure happiness I had had since I saw my home burn to ruins.

'Luciana, I will always consider you my newlywed wife. I will never allow the spectre of death to take you from me. This is my promise to you, my beautiful, gentle bride.'

From that moment on, in the eyes of the universe and in the eyes of us both, Luciana was mine.

16.

Gabriela

Soon, the visits to the park or to the cinema or to the beach were stopped. Luci wouldn't come with me when I offered, and stopped asking me to take her, even for a walk around the block or a trip to the store. She wouldn't even get in the car to go for a drive with Papá. She kept to her room with the windows closed, then open, then closed, like she wanted to hear and smell all the joys from outside, but at the same time could not stand being away from them.

Mamá, against all logic, held on to the lie that that man was fixing Luciana. It was Ximena, I think, the memory of Ximena that stopped her from seeing clearly. She had lost one baby and could not lose another. He brought gifts to Luci all the time. She told him that she was too young for him, that she was a sick girl, that she would be fine without him. I kept watch on their visits, listening as best I could, but Mamá told me that his 'treatments' were doing good things; I touched his machines in Luci's room one day and they were cold.

Luci begged Mamá to take her new diamond earrings and pawn them, to buy us another option, another way of doing things, but Mamá refused. To Luci she said it was because they were her things, and important to keep; to me she said that she had taken them to a man she knew and the man said they were worth nothing. Mamá cared for Luci in the day, and took a job cleaning schools in the evenings, keeping her late into the night, but with Papá's business so bad it only kept us where we had always been.

Finally, Luci told us that she didn't want the doctor's visits anymore. She asked me to take his latest gift of flowers to the neighbour next door, Señora Pérez, as her husband was dead and her sons never brought her anything nice. I did as she asked. It was Juan Antonio and Andrés who, knowing the man wouldn't listen to Luci's wishes, decided enough was enough; they had seen him in our home too many times, and as soon as Luci said she didn't want him, they swore he would not enter while they still took breath. But he had a power, that small old man. I have seen it many times in my life, cloaked in itself, hiding from no one, and yet so many people strive not to see it. A devil can be right in front of your eyes and yet you would swear, for your own sake, that it never existed. Andrés tried to keep him from coming through the door, but the man threatened him with Luci's death, using harsh medical and legal words that scared us all, and he forced his way into the house. Always that power, opening doors. Mamá said it was for Luci's sake, and perhaps she didn't enjoy his presence simply because he was an old man and his bedside manner was not good. But I didn't believe this for a moment. He slammed Luci's bedroom door shut and I pressed myself against it, closing my eyes so that I might better hear what they were saying.

It wasn't difficult; he was berating her, repeating all he had said downstairs, that she would die and he would let her die because she was an ungrateful girl. When I heard movement and banging I tried the door, but it was locked from the inside. There was a small thud and an unmasculine squeal; she had thrown something at him.

'It was Abuelita's ring and it's all I have! Take it! Take it as payment!'

There was silence from the room and then there was sobbing. I couldn't hear his words, only hers: 'Please, I don't want to die.'

I fled to my own room, terrified of what she had done, and so scared to admit that Luci might leave me.

After that, she stopped asking us to keep him from the house.

Luci began to shrink before our eyes. Mamá became frantic and afraid. She made drinks for that man, cooked food for his visits, sent Papá away on errands when she knew he would be coming round. Andrés and Juan Antonio ate the food and drank the mojitos, leaving Mamá full of rage, but I had another plan. I began to write to friends from home, friends who we had not lost through political division, and begged them to send us medications. It was difficult and unreliable, because doctors at home did not want to give medicine for a patient they could not see, but I knew that Cuba loved us still and would not let us down. I wrote long letters describing Luci's condition and the situation with the doctor. I sent photographs of Luci as she was when we left Cuba and as she was as she lay in bed, getting smaller and sicker every day.

Finally, medicine bottles with Spanish labels came in the post, with long and quickly scribbled letters telling us how to treat her. I read them in the street, for I was afraid of Mamá finding the letters, begging us to bring her home so she could be placed into a hospital and cared for properly. The last letter ended:

'*Señora* (I had used my mother's name while writing), *I cannot say anything with finality for a doctor cannot truly observe a patient through written words and descriptions. But it seems to me that your daughter is in the grave final stages of tuberculosis, and without the right hospital treatment she will surely die. I urge you to bring her home and let us try to save her. There is no need for her to face her end just yet.*'

So it was true: Luci would die without the help of a real doctor. And yet I knew Mamá would not allow it. Mamá who believed that a man loving her daughter held greater weight than science, Mamá who thought that God was a white man in a straw hat with a bag full of bottles and flowers in his hands. Mamá would never let Luci out of the house, let alone on a boat back to Cuba.

She probably couldn't have made it even if Mamá had let us go. Luci was only half herself, refusing to eat anything other than ajiaco and tostones, and often seemed out of her senses. Her head would roll from side to side on her pillow and she would sing songs from our childhood. There were sores on the underside of her body, even though Andrés and Juan Antonio lifted her daily and Mamá changed her sheets. We made her stand for a few minutes each day so that her legs did not become too weak. Juan Antonio lifted her like she was nothing, and we all looked away when the sheets were soiled. She was a girl again now. She could not be put on a boat. She was too weak. For better or worse, she was stuck in America.

If we had had more money, we could have taken Luci from his grasp, I was sure of it. We could have got her into a hospital and away from him. But Mamá could not work more than she already was. The boys were too young, still in school and hardly any good anyway, for young boys who looked like them lift heavy things and break their bones and get paid only half what they're worth. I looked down at my own hand and remembered how it felt to have a few dollars pushed into it, a few dollars that were easy and quick, and I sat in front of my mother's dressing table and made myself up the way Tita used to do. *Be appealing, Gabriela.* I walked far from home, in case my father might be out driving, gave myself the most extravagant Latina name I could think of, and returned home with two hands full of warm bills. But there was no space for me to exist in, then; my husband came around some evenings, lingering in the living room until he found me asleep on Luci's bed, and if it was not him it was Papá, bringing men home into the kitchen and smoking and playing their music and calling for someone to make drinks for them. Perhaps I should say I was ashamed, but I was not; I thought of St Nicholas and I watched Luci in her bed, and I would have gone out every single night had the men in my life not been in the way.

It was all I could do to begin Luci's treatments that were sent from home. I had to inject Luci two times every day, pushing the cold metal against her warm skin and letting it slip inside. I was good at it, because I was gentle and because Luci's veins were so dark and her skin so pale. Juan, who knew about my letters, sang softly while I pushed the medicine inside Luci, and Andrés held her when it was over. We did this while Mamá was at church praying to God, cursing Him for failing to save her girl Himself. One thing about my mother: she believed in God, but she was often angry at Him, and would always let Him know.

Luci's eyes grew brighter. She stopped soiling her sheets and got up, slowly, painfully, to go to the bathroom and sometimes even downstairs to the kitchen when she could smell my baking. I had learned to make American things like chocolate chip cookies and pound cake, food that had fallen out of the movies and onto our plates. Luci loved them. The boys brought tubs of ice cream from the store and we made cookie sandwiches with vanilla ice cream at the kitchen table, pretending we were all children again. That afternoon—it was a breezy day with four grown children pantomiming youth in the kitchen, father at work and mother at church. That day is what I remember when I think of Luciana. Not Luci weeks later when she was smaller than ever. Not Luci in her casket, her face staring up at us from below the eyes of God. No. This is my memory of Luci, laughing till she choked and picking chocolate chips from the mixture left in the bowl, wiping her finger in the melting vanilla, licking it off and grinning.

It was Mamá that broke the spell. One morning in the mail she saw a Cuban postmark and ripped open my letter; she read the words from the doctor at home and she burned with rage.

'How could you, Gabriela, how could you? You don't know what kind of poisons these are.'

She pushed past me and ran to my room, opening every drawer until she found the bottles and syringes. She ran to the bathroom and, hands shaking, dropped everything into the toilet, flushing and flushing, pushing the matter further in until I screamed for Andrés and he took her hands away, fearing that she would pierce herself with a needle. She fell against him, letting herself be held, cursing me again and again: 'How could you, Gabriela Maria, how could you do it?'

The medicines made her better. Luciana was gaining strength again. But Mamá was too lost in her beliefs, looking so hard at her white God that she couldn't see he was something else altogether.

17

Wilhelm

It was the family that killed her in the end. Despite Luciana's obvious slip into despondency with regards to her disease, a phenomenon commonly observed amongst patients suffering from a condition of which there is little chance of recovery, there was, after our engagement, some improvement in her general health. I attribute this solely to the fact of our betrothal and the long conversations we had thereafter about our wedding day and the many gifts she would receive.

'I shall buy for you, my darling, a dress of white lace that glides against your figure, and a veil from under which those beautiful eyes can look up at me.'

'You're going to dress me up like a doll,' she replied, smiling gently. 'Like I'm a toy, or one of those poor souls they put on strings and move around.' She was like this, Luciana, so childlike in the mind.

'And you will be the prettiest of them all, my darling,' I replied, playing to her vanity. To my shame, I spoiled her in this way, complimenting her when she was all but asking for flattery. 'We shall spare no expense; the church shall be filled with lilies of every colour, from every country, and we will drink to our marriage with champagne shipped from France. You will feel a new lease of life in you, Luciana, when you taste real champagne. It is the only true aphrodisiac.'

She looked at me, quietly taking in the vision I had painted for her. Her eyes half closed and remained that way.

'It sounds expensive,' she sighed.

I took her hands in mine.

'My darling, it is taken care of. I have valuables back in Germany, and contacts that are ready to ensure this money is delivered to me. Money, my dearest girl, is not a concern. There is so much more than you can imagine—and it is all ours, for our future.'

Her fingers picked at the sleeve of her nightgown, an exquisite thing I had ordered from Italy when she became bedridden.

'What did you mean, about Germany?'

'What was that, my darling?'

She looked up at me, and stopped fiddling with her clothes.

'You said something about Germany. But you are from Poland. Isn't your money there?'

Life proves itself to us in so many different ways, but this conversation proved to me that, beyond the borders of Luciana's failing body—and it was failing, despite my best treatments—her soul was still intact, still curious about me, her protector, still committed to my care. Her questions about my origins were questions of love, the kind of things you ask about one with whom you will spend the rest of eternity. It is only natural to want to know everything about your other half. Even in the throes of illness, Luciana was still there.

And yet against all this hope, there was a cloudiness in her eyes, a sluggishness in her manner. I had noted the various bedsores gaining prominence on her underside and on the inside of her thighs, and though I had done my best to counteract their spread, there was further evidence of neglect on the part of her family. Her father, who I now rarely saw but would often hear—and smell—late into the evenings, refused to cease his incessant cigar smoking, or that of his associates, who would stop by the house in evenings, briefly, to engage in what I can only assume was unlawful behaviour. Suffering under this, my poor bride's recovery was again set back, and this time I could not contain my anger.

As I pushed open Luciana's door to go downstairs and make a complaint, I knocked over her mother, who had, I realised, been eavesdropping on our treatment session. As she got up from the floor, I admonished the woman for her impertinence and lack of trust in me, a qualified and experienced medical practitioner.

'This house is full of toxic smoke. My patient is left in filthy sheets without being turned. She is barely eating. It is as if you, her family, don't care for her at all.'

The woman reacted as if I had slapped her on the cheek. She reddened, her ego fractured, perhaps because there was more than a small element of truth to my accusation.

'I am just scared for my daughter.'

'Shall I go now, and leave that poor girl to die in the fatal destitution of her uncaring family?'

She reddened. I turned to get my things, using the old trick to make her see I was serious.

'No, please. We trust you, I trust you, I said to Gabriela she must stop with the other medicines.'

I jolted, and stared. The woman understood the unspoken question.

'Gabriela, she writes to the island, they send her medicines from home. It is only because she loves her sister.'

I could not show how badly this admission affected me. I pushed my back against the doorframe to stop her from entering, but also to keep myself upright.

'You have brought unvetted medicines into this country from abroad? Against all the laws we have in place?'

Stunned, she had no response.

'And you have administered these illegal medicines, from a doctor who has never seen my patient and who has absolutely no knowledge of the treatments already underway, to an incredibly sick and frail girl who may not have the immune system necessary to fight off an additional onslaught of chemicals?'

The mother began to mumble and fuss unintelligibly.

I immediately picked up the house telephone and made a call. The mother, holding the cross that hung between her heavy breasts, walked backwards and forwards by the open door, as if still considering that I might actually leave. I made a second phone call, giving the address of the residence, then placed the phone back into its cradle. I turned to look at her and spoke.

'From now on, I consider it my legal responsibility to remain in this house to ensure that my patient is not subjected to any illegal practices, including the administering of foreign and untested medications. A courier will come with my things; I advise you to let him into the house without delay, unless you wish the police to become involved in this matter, and have Luciana removed to a hospital where she can be kept from you and your ill-advised interventions. I doubt that you will want to draw any official attention to your family; I remind you that whether or not you have papers in this country, any criminal activity will soon see you expelled, sent back to the place you abandoned.'

I turned and walked into Luciana's—and my—bedroom. Luciana was in an agitated state, demanding to know what the commotion was outside the room, clearly understanding that her mother was upset, and I was too. I looked over and could not help but see her as a site of war, as a delicate and beautiful shell inside which a battle raged, one faction fighting another. I immediately set about letting a little blood from her, that the most recent dose of their medication might not take hold. She flinched from the press of the blade that I took from my razor and touched to her skin, but I held her wrist still and only when she yelped like a kicked dog did I face her directly and take her hands tightly in mine.

'Luciana, I can't keep it from you any longer. Your family has been undermining the treatments that I have been administering. They have given you substances that your body may not be able to handle. Your sister may have done the kind of damage from which you can never recover.'

I pulled her close to me and held her face to my neck.

'I will stay here with you in this room until you are better. We are together now, and it will remain this way. For all that this is, let it be our honeymoon suite.'

With that, Luciana fell into my arms. She was mine and I hers. Blood stained the sheets beneath where we lay, and still, I held her.

For three days and nights we stayed together in that room, our room, opening the door to no one but the couriers who arrived, in time, with my essential belongings: clean clothes for the daytime, but also the drugs that would ease the pain inflicted on Luciana by her family. The boy passed two bags—one overnight bag with my things, the other an old medical bag filled with painkillers, sedatives and muscle relaxants—through the few inches that I would allow between the door and the frame, for I worried that Luciana's family might take any opportunity to break through. I gave back to the boy a hastily written letter for my superiors at the hospital, outlining a dire situation with the health of my wife, and asking for clemency with regards to my hopefully brief but inevitable absence. I gave him a quarter to deliver it and clarified the punishment if he did not.

The arrival of the courier inflamed the family, who now gathered in a mob outside the room, the mother hysterical, the brothers lingering with malicious intent. As I quickly closed and locked the door, the boys began to bang on it with such ferocity that Luciana was roused to a panic and attempted to get out of her bed. Pushing her gently back to stop her from injuring herself, I explained in simple words that her family felt they were more educated in medical matters than I was, and reiterated that if Luciana would like to be left to their treatment

I would certainly take my leave and turn her over to their care, though I would not expect her to see out the rest of the day. Tearfully she started towards the door but her breathing was so shallow and wet that she could hardly make it from the bed before she collapsed to the floor. I allowed her to lay there for a moment, struggling to catch her breath, assaulted by the racket beyond the door, feeling the sort of abandonment she would feel if I were to depart in that moment, then could no longer bear it; I darted forward and took her in my arms, carrying her to bed in the manner of one carrying his new wife across the threshold. She made no more effort to leave the bed; we had come to an agreement.

Throughout the rest of the day Luciana was in such heightened distress that she experienced more severe coughing fits, and at the end of the worst of these, on the second morning of our confinement, fell into a violent seizure the strength of which rocked her small bed and knocked several of her belongings from the dresser to the floor. Finding myself unable to hold my hands still, I quickly brought together a concoction of my own invention and, throwing my body over Luciana's, pinned one arm down to the bed with my hands and the other arm with the weight of my knee. Thus positioned I could hold her arm still and then, despite the movement, was able to quickly dispense the mixture into her bloodstream. Soon she was quieted, and with my own handkerchief I wiped from her face the small lumps of red matter and the black-red blood that was splattered around her nose and mouth. I rocked with her until she was fully sedated, and then I allowed the full horror of the situation to overwhelm me: she would die, this girl, my timeless love, and no manner of treatment now could save her. Despite my months of effort, the money I had spent, the tireless hours of experiments and the creation of new methods and trials, my young bride would be taken from me, all because of the people who were supposed to care for her. I wept then. I wept into the hair of my beloved, so insignificant in my arms, such a child then, unable to free herself from the tyranny of the family. Such travesties do we allow. I was powerless. All I could do was deliver her from further pain, and to this end I used the available medicines in the best manner I could.

Mercifully the family's aggression dulled, and though I knew there were bodies outside the room they made little attempt to break through to us. My threats of calling the police, both with regards to their illegal procurement of foreign drugs and their criminal neglect of their own daughter, had the intended effect. For these reasons, we were largely left alone, which suited us both. She had no need of food, of course, being by this point unable to consume anything beyond water, and I cared little for my own health. Any potential hunger was thrown aside by the spectre facing me: could I live on, having tasted the sweetness of promised love, only to have it removed from me after so little time? Had I been in possession of all my mental faculties I would of course have remembered that the first death is not the end; rather, it is the beginning of a project that would take so much of my time and energies that grief would barely take hold. But as my young wife lay dying in my arms, such logic was beyond me. I felt the weight of the moment, the fleeting happiness, the certainty of the end of a beautiful thing.

Putting aside such dark thoughts, I did my best to enjoy Luciana in those final few hours. I lay with her on the bed with my medical bag within reach and revisited the first few days of our courting; I recited some romantic poetry from memory, for in my haste I had not had the courier bring me any of the volumes that I particularly liked, and the mother had clearly removed from the room those books that I had gifted to her daughter in the months before. Luciana slipped in and out of a shallow consciousness and I allowed myself to drift into sleep alongside her, holding her body such that her head rested in my lap or against my stomach, my hand settled on her chest so that I might assess the depth of her breathing. Each inhale at this point brought forward an audible bubbling; her lungs were filling and continued to do so despite my attempts to clear them. I recalled the marmot that I operated on so long ago, back in my homeland, with boys of similar countenance around me. The animal gurgled as it lay on the edge of death, as my blade pushed mercifully into the base of its throat, putting it finally out of its misery. I pushed aside the thought; I would hold Luciana for as long as I could. I gave her heavy doses of painkillers to ease her suffering and removed the tension from her intercostal muscles. Otherwise, we simply were together, enjoying, as much as possible, our brief marriage, the connection of our souls, the beginning of our togetherness.

She died that night; her first death.

18.

Gabriela

When the door was closed Mamá was out of her mind, seized by anger and fear and grief all at the same time. Andrés, Juan Antonio and I had rushed to Luci's room as soon as we heard that man shouting, but when the door slammed behind him it was Mamá that spun around possessed, the fire of motherhood blazing within her, and she came at me, came straight for me. You would think she had never pushed me through her own body, for she was all spitting lips and pale knuckles and grabbed me with a strength not her own.

'You!' she cried, in her sharpest Spanish, as Juan Antonio struggled to get his shoulders between us. 'This is your fault! Did you hear it all? You have put your sister in the ground. Another child! Another child gone from me, and all because you could not leave it to the people who know better!'

'Mamá, please,' said Andrés, his arms now around her, keeping her safely caught. 'Luci is not going to die, he's trying to scare you. It was medicine, Mamá, we helped her write the letter.'

But she would not hear it. She pushed her youngest son away and then dropped to the floor, more Cuban now than she had been in years, words from the streets of her childhood mixed in with the names of the saints, benedictions, *please Lord we have been good and you have to help us now. Keep us in your divine light, Lord, and see your children, my children. My God, Gabriela, how could you do it?*

But then, all in a moment, the rage had passed. Andrés bound her in his arms again and took her downstairs for sweet tea. As her voice grew quiet we could hear the commotion from Luciana's room: a short snap of noise and then his voice raised, an aggressive tone and then quiet again. Juan Antonio tried the lock and it was fast. I told him no. He pressed his palms against the door and looked at his feet.

'I can carry him out,' he said, his voice a whisper. 'I can kick the door in and we can remove him from this house.'

'And then what?' I asked, that cold creep moving up from my ankles, out from my wrists, my hands already splayed, my fingers stiff. My mother's words had put rats under my skin, crawling; I felt seasick. She couldn't be right. But what if she *was* right? What if it was all my fault? Whiteness came in at the sides of my eyes and I reached out to the wall to keep from falling. Juan Antonio continued to press his hands against the door, staring as if trying to make a hole in it just by thinking.

'Then we take her to a hospital where she should have been all along.'

'With what money, Tonio? Who will pay? If we take her to a hospital she will die on a chair in a waiting room while we count for change.' It was Mamá speaking through me, her worries now mine. Had I done the wrong thing?

'Is it any worse than what he is doing to her in there?' He ran his fingers down the doorframe, holding it on either side, the straining tendons clear on the backs of his hands.

Again she spoke through me, my mother, the believer. 'He has treatments in there. She has been getting better. He has cared for her yet, hasn't he?'

This was a shock to him. Of course it was; my brother had been with me through all of it, hearing my worries, helping me write letters, my sweet Tonio who accepted everything I said because I was the older sister, the closest to our parents, the responsible one, and yet here I was betraying everything I had said before, and all so I could save myself from blame. For the first time in years I felt trapped in the gaze of God, lying for my own sake.

'He is a doctor, and he loves her. He will not let her die.'

He stepped away then, looking at me with clear shame in his eyes, and when he heard Mamá's cries from downstairs he went to help Andrés handle her. But as he went by me, he looked like a man for the first time.

'It is not your fault yet, Gabi. But it will be.'

In the heat of the evening a white boy arrived at the door and said he had something to deliver. He walked right into the house, checking his instructions on a piece of paper, and went straight up the stairs, past Andrés who was so surprised he just let the boy go. We followed him upstairs and to the room, but he was passing the bags to that man before we could stop him, and then he ran, he ran from the house, and the door was closed again before we could do anything about it. Juan Antonio went for the door this time, and started hammering his fists on the wood, placed his back against the wall and tried to kick his feet at the bottom of it, but we could hear the man pulling furniture across the room and placing it in front of the door, and Luci's thin voice was part of the noise, and Juan Antonio started to shout at him to bring her out, bring my sister out, and Mamá gripped on to Juan Antonio's arm and he nearly knocked her to the floor, and all so quickly there was commotion everywhere. I felt like a child, sitting on my bedroom floor while our parents argued, the voices enough to make your ears burst inside.

'Get away from there, you will break the door. Do you forget that your poor sister is inside there sick?' Mamá scolded. It was Andrés that answered her now.

'Mamá, what would you have us do? Let him stay in there with her, let him do what he wants? Why don't we just give him the whole damn house?'

He delivered a kick full of frustration and the wood at the bottom of the door split and a piece flew off. I moved my head just in time and it rebounded off the wall behind me. There was a small crack, not enough to see through, but we could hear that man's words, low and angry, now more clearly.

'Do you think you can take her out of that bed and wave your hands around and make her better? What are we to do, drag the doctor out of there and just leave her to die?' Mamá looked at Andrés as if she lived in an entirely different reality to him, as if he looked at the world through wholly different eyes.

'How can you believe this? He is going to kill her!'

'Andrés, that man, for his own sake and ours, wants that girl to live.'

The banging paused, and inside the room things quieted. Luciana's coughing was the thing that stopped us all. It was like drowning, like water going down a drain, and yet I could hear her getting closer to us, and for a second I thought she was going to free herself from her cage and join us, and maybe she would be thicker in the arms and pink in the face and maybe she would be able to stand up on her own, and maybe everything I had done would have saved her after all, and we would all be together again, six of us as a family. We all thought it.

Then there was a noise, as if a bag of potatoes had fallen on the floor. The coughing was now choking; she could not get her breath. There was just a door between us but it might as well have been St Peter's gates. That man said her name and moved her and it was all we could do to stand still and listen to what was true: that Luciana, that girl we all loved, could not take a single full breath.

*

Mamá took herself to church, coming home and fretting in the kitchen before she went back out again, all the stress in the house being too much for her to handle. We were all stuck in that strange water, that ocean of in-between places. Luci was neither living nor dead. We were neither acting nor grieving. I didn't move from outside her door. Andrés brought me drinks of water and snacks to eat but I could not swallow. I sat with my back against the wall and stared at the small crack in the door, listening to everything: the fierce fits of breathlessness, the slow drowning, the raspy scratching that was Luci's fitful sleep, the movement of bodies, or a body, against fabric. Sometimes that man cried out, agonised, and God forgive me I was glad to hear it, to hear that a sharp pain had caught him, because he might be safe from the fists of the boys, but he would not escape this without hurting.

Late into the first night Papá came home, and he smelled of tobacco, and Andrés cried and told him everything in Spanish, and as I listened I realised how strange it sounded to me now, how emotional and wild. Papá came with two cold glasses of rum and ice and passed one to me, and we sat with our legs touching and our glasses in our hands, because what else was there to say now?

When I first went to the toilet on that very spot he brought a towel from the bathroom and put it underneath me. I barely blinked, but he moved me, and he held my hand around the glass and put it to my lips and I drank, and he stroked my hair down where it was tangled at the back. He put his head on my shoulder and we both watched the room, hearing Luci from time to time and then not again. He stayed with me the first night and brought me a new towel in the morning, and as he put his hand on my forearm and sat for a moment, he said, in English:

'Gabi, it is not your fault.'

And, for my sins, I thought: *no, it is yours.*

Perhaps I slept. The whole house stayed caught in this lingering moment, each person blaming the other because there was nowhere for that blame to rightly sit, because the person who was guilty was still not the one who made Luci ill, and we stayed in this place until three days later, when that man opened our sister's door and simply said, 'She is gone.' Andrés and Juan Antonio took the news to Mamá, who was, as ever, at church, kneeling in front of a finger in a box, praying to a God who was not listening. She fell against the gold railing and wept with an open mouth, and it was Juan Antonio that had to carry her home, for the priest wanted to start the evening mass and she was making too much of a scene.

There are pieces of those three days, between the door closing and opening again, that I don't remember, and others that I cannot forget. There were times when I heard blood hitting fabric, the spluttering of saliva down lips, the unmistakable sounds of movement, and through none of it could I move, for any action of mine might be the wrong one. I heard him reading to her, guttural foreign words she could not have understood, and I could hear when he opened one of his bags and took out some of his medical equipment. After he did so, she was quiet and still. There was only once when she was strong enough to speak. It was the last night of her life, though she couldn't have known it, and after that man delivered one of his speeches in a language foreign to her, she said, in clear but quiet English:

'I'll be your curse, Doctor. I'll haunt you when I'm gone. You won't be able to get rid of me, not ever.'

He laughed sadly and agreed, as if it were a joke.

'Darling, you have been with me for a long time already; you were with me before we even met. It will be the greatest joy of my life to have you with me until I die, until we can be together for the rest of time.'

*

No, I am lying. It was not just that once. Hours later, as the sun was rising, and the house was silent, and none of the sounds of the street had begun to infect the day, just then I heard the last of her spirit, the old Luciana. He was lightly snoring and her breathing was raspy and wet, but clear as daybreak I heard my sister say, in our own language:

'I hope someone sees you for what you really are.'

19.

Wilhelm

Luciana's death was a hammer blow. And yet, in many ways, my years of research and my experiences had taught me that death was not to be feared; rather, death was to be embraced as another possibility, another layer of life. I remembered how I had felt around my grandmother's death, and tried to cling to what I knew was true: that Luciana's death need not be the end.

I did not tell the family about her passing until the evening of the day she died. I awoke around six, in the light of the new day, to find my darling dead at my side, and placed my head in her cold lap. I lay there for a long time. I felt a movement at the back of my head and snapped up to a sitting position to see if Luciana, saved from the grave, had touched me. Yet I could find no evidence of movement for the rest of the hour. Not wanting to deliver a false diagnosis of death if the girl was in fact still alive, I stayed there for the remainder of the morning and into the afternoon, at which point the reality of my sorry situation gripped me, and I began to weep into Luciana's thighs, causing the bedsheets underneath her to become sodden and stained. At times, I lifted myself up and searched her glorious face for signs of movement or breathing, for once a doctor has seen one in a coma, has experienced a coma, has seen evidence of life beyond the grave, how can he in good faith measure the existence of life by the beating of the blood in the veins?

I delivered the news of Luciana's death to the sister, who

I found on the floor outside our room, and I speak only the truth when I say that the woman had degraded herself in the worst way, appearing to have soiled herself as she sat kneeling in a kind of catatonic state that only my presence could pull her from. I spoke and she looked up at me, then rose, and without responding went quietly downstairs. I returned to my young wife, knowing that an explosion of emotion was coming, and so it did. Women of the Latin countries perform grief in a way that leaves those from more civilised nations shocked. It is all screaming and cursing and throwing oneself to the floor. Other Europeans hearing this from below might have been embarrassed by this behaviour, yet all I felt was pity, pity for the sister, and a strange sense of justice that she could, at the very least, feel this pain so keenly.

The other members of the family were informed of the death, and below I heard the cacophony of projected emotion heightened. I knew the peace of my final moments with Luciana—with her as she was living, at least—was over, so I removed myself from the house after settling Luciana's body in an attractive and comforting arrangement. That was the least I could do for a grieving family; to leave their daughter in a way that they would want to see her.

I took it upon myself to attend to all the funeral arrange-ments, as a courtesy to the family, though they could not extend even the most basic civility to me despite my ceaseless attempts to treat Luciana. I spoke to the funeral director, met with the undertaker, signed and delivered the certificate of death, chose the coffin and paid for it out of my own pocket—indeed, from the pool of money I had set aside for our wedding.

'I offer my sincerest condolences, Doctor von Tore. To lose one's wife is the greatest trauma one can experience.'

The funeral director offered his hand to me and I stared at

it, momentarily stunned. His words, the first kind words I had received for many years, affected me greatly. I took a moment under his gaze and let him take my hand.

As I picked out the flowers that would sit in her grasp it occurred to me that this was our wedding ceremony. She had promised herself to me, she had assented to my betrothal, and in my eyes we were already wed. But she was a Catholic, and would wish to be presented with her husband in the eyes of God at least once. So her funeral would also be our wedding day, even if I was the only one to know it.

In the funeral home, I was beset by an overwhelming and catastrophic wave of grief. All my medical training, all my cultural indoctrination came to the fore in the necessary conversation about the treatment of the body, as if it were nothing more than an empty vessel, used up and cast off and ready to be thrown upon the compost like a husk. This is the assumption that we labour under in the face of death, and I ask the reader for forgiveness when I say that I allowed myself, however briefly, to succumb to this belief. My hope drained from me and I sat in the funeral home, my head in my hands, as the director took himself off to find brochures and papers. My darling was gone; she was dead. She was no more. It was the end of love.

It was then, at my lowest ebb, at the very pinnacle of despair, that my darling pulled me from the ground and resurrected me.

I recognised the feeling; it was the feeling I had experienced back in my homeland, when I had the sensation that my promised love was somewhere around me, watching over me. Warmth melted over my shoulders and into my body; I looked up and there, standing in the corner of the room, was Luciana, vital as she had ever been and full of life, looking over me with sorrow, and yet with wide eyes, entreating me to leave my despair behind.

'Luciana,' I said, her name the only word I could utter.

'Don't abandon me, Wilhelm,' she said, her voice angelic, otherworldly. 'This is when I need you the most. This is when you, and only you, can save me.'

The apparition had never before spoken; I knew in that moment that the situation was urgent.

'I am yours in every way. I am yours and you must keep me.'

It was this sentence, these words, that told me what I needed to know. I took to my feet, my face upturned, the light of her presence making me rise physically, emotionally, in my very soul—and yet, when I stepped towards her, she was gone, as if telling me that she would, finally, be mine, if I only kept the faith in what I already knew, and took that important step forward of putting my theories into practice.

The funeral director returned to a much changed von Tore.

'Sit down,' I said, my voice calm and steady. 'I have a number of very specific requests of you.'

The presence of Luciana and her promise to me had reinvigorated my faith. I would buy her the most expensive coffin there was. I would make adjustments to it, to save my darling girl.

The funeral, being Catholic, was overwrought and distasteful—though I was surprised by the maintenance of a reverent silence in the presence of Luciana, given that the Latin peoples are not known for their ability to stay quiet. The casket was left open so that we might look upon her face, and it brought me great joy to see that she was, as I requested, wearing the white lace dress that I had purchased for her the day after our official betrothal. In her ears were the diamond earrings with which I had pierced her ears. Though she had retained her earthly beauty, I alone could see the undertaker's tricks and could understand how they would be ruining her even as we watched. The mouth, stitched closed across the gums with silk thread to stop it falling open. The eyelids, held in place by tiny pins from the inside, so that they might not fly open and terrify the guests. I had forced the undertaker to remove from his list all those actions not strictly necessary for the presentation of the face, so that Luciana would not be defiled in the usual way. But I allowed him to work lightly on her face, for I could not rob her parents of the sight of their divinely attractive daughter looking serene in their final hours with her. But why are we not accustomed to seeing the dropping of the eyes, the darkening of the irises? By what authority do we consider these unattractive? Why can we, in our acceptance of the passing of our loved ones, not bear to see the way their lips curl back from their teeth, or smell the tender scents that issue forth from their bodies as they shift from one state to another? Instead, we pay unconscionable sums of money to these dead-tenders, to mutilate and destroy the carapaces of our children, our wives, our mothers, and in doing so we commit them to the finality of death, for any hope their souls might have of returning to their former homes are dashed by us burning them down.

The thought that the undertaker might have thrown out my entreaties and committed such grievous sins to my darling girl occupied my mind for most of the service, although my interest was piqued when a heavy Cuban with greasy hair and bulbous fingers took to the pulpit and began to screech indecorously about the wrongs committed to his departed niece. I had no recollection of either seeing or hearing about this man, and yet it appeared that he was focusing all his ire and damnation in my direction.

'God will have no mercy,' he screamed through strained lungs, 'for the man responsible for this young girl's early death.'

I did not turn from my seat to see if any other eyes were on me. I was sitting at the front of the church, in the seat closest to my dear promised bride, and did not wish to look away from her for a single moment. The man continued for some time, then collapsed out of the pulpit wheezing and panting. I wished him a painful death, whenever it came.

As we stood around her grave, watching the bullish young boys lower the casket into the ground, I could not fail to notice two things. The first was that the grave, which had no doubt been dug by ignorant men simply in need of the money, was insufficiently lined against water damage, and being as we were in such a humid part of the world, the risks of flooding were large. I noted to myself that no matter how long my real plans might take, I would have to ensure that Luciana's grave was quickly protected against the natural damage that the buried endure.

The second was that the funeral was attended by those who had shown no sign of caring for Luciana in her life; a hundred or more mourners there to prove to their God that they had compassion and empathy, and yet none of them had attended to her during her illness. Some were the same individuals who had filled up the family's kitchen, smoking cigars and playing music while the girl upstairs was trying to convalesce. In my earlier state I may have caused a scene, so strongly did I feel the injustice of their behaviour, but I had moved to a place of focused serenity, seeing before me the course of action that I must follow and letting everything else pass me by. They were poor believers, that was all, who would never go beyond the things that had been taught to them. Let them have their ceremony. Afterwards would be my time.

20.

Gabriela

He had her buried under a name that was never hers. His stamp on her life, as if they were married. On my sister's grave, a stranger's name: Luciana Carmen von Tore.

21.

Wilhelm

My readers will permit me here to forgo further discussion of my own feelings around this time. I am conscious that this has been presented as a medical paper, and yet much of the contents herein have been given over to the romantic side of my life. I hope readers will come to understand the necessity of including this information alongside what is to come—that is to say, my findings and detailed notes around my actions after the funeral. I will, as a courtesy to the reader, refrain from indulging my emotional side henceforth; though mine is by its very nature romantic, I will not speak of the pain I felt at my bride being taken from my side. Suffice it to say that I was, despite my strongest convictions, heavily traumatised at the removal of my Luciana from my physical ownership, and felt most bereft at the loss of her company. I was also much concerned with the passage of time, and was battling intense feelings of trepidation and lingering grief, though I could feel the presence of Luciana's soul with me even as we drove from the cemetery. I knew she would not leave my side, and yet I could not hold her in my arms.

In the weeks following Luciana's burial, I was consumed with the necessary making of plans, for which I was happy to be back in my own home, with my equipment and my notes. The reading of my own papers formed a large part of those hazy days, so sure did I have to be that I was not losing my mind, and that the things I intended to do were substantiated by science.

For hours at a time I pored over the scrawled writings of my time in Europe as a researcher, and though the pain of being so forcefully removed from that part of my life was agonisingly apparent, it also served to consolidate my certainty. I began to recall experiments and pieces of information almost lost to memory; I remembered how much time I had spent with bodies both living and dead, confirming the processes of decay and survival, and this emboldened me. My main concern during this time was that the body might be succumbing to a level of decay that would go beyond the boundaries of that which could be undone. For this purpose, I realised, I would have to undertake a preliminary disinterment, which would be obstructed by a high level of bureaucracy. I began to file the papers necessary to move her body to a more secure location and, as I explained on the paperwork at least, to ensure that the embalming had been performed correctly. This was an extensive process, and kept me for an interminable amount of time from my real work. It also served the purpose of keeping me from Luciana's graveside, which I thought necessary as the legion members of her family would still be performing their grief and would find my presence enraging.

I was intensely surprised, then, to hear a knock at my door on the fourth day after Luciana's burial—I was keeping track of not only the days but in fact the specific hours and minutes that she had been in the ground. I let the knocking continue, for I was aware that my reputation in the neighbourhood was not entirely positive. However, I heard something of Luciana in the voice that drifted through the window.

'Doctor? Please, I have something for you.'

I opened the door and stepped out into the street to find the mother. I would not invite her into the house, and steeled myself for the onslaught of abuse to which I might be subjected. Instead, the woman seemed smaller than usual, desiccated by despair, and in her arms she held a long box of the type in which you might deliver roses to a lover. Her face, which had never been attractive, was puffier and redder than usual, the capillaries in her cheeks burst from the ferocity of her grieving. She looked somewhere about my knees.

'I will not stay long. My daughter is not happy I am here.'

She shifted the box in her arms; for a moment it seemed that she was holding a baby, a delicate newborn, but it was just a flower box. She spoke in practised words, the most I had ever heard her say in English.

'There is little I can give you in return for your care of my Luci. I do not know even if I should. Yet my own mother's voice is in my head and I cannot ignore it. So—here.'

She thrust the box into my hands and dropped her gaze to the floor. In that moment I saw her as a schoolchild, pushing a love note into the hands of a boy and then blushing while she awaited the answer. It was almost charming.

I removed the lid from the box. In it were the long tresses of Luciana's glorious, thick hair. The smell of her was on it and escaped into the surrounding air; I experienced her intoxicating scent for the first time in days.

'When we came here, she cut her hair like the American girls. So much of it. I could not throw it away.'

I let my fingers play with the strands, stroking it like a kitten. I felt the woman's hand around my forearm and met her gaze, her eyes boring into my own.

'I know you loved her. Whatever you—however…I know you loved her. Keep this of her. It's all you have left.'

With that, tears leapt to her eyes and she squeezed my arm, looking for a moment as if she might throw her whole body into my embrace. But instead she turned and walked away, wiping her nose with a handkerchief, and I did not wait to watch her go.

In the following weeks, I was able to construct something of a shrine to Luciana around the fireplace in my bedroom. I procured a wig-maker's mannequin and draped my darling girl's hair over it; I also pushed into the head the second grandest set of earrings I had bought for Luciana, knowing that the very best were still in her ears as she lay in the ground. I hung all of the necklaces that I had bought for her around the neck of the mannequin, and though the very presence of a vague Luciana was a comfort to me, it began to feel obscene that the girl in my room had no face, so I lightly sketched upon it a vision of her features. For all my talents, I am not a portrait artist, so I am sure that to other eyes, the likeness I inked on the face of the mannequin was, to my displeasure, unfamiliar. For me, though, it was enough even to have the spirit of Luciana's body there in the room. Indeed, I brought the mannequin's head to my bedside table and began to make my promises to it before I slept.

Throughout this period Luciana appeared to me often; not only for a moment, but for hours at a time, appearing as the sun fell in the sky and staying with me all through the night, sitting quietly on the chair in the corner of my room to watch over me as I slept. I would talk to her and tell her of my plans, of the theories I thought the strongest, the course of action I thought best, and she would nod at the ones she agreed with, and let her gaze drop when she thought my science was departing from reality. In this manner she guided me through the difficult period of uncertainty and self-doubt that followed her death. On several mornings, I woke to feel a distinct weight next to me on the bed, but when I turned over to prove to myself that someone was there with me, the feeling would disappear. For this reason, I began to wake early and, feeling the presence, simply lie, basking in its warmth, until my need for her touch was satisfied.

However, it became clear that I would need to build a significant amount of equipment in order to perform my grandest experiment, and all the while, Luciana lay in the ground, the forces of nature all around her, committing her to a fate worse than her first death—a permanent extinction. I began to lose sleep due to the vicious and consuming dreams of what might be happening to her body. I woke in sweat-drenched bedclothes and could barely stand to eat. How much longer would I suffer through this interminable situation?

Finally, the disinterment permit came through. I could lift my Luciana out of her sodden grave and place her into a tomb fit for my beloved.

22.

Gabriela

We broke into pieces after Luci was gone. My poor Mamá—to lose one child is enough; to lose two is more than any parent should have to bear. Not even the house was left solid. That man had forced his way into our home and treated it as if it were his own. This caused a trauma that our house could not endure. I knew for Papá it was no longer a castle. It felt like a house made of sand.

Every day I went with Mamá to visit Luci. Every day we took new flowers. She even took a small statue of Nuestra Señora de la Caridad del Cobre to watch over her body. We said she was being silly at the time. Now I can see it was the right thing to do. It was painful each day to see that man's name attached to that of our sister. Even the announcement in the newspaper had listed her as Luciana del Carmen von Tore, and I had to write two letters and go to the office in a rage before they would print a correction. It was so small that most of the town did not see it.

Clarification:
Death reported last week of Luciana del Carmen von Tore.
Name of the deceased should read: Luciana del Carmen
Herrera Madrigal.

Very soon after, Papá rented Luci's old room to a friend. Mamá was so angry we thought she might leave forever. Papá's grief was bad for business, and now he owed money to a sweaty man who would come round to the house late at night and speak in a low voice. Papá always looked tired after Luci's death, and when the fight came about renting the room, he simply told my mother to think of another way to make the money if she could. The man moved in the next day. He was tall and pale and hardly ever spoke. He slept in Luci's sheets, for we had no more to spare.

Several weeks later we received a letter about Luci's body from a man at the county office who knew Mamá. He said that man had got some papers and they were going to let him move Luci's coffin to some other place. We all thought it was over; looking back, I can't believe we were so naïve. But how many families think that their daughter's death can only be the beginning of their pain? No, God forgive me, I thought that our Luci was safe in the ground.

'Why does she need to be interfered with again?' Juan Antonio would not hold his anger. 'Is he going to buy her a four-poster bed? Maybe bury her at sea?'

I paced the kitchen between Mamá, who watched me, and Papá, who had his head in his hands.

'She needs to be left alone,' said Andrés, who had helped lift her out of the church and placed her into the ground with his own hands.

'She is not his to play with,' said Juan Antonio. 'If she belongs to anyone, it is us.'

With this argument we went to the county office, only to be told that if Luci's remains were the property of anyone, that person was her husband.

'You must be looking at the wrong papers,' I said to the curly-haired older woman behind the desk, trying to smile politely. 'She was not married.'

'Her husband was here yesterday, and he was given the permit. This decision cannot be reversed, miss.'

She turned her back.

'My sister had no husband.'

'Mr von Tore collected his permit, miss,' she said again, not turning around to look at me.

Juan Antonio pressed all ten of his fingertips into the desk and pushed his face forward, just a little.

'I think you must be incorrect,' he said, speaking very slowly, as if the woman did not understand English. 'My sister Luciana did not have a husband, and her body belongs to us.'

The woman stood, looking at Juan Antonio as if he had assaulted her.

'I'm going to have to ask you to step back from this desk, sir,' she said, speaking slowly and with her hands out, like we were trying to rob her. 'The permit has been handed over to her next of kin, her husband, Mr von Tore. I suggest that you accept this and go back to your home.'

Juan Antonio started to argue, but Andrés could already see the security guard looking at us from the doorway. We would have no luck there. We went home, and in Mamá's kitchen the boys began to plan how to threaten von Tore so that he might leave Luci alone.

Mamá spoke without looking up from her sewing.

'Chiquitos, there is nothing to be done.'

'Mamá. How can you say that? He is going to dig up her body. He is going to cement her into the ground. He is acting as if she is his property. How can you let this happen?'

Papá looked up from his hands, a tired old man who has buried a baby, buried his hope, taken his grown daughter from his home and buried her too. There was none of the man who had walked around town wanting to be looked at, the man who had brought our neighbourhood a miracle. His eyes were grey, his face was pale, and, for the first time in a long while, he agreed with our mother.

'Luci is dead. She belongs to no one but God.'

'But the body—'

Mamá put down her needle and thread and rubbed the palm of one hand with the fingers of the other, sighing.

'The body is just a body. It is not Luci, and it will not be again. Now listen to me, all three of you. You will put all these plans of aggression out of your mind. Three Cubanos threatening a white man—you cannot do something so stupid. You already made fools of yourselves at the county office, and now I will have to endure the stares of our neighbours when I walk down the street. Along with their pity. It's too much for me to bear.'

'But Mamá—' began Andrés.

'But Mamá nothing,' she replied, locking eyes with him. 'He is just a man in love.'

'That is love, is it? What he did to her? That is what love looks like?' Andrés was shouting now, standing, and Juan Antonio shouted back, came at him like a firework, telling him not to speak to our mother that way, and they both popped and fizzed, snapping and pushing and then burning out quickly. They both stood, pathetic then, useless with aggression that had nowhere to go. Mamá picked up her sewing again and did not even flinch when the needle pierced the skin on her thumb.

'Love is selfish. Love does not care for what anyone else wants. Let him love her in any way he wants. He did not hit her, he did not hurt her, he did not chop her up and put her in the ocean. Let him move her to some other place. There is nothing left of her there at all.'

23.

Wilhelm

I was able to ensure, by pressing a rather large amount of money into the hands of several people at the county court house, as well as the original undertaker, that I would be allowed access to the morgue following the disinterment of Luciana's body, and that I would maintain ownership of it for the entire night following her removal from the grave. I would have Luciana's body in the morgue, from dusk till dawn, with no interruptions and no one else present. The body would be placed into the new concrete tomb the next day; this was my legal contract with the county authorities.

My agreement with the undertaker, who sneered in the most unappealing way when I made the suggestion, had two stipulations: one, that I should be left completely alone, with not another living person in the building, and two, that all the apparatus in the embalming room should be made available to me. On statement of these conditions, I was forced to endure the expression on the man's face, the silent judgement about my assumed intent. I could not, of course, clarify what I intended to do, for the deal would not have been made, so I stood there in the spotlight for crimes I had not committed and did not intend to commit. He demanded an additional sum to ensure that my demands were met, and I handed it over, cursing the man and his apparent lack of morals. It occurred to me that this was not an arrangement out of the ordinary for him. I promised the man another sum if I could be sure, when I placed Luciana into the concrete, that no similar courtesy had been extended to any other paying customers—at least as far as my property was concerned.

I was surprised to see that no member of Luciana's family was present at the removal of the body, as in a place like Key West, where salacious gossip is the highest currency, rumours travel fast. In addition, I had seen a Cuban at the county office. I suppose it should have been no shock to me that Luciana meant nothing to her family after her death; all they ever placed on her grave were cheap flowers that were blown away by the time the day was spent. In the end, the only people present at the removal of the body were myself and the two young men paid to complete the task. The coffin, which had sustained some damage, was easily transported to the funeral home, and there the undertaker assisted me with the removal of the inner casket. He helped me unscrew the lid, but I insisted upon being alone to finish the job. I could not stand to share Luciana with another. He took his leave and I was left there with my darling and with a set of keys; I locked the doors behind the undertaker as he left and had to take a seat for several minutes, such was the intensity of the feeling of being in Luciana's presence again. My time was short, however, so I began my task.

As I pushed the coffin lid aside, I could see immediately that some of the lining had adhered to Luciana's face, so it would be necessary to cut this away before I could open the casket entirely. It did not escape me that, so veiled, my darling's face was that of a bride standing at the altar. I took her hands, kissed her lips and took a lungful of her smell, which was, of course, tinged with the slight odour of decay. I disinfected the body quickly, with gentle care, and wiped away the myriad fluids that had been expelled from her in the weeks since her burial. Despite my excitement to be once again joined with my lover, I could not fail to see that despite my best efforts, decay had begun, and Luciana's body was not as it once was. Before her illness took hold, she had been a strong, firm, flexible girl. In front of me was a body that had started to succumb to the conditions in which it had been placed. I fought off a wave of anger; if only she had been given to me, she could have been resurrected exactly as she had been. I quickly gained hold of my senses. The clock was ticking. I did not have much time.

My first task was to remove the lining of the coffin from Luciana's face while causing minimal damage to the skin below. With the application of a mild soap solution—Luciana had always had sensitive skin—I began to work at the remnants of silk that had attached themselves to her face, hands and décolletage. The silk had become adhered to her body by the presence of liquids expelled in the days following the departure of the soul, and for this I blamed the shoddy workmanship of the undertaker, clearly a charlatan despite the amount of money he charged for his unsatisfactory service. But how many of his victims would ever discover the results of his unprofessional handiwork?

With the tweezers I teased off the material millimetre by millimetre, squinting by the light of the candles around me, keeping the light low so that I might not be discovered, and wiping the sweat away from my forehead with a tissue folded in my left hand. This, however, took several hours, such was the delicacy necessary to preserve the girl's looks. Despite my best efforts, some facial tissue and some portions of the upper layer of my darling's skin came away from her face with the removal of the silk, leaving the hypodermis exposed. Panicked, I covered the rest of the silk in dampened gauze. I cursed myself for leaving my beloved so long at the mercy of nature. And yet the fault really lay with the undertaker, who did not treat the body as requested, and allowed the coffin lining to adhere to my wife.

I laboured all night cleaning my darling; removing rotten tissues where her body had been tossed around in the coffin, causing fissures that were left vulnerable. I pulled open the undertaker's stitches and saw with dismay that her smaller organs had begun to consume themselves in their own acid. I stuffed the gaps in her abdominal cavity with sterilised gauze and rags, bulking out her small frame and providing some additional padding against the shrinking caused by the desiccation process. When I saw that the sun was beginning to creep up towards the horizon, I arranged Luciana in such a manner that I could, via a series of pulleys and with the help of a sheet that would hold her entire body, lift her out of the putridness of her original coffin and place her inside the specialised inner casket that I had spent weeks building. With no small effort on my part, and more than one terrifying, heart-stopping moment where it looked like Luciana might fall and injure herself irrevocably, I managed to manoeuvre her into the incubator tank. This was an inner coffin with an interior and exterior wall, between which was a series of pipes filled with a combination of liquefied gases. The purpose of this layer was to drop the temperature of the body and thereby offer some cryogenic protection against the natural process of decay, at least to her outer layer. This was an invention entirely of my own, applying the principles learned in the experiments conducted under Dr Magnussen. The base concept was simple enough: by creating a mixture of nitrogen and oxygen made liquid, I was able to partially freeze the body within, stopping the functions of decay from occurring. In addition to this, I had prepared a solution that contained a mixture of preservatives, nourishing and antiseptic in equal measure. Liquid formaldehyde was one of these, and the others had been shipped from Europe to circumvent certain laws in America that remained despite the advancements of medical science. By coating Luciana's body with this solution inside the inner chamber, I knew I could place her in a suspended animation whereby the shell of her body would be protected from further putrefaction and decay.

Before I closed the inner casket, I allowed myself an hour to hold my wife in my arms. She was much colder than she had been before her death, but curiously her smell, when she was removed from the stinking original casket, was much the same as it had been, and I lay there with her with my arms in the fresh, sterile silk of her new coffin. I could almost feel her heart fluttering, as if trying to give me a signal that the umbilical cord between it and her active soul had not been entirely severed. In fact, lying there with her, my own body temperature soared, and by the time the undertaker arrived, not a minute after dawn, I was covered in perspiration—a condition exacerbated by the physical task of closing the new inner casket before the man could look at my darling. I gently stroked the coffin, whispering sweet nothings to my resting bride while I waited for the arrangements to be made, and we quickly drove Luciana to her new tomb before the day had truly begun. With the help of a winch, we lowered the casket into its new tomb, a single piece of concrete with a matching concrete lid. As a small folly, I had ensured that a piece of glass had been set into the tomb, so that I could look in and see the coffin. I felt a peace in my heart knowing that she was thus preserved, and yet still, in my soul, there was a restlessness that would not be sated until I had rescued her for good.

24

Gabriela

We didn't go to see it, when he took her out of the ground. Mamá had given in. She asked us not to go and watch what he was doing, because Luci was not there, Luci was with God, she said, and there was nothing holy about an empty body; she could speak to her daughter whenever she wanted. The truth was that Mamá knew there would be gossip if we were there, and she could not hear the Madrigal name in strangers' mouths any longer. But Andrés, Juan Antonio and I—we knew something was wrong. The reasons he gave for taking Luci out of her grave made no sense. Why not leave the girl in the ground, where she could rot like a person is supposed to rot?

Only Andrés went the next day, in secret, and he came back and told us he had encased her as if she was something dangerous, as if she might spill out into the world and infect everything around her. It was a concrete tomb, big and ugly, an imposition on the rest of the graveyard, something alien that had landed and taken over the space. Andrés then went to the funeral home, and asked to speak to whoever had signed the papers for this move; the undertaker swore to Andrés that he had watched the whole thing, that he had seen Luci's body placed into the new tomb. He swore on the Bible that she had been closed up, that she had not been taken away, that our sister really was in that strange structure, that tomb that had nothing of Luciana about it.

*

Grief does not go away, but it does change, slowly. It turns from a hollow pit inside you to something you carry with you instead, a something, a shard of glass with its sharp end buried in the marrow of your bones. You can't push it out, but you do grow around it, like a tree engulfing a knife thrust into its bark. In the months and years after all of this happened, I continued to take flowers to Luci's grave, her real grave, once a week. There was nothing there but a hole where the headstone had been, and the turned-over grass of a grave filled and emptied and filled up again, but to me she was there. To me, the new tomb could never be where Luci lay. At the graveside I would talk to Luci as if she was hovering just overhead, looking at everything we did, and after a while she began to speak back. She spoke in her real voice, her voice before sickness, and I swear I could hear it; I swear it was a real thing in the world. Soon enough I didn't have to speak out loud, for Luci would hear it regardless, and soon after that her voice was part of me too, the two of us speaking to each other in my mind. I took her in, my dear sister, our Luci, and this is the place she continues to live—not in her first grave, or in a concrete tomb, or anywhere else she might have ended up. This is where Luci is, and where she always will be.

The months after he moved her were difficult to bear. We expected it all to be over then, but the story became gossip, became a tale for people to share over dinner. On the street, strangers ran up to our mother, who had grown quiet and smaller than we ever imagined she could be, to talk about her dead daughter, her 'miracle treatments', and the man who was so in love that he'd dug up her body and moved it somewhere better. I would wait for her to tell the real truth, to tell them what that man really was, but each time my mother just hurried on, making herself smaller still. Afterwards they would say she was rude, that old Cuban, a woman who would not even give you the time of day. The stories even followed her home;

neighbours would come over to borrow a dish and instead tell my mother that he, that man, had been visiting Luci's tomb every day. When my mother asked them to stop telling her, they whispered about her in their yards. But worst of all was still to come: a year and a half after Luci's death, the mailman told Mamá that his daily visits to the tomb had stopped, that no one had seen that old Polish man in the graveyard for weeks. I found my mother at the church, crying, praying to God, crying that her baby girl had finally been forgotten—even by the man who was supposed to love her eternally.

It would be a lie to say we didn't hear the way people talked. At least I heard it; Andrés did not say, neither did Juan Antonio, and my father—well, he barely spoke at all. They closed their minds against it, closed themselves up against it. But I couldn't help but hear; the way people speak, they like to pretend such a story shocks them, but really, they love the way it feels on their tongues. Like slices of ripe mango. I saw the pieces in the newspapers, heard the ghost stories about my sister, turned over and softened and shared over coffees. I told my friends not to speak of her to me, nor of him. It was too soon, and my sadness was still so heavy. In this way I hurt myself, and hurt Luci most of all.

But like Mamá, I couldn't escape the knowledge that he had stopped visiting her tomb. It seemed like all Key West was desperate to tell us; no one thought about the things we had felt, about the real girl who had lived, and then died, and who once ran around our streets with the same body they whispered about. By then the real Luci was an abstract, a pretty girl with a sad romance, a girl forgotten in the ground after all. The rumours, of course, talked of every possibility. He had killed himself in that strange house. He had moved away. He had shut himself up with his loneliness. The worst was the idea that he had stopped caring about Luci at all. I thought that was the truth of it. I thought in death she could offer him nothing of her beauty, so he had moved on. When I first heard he had stopped visiting her tomb, it sent me to my car weeping. I held the steering wheel and cried and cried. This man, this monster—all I had wanted was for him to leave my sister alone. So why did it upset me so to think that he finally had? That day, I stopped listening once more.

25

Wilhelm

E very evening after Luciana's second burial, I went to visit
her at dusk, just as the sun was crawling towards the
horizon. I felt it the perfect time to remind Luciana that
I loved her, to peer into her window and assure her that I was
doing everything possible to work towards her resurrection. I
told her over and over that, when the right day came, I would
take her body from its resting place and restore her soul to it. I
promised that I would give her the wedding day she had always
wanted; that I would place her veil over her face and hold her
hands and from then on I would keep her forever, my promised
bride. The cemetery was often quiet at this time of the evening,
and I could sing to her, gently, songs from my homeland, about
love beyond all.

Luciana, for her part, began to sing back.

I know that many will find this difficult to believe. I ask those
people to suspend their disbelief for a brief period, though I
appreciate the challenge of doing so when discussing subjects
about which one feels certain facts are immutable. But I knew
that Luciana's soul, when not wandering, did periodically rest
in her body; indeed, if I had not left my home at a certain hour,
Luciana's spirit appeared to me standing by the door of my
house, as if reminding me that I had a date set with her and
should not be late. So to hear, one day, when the cemetery was
empty but for me and my love, the thin but unmistakable voice

of my darling emanating from the tomb I had built for her—well, it was not such a shock to me. As a matter of fact, I grew to expect this from her, and it became our goodbye call to one another.

The astute reader may ask why I did not take an easier route here to join my darling, as we would of course be together forever in eternity. Perhaps it was my own cowardice that prevented me from simply putting a rope around my neck and releasing my soul into whatever realm Luciana existed. Having received proof of a post-death consciousness, it would not have been irrational to consider that I too could enter this metaphysical state. Neither would it be illogical to hope that I would be beside Luciana there. Yet I had no evidence that my soul would endure after death in the same way as Luciana's and my grandmother's, and though I considered this route a number of times, I was simply unable to commit myself to death with no certainty that I would be with her. All I had, in this regard, was faith—and faith is no alternative to science.

For twenty-one months following Luciana's removal into the tomb, I worked day and night at my laboratory. I was forced to give up my job at the hospital, for a variety of reasons, which I will not enumerate here. Chief amongst them, however, was my unwillingness to give over any of my time to any other task that did not involve Luciana. When one has a singular goal, even sleep feels like a betrayal of the greatest magnitude. I would have stopped sleeping, stopped eating, stopped any other matter of life at all if I could have, just to hold Luciana close to me a minute sooner. Yet living involves self-gratification, and I was forced to sleep, eat and attend to the other annoyances of daily life yet still.

Once every four weeks, however, I would forgo sleep and make my way to the cemetery in the dead of night to make my necessary checks on Luciana. Once I was convinced that the area was empty and secured, I was able to lift the lid off the tomb by application of a crowbar. This allowed it to be pushed to one side, giving me access to a small valve that I had inserted into the lid of the casket. I screwed the cap off this valve and, checking around for spectators once more, opened my mouth and pressed my face to it. There was the astringent, chemical smell of the various preserving liquids mixed with that of the body of my love. I breathed it in deeply. Each body has a particular smell, and Luciana's perfume only grew in intensity after her death. It appeared warm, as if the sun of Key West had penetrated the concrete shell around her and touched her skin. In this manner I was able to ensure that Luciana's body was still, in its way, alive—and, of course, I used these opportunities to refresh the solution of liquids that was keeping her cold and free from decay. The reader will forgive an old fool if I admit to stealing a kiss from the top of the coffin lid and singing quietly to my darling. If love is foolish, I was its helpless victim.

In truth, I felt a growing sense of unease about my plan and my theories. One evening I failed to keep my appointment at the cemetery. I was wracked with the worst type of self-doubt; I had eaten only boiled eggs and pickled cabbage for days, and so active was my mind, I found it increasingly difficult to sleep. I had in front of me all the proof I needed that my plan would work, and yet I was paralysed by indecision, and by the creeping, insidious thought that my daily trysts with Luciana's sleeping body were enough, that love could remain this way indefinitely. I had forgotten to buy light bulbs—such occurrences were becoming more commonplace as I slipped out of this realm and into some other—so was working long into the evening by the light of three candles at my desk. There was no wind outside; it was one of the calmest Florida evenings I had ever experienced.

And yet suddenly all three of the candles before me blew out, violently, and I was plunged into darkness.

A quiet but persistent whimpering then began.

I stood, saying Luciana's name, grasping at the air in front of me, looking for something to hold on to. My darling felt rejected, abandoned. I had broken our date and now she was thrust into doubt as to the strength of my love. I had promised her the world, I had promised to be her saviour, and I had yet failed. I stepped sideways, banging my thigh against a table, then tried to move forward, to find where my Luciana was, and fell heavily against the floor, my knees bearing the brunt of the fall's force. The whimpering stopped for a moment while I rubbed my knees and brought myself to a sitting position (I was not a young man and this was difficult), but when I settled, the crying began again in earnest, indeed increasing in volume.

'Luciana, my darling, my bride, I'm sorry!'

I opened a drawer and searched blindly for a box of matches. I found them, brought one out and struck it. It was blown out immediately. My darling would have her voice heard. It was the deep crying of a child who has been denied her favourite toy; the heartfelt keening of a girl who has run into a store and lost her father's hand. She was petulant, my young darling, in death as in life. I continued my profuse apologies, but the noise grew louder, so much so that I worried that any individuals out on the street might hear the sound and call the police.

Suddenly the crying stopped, replaced by a heavy breath-ing; the child half sated but so close to crying again. I heard a single sob and responded.

'One week. A week from today I will save you. A week from today I will bring you home.'

The noise stopped.

It was set. She had decided.

*

It was a fierce night, the moon obscured by clouds and the rain vicious from before dusk. At first I considered this a hindrance, but it would in fact be a help, ensuring that there were no bodies out on the streets and washing away any evidence of my presence in the graveyard.

Luciana herself had laid out her plan in the previous evenings, by manner of indicating to me whether or not she was happy with the suggestions I had written down. If she did not agree, she would blow out the candles. If she thought them satisfactory, she allowed the light to remain. In this way her soul guided my hand, forced me to act how she wished.

There were some preparations necessary, and I spent several days turning one of the rooms of my home into a ward-morgue, sterilising and sealing the area and moving the furniture into other spaces in the house. I filled the home with flowers, to welcome Luciana and also to obscure the odours that would undoubtedly overwhelm my small abode. I took care to make the home as welcoming as I could to my young bride—for I know that an old man's sparse hovel is not the place into which a young wife would want to step.

I had also traded my smaller car for a roomy station wagon, and had made sure to be seen using this for some weeks prior to my rescue of Luciana. I made strict measurements of the car, and found that, with the removal of the back seats and the passenger seat in the front, as well as the addition of some stabilising shelves, there was enough room from front to back for the cargo I would be carrying.

As I made my way to the cemetery in the driving rain, I felt a strange calmness—certainly in comparison to the enormous anxiety I had been struggling against in the weeks prior. In taking my hand, Luciana had freed me from the self-doubt and the indignity of inaction, and in this way she had saved me, as I was about to save her. The thought brought a tear to my eye as I turned into the graveyard.

I wore a dark coat, buttoned up to the neck, a black hat on my head, and around my face I tied a handkerchief, also dark. Luciana had intimated to me that no cover would be necessary; that her placement in the cemetery would shield me from the street outside, but also that anyone looking into the cemetery would consider me just another gravedigger at work. The handkerchief would keep my privacy, in the case of any disturbance. The gates were locked, but a short application of the crowbar remedied this situation. I had brought from home a heavy-looking chain, which I wrapped around the bars of the gate to discourage any passers-by from following me in, and blankets to cover the coffin as I moved it. The disinterment was simple enough, facilitated by several car jacks and the aforementioned crowbar, but in my commitment to the project of rescuing Luciana, I had grossly underestimated the physical strength necessary to complete the task; or, rather, I had grossly overestimated the strength that my ageing body held. With some effort the tomb's cover was removed, but of course could not be damaged, as it would have to be replaced. With the help of a quickly installed pulley-and-lever system, and some rocks tied to the end of the ropes to substitute for the strength I did not have, I gingerly let the lid down to the ground, on its side. The levers, specially purchased for this task, from a store that more usually supplied to mechanics, were able to bear the weight; without them, it would have been impossible for me to complete my task. With the same tools, and the last of my own energy, I was then able to hoist Luciana's coffin, which was made heavier by the equipment I had placed inside it, out of the tomb, inch by inch, and onto a substantial cart that I had managed to purchase from a local woodsman; this would be my vehicle for transporting her to my car. It was constructed of a door, with two wheels in the middle and handles on one end, but it would be more than sufficient. Here the pulley-and-lever system was of limited use, and, fearing that Luciana might fall if not placed properly onto the cart, I lifted and moved, lifted and moved. On the third of these movements my shoes, which were unfit for purpose, slipped on the wet ground by the tomb and I fell to my knee. My hat was knocked onto the ground, and in my scrabbling around, I pulled the handkerchief from my face and into the mud. Luciana's coffin, which was balancing precariously in the midst of the process, toppled sideways, and the bottom right-hand corner of it fell first onto me and then onto the ground below. I cried out at the thought of my love being damaged in her container, then I smelled something I knew too well. The lid of the valve in that corner had fallen and the liquid inside was leaking out, creating a puddle around my knees and soaking into my trousers. The odour was much more pungent than I was used to, having only smelled it through the coffin's small valve, and for a moment I sat there, almost defeated, certainly overwhelmed—a greying lover sitting in a pool of his darling's fluids in the driving rain. For a moment, I considered giving up. Cowardice overtook me; I could simply leave, abandon the project and claim the next morning that it was grave robbers, after the jewellery that Luciana was buried in—or, more darkly, after the body of Luciana herself, for nefarious purposes. This was my lowest ebb, perhaps for decades. Everything was conspiring to urge me to abandon my wild scheme.

At this point, I began to hear Luciana singing, in my native tongue, that beautiful melody which we had been using to communicate; my darling girl knew she was almost home. More than that, she knew I was so close to abandoning all my ideas of rescue—and she responded not with violence or anger, but with compassion. With forgiveness. I allowed myself to cry openly, with no one to see me and no one to judge an old man in love.

How long I sat there in Luciana's thrall, I could not say. In time, though, I began to sing with her. She was so close to rejoining this world; I knew I must act. We both quieted. I pushed myself up, feeling every one of my many years, and with all my effort, hoisted the fallen corner of the coffin onto the cart. From there, slowly and carefully, I pulled the casket into place. Whatever happened after that point, we would be together.

The tomb's lid was replaced, trapping a substantial amount of rainwater inside. I removed my pulley-and-lever contraption from around the grave, and threw it, too, onto the cart. I secured the coffin with straps so that it would under no circumstances fall again, and then began our journey back to my vehicle. The weight of the coffin and the equipment on the cart's small wheels drove them into the rapidly loosening earth, meaning that to move it even a few feet required strenuous effort on my part. As the ground grew muddier, I dragged the wagon, with great difficulty, along the alleyways of the graveyard and to my car. Thanks to the height of the cart I was able to push the coffin into the substantial trunk of the station wagon directly from it, though this expended what little strength remained in me. I allowed my body to press against the lid of the coffin, and it was warm. So warm I could have sworn it had a heartbeat. I hoped then that Luciana had had the company of other souls in the realm beyond this, that in the months since her first burial she had spent her hours in communion with the first-dead, telling them of her saviour, of her loving husband who had uncovered the secret of resurrection and was going to save her from non-existence. I then retraced my steps, ensuring that the rain was sufficient to cover my tracks, took back the blankets, now totally sodden, and folded them up. I glanced back at the many graves that lay untouched; it was more than I could bear, the indifference of the living. We are engaged in a genocide, a massacre of all who have ever lived. I took a moment to mourn those hundreds of unnecessary dead—and the millions more in graveyards all over the country. I walked slowly to the car and said a prayer for the unrescued dead as I passed over the threshold of the cemetery. Without looking back, I drove Luciana home.

Though I would have liked to hasten Luciana's freedom, two forces of nature were working against me. The first was my own old age; the physical exertion necessary to free the coffin from its tomb was beyond what I could easily achieve, and were the reward not so great I would have undoubtedly failed to do so. I was thoroughly exhausted on arrival at the house, though I could not sleep until I had attended to the second challenge: the necessity of thawing out my darling.

Upon arrival at home, I brought Luciana from the station wagon into our home with the help of the cart and installed her inside the room I had dedicated for her. Due to my extreme fatigue, this was a much more difficult process than I had anticipated, and I had neglected to consider the width of the doorways and whether the wagon would fit through them. I was forced to slide Luciana's casket off it at the front door, and from there could only push or drag the coffin along the floor, navigating it into the prepared room in ever-shorter bursts of movement. I hid the wagon around the back of the house and locked the doors against visitors. Having taken some time to recover myself, I lifted the lid of the casket with a racing heart. To the touch, she was now sufficiently cold as to cause pain in the pad of the finger. The partial freezing that I had used to save her from further decay had to be undone before I could safely remove her body from its coffin, as even half-frozen structures are significantly vulnerable to injury. While I had taken precautions against crystallisation of the liquid in her body, there was no way to hasten the reversal of the procedure—none, at least, that would deliver her safely to me in one piece. To this end, I had to leave her to thaw in a gently warmed room while I slept. I replaced the casket lid and secured it; perhaps this was superstition, but I did not want to lose her to theft or injury at this final stage. By the time I woke, she would be ready.

I dragged myself into bed where I fell into the deepest sleep of my days. However, on waking, I had the overwhelming realisation that this might be the last time, ever, that I woke alone.

It was night again by the time I roused; almost twenty hours had passed. I ate a little, my stomach too nervous to accept much-needed sustenance, and tended to the space, ensuring soft candlelight would greet Luciana, lest the harsh electric bulbs damage her long-unused retinas. I took the time to draw a long, hot bath, as I had fallen asleep in my clothing the previous night and did not consider myself in a fit state to receive my darling once again. I washed myself aggressively, almost searing my skin in the heat of the water, then towelled my body vigorously before perfuming my skin; yet still the odour of the valve's contents would not be overwhelmed. I placed aromatic oils around the house, hoping that the combination of smells would be agreeable to Luciana.

The reader at this point will not begrudge the author, I hope, a little vanity. I dressed myself in my most pristine and presentable outfit: a tailcoat and trousers that I had had tailored to my exact measurements, with fabrics from abroad, by an Italian professional who, by coincidence, shared many of my life's experiences and had settled in the same area. We had struck up something of a friendship, and though I never admitted the fact of my nationality to him, I suspect that he knew it. Yet he was nothing less than courteous and, dare I say it, chivalrous to me, and when I told him I needed a suit fit for my wedding day, he created for me the most handsome outfit I have ever seen—with a comforting emblem hand-sewn into the underside of one of the lapels. I trimmed my beard, dressed in this suit and perfumed myself again. I looked, if I may permit myself to say so, almost striking.

The home, then, was ready for its mistress. Flowers, art, feminine accoutrements, the schnapps Luciana loved so much—everything a young woman could want, I had provided, and thanks to my arrangements with regards to payments from Europe, there was plenty of money available for whatever she might need in her second life. The room in which she rested, growing warmer by the minute, would also function as a medical room, with all the chemicals, solutions, sterile instruments and helpful additions I might need.

I took a short while to gather myself, taking a sharp shot of schnapps to steady my nerves. As a rule I did not drink, but I allowed myself this small indulgence. I closed the curtains, locked the door and readied myself to free my bride.

I unscrewed the coffin lid, lifted it, and rested it against the wall.

Turning to my wife, I forced the horror from my face, lest she see the intense and inescapable despair that had descended on me in that moment. I placed my hand on her hair, the other on her stomach, and leaned in, whispering brief words of love, of gratitude, of yearning.

While my theory had been proven, and my methods had worked, the fact of twenty-one months in the grave had caused immense damage to the image of my darling Luciana. While her arresting aroma was still prominent, so too were the odours of decay. The silk sheets on which she lay were now sodden with my cryogenic solution and her own bodily excretions. Having been placed for some time in the ground and then in the tomb, Luciana's body had been ravaged by maggots, larvae and other small insects feasting on the first evidence of localised putrefaction. My darling's skin looked waxy and queer, with pallor in places and purpling in others due to the advance of hypostasis. She was now smaller than when she was alive, due to various decomposition processes that, while slowed somewhat by my treatment, could not be avoided completely, and though she in life was something of a lithe creature, here she was almost a child, so much had the weight of her body been removed from her. And yet—my partial cooling and my treatment with fluids had worked to save Luciana from the advanced decay in which her body would otherwise have been; her skin still had the flush of life about it, and though her cheeks were sullen they were not dried or rubbery; she might have been captured in a jar like a creature in amber, kept to gaze upon in wonder. There was work to do.

I stared into the shadowy depths of Luciana's eyes, expecting to see the slow flutter of her eyelids as her soul came back into her body. I stayed there, the gentle welcome on my face, soft words escaping my lips, but she did not stir. Of course; she was not ready. Her body was not as it should be.

Talking and singing to my darling constantly with reassuring words and platitudes, I pulled on my latex gloves and began my work.

The first task was to remove from Luciana the remains of her bridal dress, which had been eaten away from around her body, and the remaining layers of silk from the first casket's lining. While I had worked these away from her face previously, I had not had time to properly attend to the rest, which had unfortunately become joined to the tissues of her hands, arms and feet. Beginning with the dress, using tweezers and working with the utmost care to ensure that the remnants of the fabric did not remain adhered to the upper layers of her skin, I detached from her torso the portions of lace that were covered in slimy mould and overgrown with a kind of moss, knowing that this would be the easier task of the two ahead of me. Clearly this growth had occurred in the months before I was able to drop the temperature of Luciana's casket, for the cryogenesis should have prevented any spores from the outside world taking hold inside the coffin. I dropped the overgrown material into a bucket by my feet, and into this I also squeezed the liquids that had been sponged off in the process. All the portions of lace that were too firmly adhered were left soaking in a solution; I was loath to tear them off and cause injury to her delicate skin, which, in death, had taken on a hue which I found most becoming—even more so than in life. I changed the bucket and took another shot of schnapps, finding myself grateful for its strong smell and even stronger effects.

To the remaining silk. The lack of fat around her clavicle area made the skin difficult to attend to, but for the sake of Luciana's vanity I painstakingly worked around these areas, knowing that a woman's confidence relies upon the reaction of men to these parts of her body when she allows them to be displayed. Again, the bucket filled, and again I emptied it into the toilet, noting that beyond the flimsy closed curtains the light of day had begun again. Time is a vicious mistress.

I worked at Luciana's hands for several hours, again resorting to leaving portions of the material to soak, for fear of causing further damage. Gathering all my strength, I lifted Luciana's body and washed it gently, fighting against the fluttering of my own heart while holding her body so close to mine. Taking the sponge, I removed all the antiseptic solution from the innards of the coffin, and, turning my darling gently, removed the sodden rags that had found their way out of her various stitched areas. Lifting her forward, being very careful to listen for the telltale crunch that would let me know that parts of her had not been adequately defrosted, I held her head against my chest as I used chemical cleanser to disinfect her outer portions once, twice, three times, then took the softest of cloths and went over her entire body, drying her as best I could. I applied perfumes wherever her skin was not soaking for the removal of the material, and took some time to massage my darling's feet, wanting to offer her some relief from the ordeal she had gone through. I removed the seemingly endless wads of cotton wool from the small orifices of her head and the anal opening, and packed these areas with fresh material, to give her the dignity of remaining clean. By the time the day was full, I had fallen asleep in my chair, my face resting on the feet of my lover, half out of the grave and half still in. In my dreams I kissed her toes and took her hands in my own, and in all ways possible she was mine.

This was my pattern for several days. The removal of the casket lining from Luciana's skin formed the majority of my work in that first week, such was the importance of ensuring that her delicate beauty was in no way disturbed, for when she woke entirely, I wanted my darling girl to see in the mirror the face that she, and I, had always loved—not an undeveloped negative of it.

I could not fail to see the natural post-mortem processes that had occurred before I was able to place Luciana into her second coffin, and these dismayed me. As well as the sunken cavities that now comprised my darling's eyes, her lips, still held together by the undertaker's wire, were dry and shrunken, curling slightly inwards and sticking to her gums. Though I had thought to place the moisturising solution all around her, those initial few months had allowed a certain amount of desiccation to occur, and her skin pulled back from her nails, from her hairline, from her other bodily openings. Her hair was brittle, and her hands, curling slightly into claws, were almost completely fixed together. I held her, noting these flaws that could not be undone, and pledged to love her still, and moreover, to restore what I could of her beauty so that I would not notice her fundamental deficiencies. Indeed, as I held Luciana in the dying light, and stared into the empty black holes of her eyes, it seemed to me that matter was gathering there to form fresh pupils, to look back at me with renewed love and hope, to stare back at me as my beautiful bride, finally alive again.

I fetched a sharp pair of medical scissors from my bag and pulled Luciana's lips back so that I might cut the wire that held them together. The wire nicked the soft inner flesh of her mouth, but she did not bleed. I pulled each portion of padding out with tweezers, my hands failing to function as I brought out the last piece, for I knew I was about to take my bride. I brought her closer to me and kissed her lips, tasting for the first time in many months the flavour of the woman who had been promised to me for so long. As I brought my mouth from hers, I gently wiped away the remnants of skin that clung to me, and took a deep breath. I kissed her parted mouth again, releasing my full lungs into hers, breathing life, watching her chest rise with my love. Whispering softly, I retrieved her bridal veil from the mannequin I had created, as well as the white bridal gloves I had purchased without her knowledge. Prying apart her hands, I placed them into the gloves and arranged the veil around her head, covering her eyes coquettishly. Behind her head I arranged a golden silk scarf which I had gifted to her in life, as well as the heads of yellow roses, trimmed of all their thorns. She might have been a fresco in a church or a picture on an altar. I laid her down gently and sank my upper body into the coffin beside her, lifting her head to place my arm beneath it, so I could embrace her in the manner a husband embraces a wife. Again I pressed my lips to hers; again I filled her up. She took on a temperature closer to my own, and I would retain that I could see the colour spreading in her, could see the vivacity of her living days returning to her then and there, so potent were my feelings. I dropped my hand down to where hers lay, below her navel, and the gloved fingers tickled my palm. I placed my hand on the flat of her navel and felt her lower body shift. Breathing into her, I swear she shifted towards me, asking for more, to be brought to life in such a manner, and I kissed her with great vigour, feeling the youth of her body return to it. She looked spectacular, she felt spectacular—I could not resist. Under her spell truly and irrevocably, I took hold of her as a husband should, as if she had never died her first death.

If I had any remaining doubts as to the veracity of my theories, that single night banished them from my mind. From then onwards, my singular goal was to understand the condition of Luciana's body and bring it back to a state of living whereby her soul might re-enter it for her second life. The first process of this was to bring her to a state in which she could repose without the risk of further decay—and in which such a daintily vain girl might be happy to live once again.

My darling's body remained delicate; my days of careful treatment had not yet expunged all the evidence of her death from her physicality. It took many days to remove the final portions of clothing from her body, and when this process was complete I was dismayed to find many small, and some large, lacerations of the skin—some of which stemmed from the removal of the clothes, and others that were certainly the fault of the undertaker who had handled Luciana at her passing. I treated these damages as if they were living tissue, cleaning out the wounds with iodine, adding lotion and covering them in sterile bandages. In some cases, it was necessary to use stitching, which was not ideal but was required in several places. I made my way over the body, dealing with the minutiae of the lacerations. It was necessary to bind the toes, ankles, feet and calves in sterilised, moisturised bandages, and for this I blamed myself; my lack of care when removing Luciana from her grave had caused her to crash violently into the bottom right corner of her casket. Of course, there was additional skin damage from the moist environment that she had been laid in; I applied bandages from her thighs down to the bottom of her feet in the hope that this would assist in the regeneration of these parts.

On close inspection of the abdomen, I found that there were maggots feasting on the blood that had escaped from the many small tears. There were also a significant number of larvae around the ears, and near almost all other openings and tears on the head, including many in Luciana's hair. I painstakingly removed these and sterilised the areas on which they had been feeding, but they were numerous and persistent. I had been very much at pains to save Luciana's hair, of which she was so proud. It was unfortunate that Luciana had cut her hair into the American style, which was much shorter and blunter than the popular styles worn in Spanish countries. It had taken her passivity during her illness for it to grow long, almost down to her clavicles, but still the effect was a boyish one. When she had first appeared to me beside Oma, and in all subsequent appearances up to the time of our meeting—and, indeed, in all of the appearances since her death—Luciana appeared to me with the wild, thick, black hair of her heritage rather than the jagged cut she had taken on in life, and it was undeniable that the more natural style suited her more. I went to great efforts to wash Luciana's hair, as much of it was glued to her scalp with the body's post-mortem discharge. With the assistance of a demure young woman at the beauty store, I had chosen two combs, one wide and one fine, and had purchased a reviving shampoo along with the accompanying conditioner, none of which came cheaply. I washed Luciana's hair with these solutions several times, and brushed it with one comb then the other, wiping the implement free every few seconds of the small bodies that therein resided. Yet this was still not enough; the hair seemed to become riddled with more growth every day, including a proliferating cobweb mould, creating a strange halo around her scalp. So it was with regret that I was forced to cut the entire head of hair back to an even more masculine short style. This still did not solve the issue, so with great care I took a straight razor and shaved all of the hair from Luciana's head. I was keen to avoid causing further trauma to the skin, and therefore the process took me several hours, including short breaks in which I was able to calm my trembling hands. From one of these breaks, I re-entered the room and saw my bald-headed darling laying there and I am ashamed to say I felt disgust. All of her femininity had been shorn from her, and in the place of my feminine beauty lay instead the figure of a boy, sharp about the head and face and far too male-looking to be considered attractive. I covered her face and torso with a silk blanket while I finished the rest of my task. Having shaved the head entirely, I treated the scalp with a bleach-based solution, to kill all remaining larvae both on top of and under the skin, and then applied moisturisers heavily on all areas. I also took pains to block up the holes in Luciana's ears; I felt certain she would be able to hear without them, having mastered the art of speaking to me without her body, and the risk of small bacteria invading her through these orifices was too high. Realising that her head would not be the only site of infestation about her person, I sharpened the razor and took to removing all the hair from her body—a task that was as distasteful as it was laborious. Yet I knew that she would not be safe from lice and other pests until all the hair had been removed. After several hours, when this task was complete, I took a strong glue and applied to Luciana's head the wig that I had had made from the hair that had been given to me by her mother. As this hair was cut from Luciana when she first came to this country, it was long and vibrant; the wig had a natural curl and as I applied it to her scalp, I arranged the tresses gently around her jaw and neck, restoring to her the appearance of a seductive woman. I uncovered her face and body, sure that I would once again feel attracted to my beloved bride.

I treated the skin across the entire body with emollients containing additional minerals that would have leached out of the body in the months following her burial. I took the time to massage this tenderly into every part of her skin; I knew that massage was a vital part of the reviving of cells, and I will not deny that I enjoyed pampering my darling thus, singing to her and telling her of the adventures we would have upon her eventual return to her body. I watched the colour bloom in Luciana during these long massages, and I knew that under my touch the cells were finding new life, new power, new energy. After this I applied a fine powder all over the body, making sure to apply this into the crevices and folds so that mould could not find moisture there on which to grow. I made sure to speak to Luciana throughout these processes, averting my gaze from her most private areas, as any doctor would to preserve the dignity of their patient. This powdering left the body clean and free from acid, and also removed the crusts of discharge that had formed upon the epidermis.

Having clarified the quality and cleanliness of the skin, I then went about the body to ensure that any damage had been attended to. As I mentioned, my own clumsiness upon her second disinterment had caused some trauma to the lower legs, and I found that the ankles were left at an unpleasant angle, so much so that walking might prove difficult for Luciana when her soul finally returned to her. With confidence that my patient would feel no acute pain (one of the few advantages of working with the dead rather than the living), I cracked the ankles back into place and fixed them with splints, so that the recovery might begin while I prepared the rest of the body. I also noted that Luciana's nose, which had been broken as a child in some sort of incident back in her native country—I can only consider that parental abuse may have been involved, although Luciana, a loyal girl, would never say anything to implicate her mother or father—had shifted slightly, perhaps from the actions of the undertaker, or more likely under the pressure of the weight of the coffin lid when she was first placed within. Spurred on, I did a little reading around the methods of cosmetic surgery and, having educated myself in a subject which had hitherto never been my focus, I settled Luciana's head on my thighs and swiftly brought the bone of her nose back into place, where it may have originally been. Significant bruising appeared in the subsequent days, and though I hoped that this would abate, it never left entirely—there was nowhere for the blood to go, no propulsion to remove it from where it pooled beneath the face. Still, the purpling of the skin was a small price to pay for the restoration of Luciana's original beauty; indeed, the adjustment had brought to her a greater level of attractiveness than I considered possible. She was pristine.

As farmers burn their fields of corn to prepare them for fresh life, so too does our first death prepare our body for the second.

26.

Gabriela

I didn't know it at the time, but in those first few years, anger was our saviour. It gave us a focus, a reason to burn. When there was nothing left to be angry at, when there was nothing to fight against and no one to hate, all we were left with was the hollow ache of grief, the waking up in the mornings and remembering the dead, the empty seat at the family table and the silence left where once she would speak. The impossible task of trying to carry on when the person you love most in the world is gone.

There are years of this account to fill, I suppose, but when I look back, all the things I could write seem either too far away, like someone else lived them, or they seem ridiculous, a person going through the motions with no real life in her hands, nothing to give in or take out of the world. Just endless empty days, during which I could never have imagined what was happening to my sister.

Yet things did happen, to me and around me. After Luci's death, I threw myself into Felipe, and found his arms still waiting. He located a small apartment that we could live in, and built a home around me, holding me delicately as I grew listless and distant, waiting patiently for me to wake up and come back to him. We had no money for furniture, so he took things from the street when the neighbours had put them out. Mamá gave me some things she'd taken from Luci's room before the new lodger moved in; it was a kind of forgiveness, or an apology, maybe. Papá didn't want to see them go, because he knew they would not be able to replace them, but all the bravado had gone out of him. Now, he was just a small, old man in a big and terrible world.

Felipe worked hard, and treated me kindly, and eventually I began to respond to him, to remember he was there, to recognise that I had a home now. I started to make that home more like our own, and I lost myself in Felipe at night, and enjoyed it. My parents both lived long enough to meet our little daughter, Isabella, whose second name was for Luciana and whose third name was for Mamá, for it would have killed her in a second if my child did not have at least one name for God. When I found out I was pregnant, before I told Felipe, I took out my old jewellery box, the one that contained within it the something that once lived inside Luci. I unwrapped it from its covering, which may once have been white but was now the rust colour of old blood. It was there, the curled finger, but now it was dried, almost rubbery, and I had to pull the handkerchief away from where it had stuck to its surface. A twin of my own little something, Luci and I now close once again, both mother and daughter at the same time, half one thing and half another. I felt a cold stab in me, on the inside, and held the thing closer, wondering if I would be so brave without Luci guiding my hand. But in that moment I realised I wanted the baby; that it was only desperation to be close to my sister, to go through the same as my sister, that was stopping me from becoming a mother. So instead I held the only part of Luci I had left and prayed for her strength to be given to my baby. Chabela came out looking like Luci. Papá, my small and quiet Papá, covered her in floral cologne. She was so big she almost tore me in half. Felipe loved her so fiercely I had to pluck the baby from his sleeping grip.

Mamá had been so happy since the pregnancy that I barely noticed she was sick. But after the baby came, Mamá grew grey around her eyes and mouth, and took to her bed in the afternoons because she no longer had the energy to stay standing up. I would go over to the old house every day and sit with her, and if she was strong enough I would let her hold the baby. I thought it was grief, the same thing draining the colour from the rest of us, even when we were growing life. I was getting Isabella settled in her arms one day when my hand brushed against her blouse and found it wet.

'Mamá, did you spill something? You're damp here.'

'No spill, Gabi. Isn't she beautiful? Just like your sister, before she ruined her nose.'

She shifted the baby so her arms covered up the stain on her clothing, but I pushed my hand between her arm and her body. She reacted as if I had stuck in a knife; the smell was like old fruit at the bottom of the bowl, sweet and acid, grey mould growing over food. It was so honey-rotten I had to put a hand over my mouth to keep from retching.

'Mamá? What is this?'

I took Isabella from her and laid her on the bed, and with one hand on the baby's belly to keep her from rolling I pulled up Mamá's blouse and the worn material of her old brassiere. There, at the side, on the breast that had fed five children, two dead, was a hole, no, a filled circle the size of a quarter, pus yellow and angry and sore, with a raised red border so vicious I could barely stand to look. This was the smell, her body trying to push the bad things out, her skin trying to keep them in, and when she slapped my hand away and the brassiere fell over it again, it caused a thin trail of blood to stain her blouse.

'Oh, Mamá.'

She turned away.

'It's nothing, Gabriela Maria. There is no need to make a fuss.'

The baby cried and Mamá picked her up, and I wondered how I hadn't noticed that she held herself so strangely, keeping distance between her upper arm and the side of her chest, or how she grunted when she lifted the tiny weight of the child, or how tears sprang to her eyes when she smiled into Isabella's face and said, 'Mi Chabela, my beating heart, how beautiful you are.'

'No need to make a fuss,' she said again, but it was not about need, it was about money and time, and she was right about one thing: there was none of either.

Downstairs Papá sat on his folding chair in the dust outside the house, and when I began to tell him, he said, 'I know, Gabi. I know,' and I sat on his lap and held him while he cried. First one child, then another, and now his wife; he was incapable every time—but now, more so than ever. His hands had begun to swell at the knuckles and at the wrists, and his fingers were no longer straight, and his back rounded to make him look at the floor. Andrés said it was from years rolling tobacco leaves; I think it was from the weight of having everything on his shoulders for so long. He could not work and did his best to care for Mamá, though his hands could not hold the spoon to feed her and he would never take her to the doctor because they could not afford it. I did what I could and brought money to them, but it hurt his pride to accept it. He stopped talking about the possibilities in America, he stopped talking about Luci, and after Mamá died he stopped talking at all. He fell down on a dusty street on a rainy afternoon and he would not get back up again.

Juan Antonio sold the old house and we shared the money between the three of us. We could not bear to get rid of the piano, or rather *I* could not bear to get rid of the piano, but we didn't have room for it under our roof, so Andrés took it into the backyard of the beachside house he shared with a few other surfers and it was kept under a tree. Back out under the stars, just like its predecessor. Soon Tonio had a girlfriend and soon that girl was pregnant, so they had a wedding to keep God, and the soul of our grandmother, from being angry. Andrés didn't marry or even date, and I knew it was because he was making a life, however secretly, with one of his bare-chested surfer friends. We may not have had parents left to see, but God was always watching. Some days I was sad Papá was not around to see us all this way: housed and secure, making our way in this foreign country, and if we dreamed of Cuba we did not mention it, because there was no going back, and we all knew it.

When Isabella was big enough to go to school, I took a typing class with some of the money from the sale of my parents' house and found that I had fast fingers and my listening ear was good, so I got a job as a secretary, and for the first time we were a two-income household. I finished just before Isabella's school day ended, and every day I walked over to take her from the arms of her teacher, and together on the way home we stopped for ice cream or lollipops or even just to buy a mango and have the man cut it open for us so we could sit on the step outside the shop and eat it with our teeth pressed into the flesh, laughing at our sticky mouths and trying to kiss each other after. She got bigger and Felipe wanted more children, but by then there were things you could do, and things you could take, and I did all of these things, and there were no more babies, because to have one is a ludicrous miracle, and to ask for more is just asking for trouble. Chabela, she was my sister then, and my friend, and kept me from loneliness. If we were outsiders, we were outsiders together. When she began to make friends, and to speak with an accent so different to mine, I was half sad and half proud—my little gringa, all grown up. But I was so scared when she was out of my sight, in a world I did not really understand, that I would pray as I watched her go. Yet the praying felt incomplete; call it superstition. It was only when I took out my jewellery box and took out that rust-wrapped relic and held it in my hand that I felt like God was really listening. I began to carry it with me, in my handbag, in my pocket, always somewhere close by. It was a habit I just could not break.

With my wage and Felipe's, we bought our own house, which was small and sweaty, but it was ours. Eventually Andrés moved into a new place with his surfer, just the two of them, and he wanted rid of the piano from out of the yard, so I decided we should have it, that old and wrecked thing; we could take something broken and make it good again. Chabela, she could learn; maybe she would be better than any of us ever were, making real music instead of just noise. But Felipe said there was no room in our house, and what did we want a piano for anyway? It wasn't even the original one, just a poor replacement, and badly kept at that. He was right, and even I could see it. So he took an axe and chopped it up and Isabella and I sat by the fire on one of the chilly nights of fall, and I told her about her Aunt Luci and her wooden sword and me trying to fix her mistakes but only making it worse.

27

Wilhelm

I fear that in my pronouncements I may have given the impression that romantic notions overwhelmed my scientific mind with regards to the possibility of resurrection and the state of Luciana's body upon her disinterment. To counter this, let me state that I was in fact acutely aware of the challenges that lay before us, and of the extent of the irrevocable damage that had been done to the body in its post-mortem state.

Upon first death, many tissues in the body die too and cannot be enticed to life a second time—at least, not by any medicine that we currently understand. There had been, as I have mentioned, a level of damage to Luciana's facial tissue, and following her death many of the cavities of the body had become desiccated and hollow. Yet the strength of my belief in my ability to revive Luciana saved her from the murderous embalming process in its entirety; I had paid the undertaker to leave Luciana's organs not only in place but connected to her systems. It has long been understood that the heart is the seat of the soul (ignoring the belief, during the Middle Ages, that the soul resided somewhere in the lower abdomen, amongst the propelled filth of the digestive system) and it was my personal belief that the lungs would be necessary to allow Luciana the strength to walk and move when her soul was returned to her. I did not have any evidence that she would be able to eat food in the manner of the living, but I erred on the side of caution and allowed all of her organs to remain, including her stomach, intestines and bladder. My experiments had shown that the link between the metaphysical and the physical body is stronger than medical science currently entertains, and indeed the readmittance of the soul into the body produces a physical improvement that cannot be explained by science alone. It became apparent to me in the weeks following Luciana's restoration that the life force of the soul had a physical and perceptible influence upon the atoms of the body, stronger indeed than that seen before death. I attribute this to the strength of the power of the soul being increased when the body declines, in a similar way to that in which a newly blind man's hearing or sense of taste improve hugely upon the removal of his sight. When one part of a person wavers, the other strengthens. The influence of the post-mortem soul on the rescued body cannot be overstated, and as my married life with Luciana continued, I saw improvements that I cannot attribute to anything but metaphysical intervention.

I continued to treat my darling with injections of alimentary fluids and also persevered with the dermal application of these solutions. Concerned by the concave nature of her navel and the surrounding areas, I unstitched Luciana's body and filled her abdominal cavity once again with sterilised rags, padding and pieces of fabric, purchased from my friend the tailor and therefore of the highest quality, taking care to keep her organs in place and in full functioning contact with the rest of her body. This brought to her body a very satisfying plumpness, of which she was not possessed in the latter days of her illness. I also began to feed her orally, with the help of a thin funnel held in place between her teeth, first with easily digestible fluids such as milk, and then with a liquid food solution, puréed and strained so as to be tolerated by her beleaguered system. Here I found that Luciana was as fussy in death as she had been in life, and if she did not enjoy the taste of a certain type of this liquid food, she expelled it violently through her nose and mouth.

This necessitated a cleaning process that was both arduous and frustrating. The following day I would administer a different variant of the solution, and by tiring trial and error I found an entire menu which was satisfying to Luciana. Finally, she appeared happy with her feeding, and gained fifteen pounds in several weeks. Around this time, I removed the splints from Luciana's ankles and the bandaging from her nose, and was satisfied with the reaction of both. I also carefully removed the bandages from across her torso and legs, and found, to my amazement, that the lacerations there had completely healed. It was clear that the tissues of the body were regaining their strength, and although recovery from these small injuries was twice, perhaps three times as slow as it might have been in a first-life body, it was miraculous that they were healing in totality.

As my work with Luciana went on, I became concerned that exposure to the cloying and changeable Florida environment would have a negative effect on her looks, and to that end I ordered a large amount of the softest white silk I could find. My intention was to oil this material and wrap it around Luciana's skin whenever I was not tending to it directly. This would provide a barrier between the delicate tissues of Luciana's skin and the humid air, which contains much to degrade a vulnerable body. I gently applied it to the skin on her face, touching it lightly to her cheekbones and nose, so as to not leave a layer in which bacteria might flourish, and on top of the silk I applied a thin layer of wax as an additional protectant. I was satisfied at this and allowed Luciana to rest covered for three days while I attended to other parts of her. However, when I came to unwrap her, I saw that the silken outer coating which I had applied to my darling had become, despite my best efforts, noticeably adhered to her face. This alarmed me so much at first that I had to take myself from the room to calm down, so worried was I that I had caused my beloved an injury. And yet when I returned to the room, in the gentler light of the dying day, it became apparent that the silk had actually improved the look of my darling's face; indeed the material with the wax solution looked like a stronger layer of Luciana's own skin. As I had intended, it also provided a sterile protection against insects, pests and microbes, which were ever-present and tenacious in their attempts to breach Luciana's body. Despite the fact that I had kept Luciana inside the cooling casket which had saved her from the worst excesses of burial, I knew that one day I would have to remove her from it, and so I applied a second and third layer of the oiled silk to her head, neck, chest and arms, making sure to bond the material to every crevice of those areas, and then cover the layer with the wax once again. In this way I created a firmer, more resilient skin for my darling, and could rest more easily in the knowledge that none of the small creatures that dine on the dead could attack my beautiful bride.

The months passed me by without notice, so dedicated was I in my endless task of caring for Luciana. I was only able to feel the change into winter when, one day, washing her hair, I found that my hands could barely move to massage the shampoo into her scalp, so cold had the room grown. It occurred to me then that time was moving forward, and I was neglecting to celebrate any of it with my wife. While I had never had much interest in Christmas, which seemed to me a quite brazen display of empty consumerism, I thought it would be pleasant to mark the New Year with my beloved. I prepared sauerkraut with my own hands in advance, and on New Year's Eve itself set up a small table and made pains to remove Luciana from her coffin and place her in a sitting position alongside me, so that she might join in the meal. I took her hand gently and kissed her lips; in the preceding days, I had grown frustrated with the manner in which the new silk layers on her skin prevented access to her mouth and had torn a hole so that her lips now could be penetrated; it made her less safe, I know, but a husband must have his intimacy.

I explained to Luciana the tradition of eating sauerkraut to bring luck (with money, but also in life) for the succeeding year. The salt had permeated the cells of the cabbage and the vegetable was pleasingly fermented. I had cut the cabbage so thinly that there was no need to turn it to liquid. Instead, I held Luciana in my arms and fed her a small, thin slice at a time, telling her about the many ways in which we were lucky, and would continue to be so. In such a manner, we entered our first new year as man and wife. It was a calm and gentle night, but holding my darling in my arms as the bells rang for midnight brought me such serenity and happiness that I was overwhelmed. Luciana shifted in my arms to show me that she, too, felt the importance of the event, and that she felt content in my embrace.

However, the turn of another year brought consternation. I was growing frustrated with our daily routine, and was keen to accelerate our small achievements. It occurred to me that the labour necessary to apply all my solutions to Luciana by hand was more than one person's work, yet finding myself an assistant was, of course, out of the question. I hit upon a solution of ludicrous simplicity: the bathtub. With relative ease, I was able to lift Luciana out of her coffin, bring her to a standing position, then lift her once again into the bathroom. I laid her flat in the bath and filled the tub with a solution primarily consisting of blood and plasma, which I had procured via a trip to the hospital late one evening (the specific components of this solution and its various additives can be found amongst my papers, filed and labelled extensively in my home). The hospital stored large amounts of plasma for the treatment of blood cancer patients, so it was simple to take as much as I needed. I left Luciana in this solution for ten hours, and thus spent my first night without her in the best part of a year. I hardly slept. The following day I lifted her out of the bath, retaining the liquid in which she had been laid, for I would need to infuse it and use it again; too many trips to the hospital would of course arouse suspicion. Her body was pleasingly warm and much easier to manipulate. After I had cleaned and dried her, returning her to the coffin, I injected my darling with glucose liquid infused with saline, calcium, magnesium, vitamins; I should, in retrospect, have been treating Luciana thusly from the moment she stabilised, and it was a source of great pain to me to realise that I may have wasted months expecting her to return to her body when of course she would be waiting for me to complete the transformation for her.

I performed this reviving procedure on Luciana weekly, giving her several days of rest and recuperation in between, for I knew from my experiments how taxing such a process could be on the body—and the soul. Again, my darling gained weight, this time a significant amount. Her body again took on a more lustrous look; it was a great joy to sleep with her pressed against me at night, and to lay with my face in her hair, which smelled once again of youth and vibrancy.

However, in bringing Luciana's cells and tissues closer to life, and at higher temperatures, she began to be beset by many more living things, despite the silken layers on her skin. Bacteria, mould and hordes of insects began to take hold, especially on the underside of her body and in the small folds where heat and moisture flourish. I was horrified to find, one day as the spring set in, a small bouquet of mushrooms in one of her more intimate parts, and though I removed them quickly I realised that the forces of life could not be escaped completely. In bringing Luciana to life again she would have to fend off these attacks herself. Until she did so it would be my task to examine her daily for any signs of these infestations, and to powder and dry her thoroughly to protect her from such indignity. I took the decision to dress her in clothes I had to purchase from the local stores in town, no doubt inflaming the gossips of the town, for what use has an ageing doctor for clothes for a young woman? I hoped that they would assume some perversion on my part and that their enquiries would go no further.

Dressing Luciana in the outfit I had purchased for her, I could not help but feel a barrier had been placed between us, such of the type that occurs when a couple has been married for a long time. Our immediate intimacy was removed, and this brought me a great sadness. To counter this feeling of acute loneliness, I allowed Luciana several hours each night during which she would be unencumbered by clothing, and this brought, to both of us, a greater feeling of ease. I dressed her each morning, even purchasing further outfits so that she might have some variety, to encourage her, in any way I could, back to life.

The reader will permit me at this point to talk for a moment on the subject of my personal situation, distasteful as I have always found this. My financial reality since arriving in America had always been one of self-sufficiency, as I was able to work, for an adequate wage, at the hospital. As I have mentioned, my income was supplemented by a pension of sorts from my time working in medical research in my homeland. However, when I took on Luciana as my charge, I was unable, after a point, to continue my hospital role. This coincided with a significant increase in my outgoings, as many of the medicines, solutions and pieces of equipment had to be bought from abroad and shipped to America, and even those that could be purchased locally were bought at a significant cost. As Luciana's repose wore on, it was necessary to purchase larger and larger amounts of the chemicals used to keep her safe, clean and reviving, and though I was able to procure much of this from the hospital in the first year or two of our married life, I began to grow nervous that my movements were being tracked, and that the increased security at the hospital would result in my incarceration, which of course would leave Luciana with no protection at all.

Around this time, I received the news that my regular payments from Germany were to cease. Many of the contacts I had been relying on for the seamless transfer of these funds had moved on, passed away or simply were no longer contactable, and in order to rectify the situation it would have been necessary for me to travel to Germany, whereupon I likely would have found myself under suspicion and with little chance of proving my real nationality, given that all my official papers were in the name of a Polish national, or indeed a naturalised American citizen. I also could not countenance the idea of leaving my darling, and to travel with her was, at the time, completely out of the question. Thus, the payments from Germany dried up and there was no way to reinstate them.

All this conspired to mean that my funds were dwindling rapidly, and I had to resort to selling my own blood at the local clinics as regularly as my body would permit. This procedure required several days of recuperation, as my age was advancing and recovery was slow. During my appointments, I was unwilling to leave Luciana unattended at home, which, despite being outside the main area of Key West, was far from shielded from the public gaze. To this end, I was able to barter with a local resident who needed some medical advice and had a small number of German shepherd dogs. Having no insurance, the man was unable to take his wife to a doctor, but had heard that I was of some medical training and offered me one of his dogs as payment. On the condition that I would come to his home (I of course was reluctant to allow any strangers near Luciana's room) and that I would be able to pick which of the dogs I was to take with me, I accepted, and so Luciana and I came into possession of a male German Shepherd, whom I named Gorky.

The dog was a beautiful specimen, purebred and entirely well kept.

I introduced Gorky to Luciana gradually, and always with the dog leashed properly and by my side. By familiarising the dog with the smell of his mistress, I was able to slowly bring the animal into our home, until eventually I could allow him to spend time in Luciana's room off the lead. However, the point of the dog had been to ensure the home's security when I could not be there myself. When I left, I would place the lid of Luciana's casket back on top of my darling, apologising profusely to her as I did so, for I knew that she was never happy when she was trapped inside and indeed felt a keen loneliness every time I was forced to leave her. Thus secured, I locked Luciana inside her room for additional safety and trained the dog to bark viciously any time he sensed the movement of anyone but his master.

Although I was emotionally bereft at leaving Luciana on these short excursions, it is my conviction now that these periods of loneliness were in fact instrumental in her final resurrection. In much the same way that a small child can be kept from walking independently by parents that too readily reach forward to stop the child from toppling over, so too was my constant presence preventing Luciana from fully reclaiming her body.

My girl, still charmingly petulant, so hated being trapped in the confines of her casket with no company other than that of the dog that she decided once and for all to return to life—to be my living wife once again.

I returned one day from my appointment at the local clinic. These appointments, though they were not long in and of themselves, had to be followed by a trip to a nearby restaurant to increase my blood sugar, and then by a small period of respite in the park near the clinic, for I found the process to be exhausting; I had had to lie about my age in order to be accepted, and even then it was only my beard, hiding as it did the myriad wrinkles on my face, that allowed the clerk enough self-delusion to take me at my word.

Luciana, by then, had been alone for several hours. I entered the home stricken with fear, as I had heard the dog barking from the other end of the street, and had hurried home, as much as was possible in my weakened state, terrified that I would find a strange man inside interfering with the body of my beautiful bride. I was relieved to find the doors were secured and there was no one inside. Yet the dog was reacting to the presence of a stranger, or to some movement about the home that was not my own.

Unable to settle the worrying murmurs in my chest, I unlocked Luciana's room and was satisfied that she was alone. I then removed the lid from her casket, and nearly dropped the wood, so striking was the transformation that I saw inside.

Luciana, my bride, my darling girl, had finally regained her body.

The skin, which had by now developed a startling pallor, had softened and warmed beneath the layers of protective silk. Her jaw had loosened, her neck had become less stiff, and the fingers of her hands were more naturally curled, no longer settled into the claw-like grip into which rigor mortis had rendered them. Her lips, though silken and covered, shone deep red through the layers of protection. I lifted her eyelids with my thumb and saw, though her eyes were still sunken, a deepening of the colour, as though something had changed therein. It was in leaning over her body that I noticed the most arresting indication of life: several drops of blood below her nose, at the corners of her mouth and at the openings of her ears. I quickly swabbed this blood onto cotton and then onto plates for later examination, only barely remembering to preserve it for scientific integrity as excitement took hold, and I ran, or rather stumbled, towards my medical bag for my stethoscope, where it had remained from when I had attended to the local man's wife.

I stopped, taking a moment to look upon the face of my darling, and told myself that whatever I found there, I would know that my bride had returned. I pressed the stethoscope to her chest.

Where I had expected breathing, perhaps, there was none—a significant blow. Yet when I had managed to quiet the dog and the sound of my own heart thundering in my chest, I was able to hear a low but defiant movement of liquids, and an irregular flutter, then the movement of liquids again. A tear dropped from my face and onto Luciana's, and I wiped it away with a piece of cotton.

'Schön ist die Nacht, die lauschige Nacht.

Es leuchten die Sterne.'

I sang it gently, barely hoping. Beneath my gaze her lips moved.

'Ich hab dich gerne, nur dich, dich allein.'

With shaking hands, I examined the rest of her body. There was a warmth there that was not the warmth of my own body, nor of her heating baths; it had been days since the last treatment, and she usually returned to a cooled state in the middle of the day. Small cuts around her arms were, too, splattered with fresh drops of red, and when I removed, with care, her lower garments, I was astounded to find the inside of her thighs smeared with fresh menstrual leakage. I ran my finger tentatively along the soft inside of her thigh and brought the finger to my face; that astringent odour, the small solid knots of matter—it was blood unlike the rest. I placed my hand instinctively on Luciana's abdomen then and felt the hollow there, as if I might feel heat from the activity in her uterus, and the enormity of the discovery overwhelmed me. I ran my hands along her legs; the saphenous veins on her legs had, too, spilled some of their contents and had to be patted with cotton and silk. Staggering backwards, I took my seat, and the dog rested his head on my knee. Minutes passed before I could regain my senses and make a rational assessment of the situation. I turned to Gorky and said,

'Your mistress, dog. She's alive.'

The following weeks and months were ones of unbridled joy for both me and Luciana. With life thus restored to her body I was able to free her from the constraints of her casket and reduce the frequency of her treatment baths significantly. I was also able to move her into my own bed, where I could keep her warm with blankets, sheets and my own body, as any husband would.

I decided at this juncture that it was acceptable to leave Luciana exposed to the open air for the majority of the day. Despite my moisturising treatments, the increased temperature of her body and the life in her cells, I knew that tissue desiccation would continue regardless, and mummification would finally take place; no amount of application of liquids would fend off the inevitable. Yet the movement that Luciana was capable of brought me hope that this process would be kept at bay for several years, perhaps even a decade, and at some point we would be able to travel back to Europe where we could finally settle to live out the rest of our natural lives.

In an effort to encourage her more quickly towards full recovery, I constructed a large fence, of eight feet, around the small yard space at the back of the house. I am no gardener and had little interest in tending to this area, leading to its neglect in the years of my occupation of the home. However, I began to notice that the air inside the house, and especially in Luciana's room, had something of an acidic odour. Fresh air is a necessity for the preservation of good health, so I set about creating a pen into which Luciana could be placed daily. My primary concern here was the preservation of her privacy, so as well as the fence, which would keep out casual intruders, I constructed a small veranda out of wood, and though it was mostly enclosed, I built the two side walls out of a fine mesh that would shield her from any onlookers. This took several weeks, and the veranda was mostly constructed from reclaimed materials from several junk yards, but once completed it proved quite agreeable to Luciana. She was much easier to move, although still heavy for me; while Luciana had been arrested in time, the same could not be said of myself. I spoke to her, one afternoon, of my terror that when she would regain her body, she would not want me—me, a wizened old man who only lived for her. And she spoke back.

'You are beautiful, more so now than ever, my darling,' I said, as I worked at her skin. 'I have never been attractive, and am certainly not now.'

'How could any physical ageing come between us now?' It was her voice, unmistakable.

For the rest of the day I could do little but stare at the face of my sweet, sensitive girl, willing her to speak again.

I found myself compulsively checking on Luciana even in our quietest moments together. I became paranoid, terrified, that she would be snatched from me by some turn of fate.

With the benefit of hindsight, I can see this was prophetic.

Of her menstrual movements I could make little sense. My examinations pre-death had told me that the trauma of the tuberculosis and the rapid weight loss that came along with it had arrested Luciana's menstrual cycle, and thus killed any hope of her bearing children. I had not expected even in my most optimistic projections that Luciana's cycle would begin again, and though blood would appear in small amounts on her inner thighs in the following months, its irregularity made it difficult to conclude with any certainty that that particular system of her body was functional. And yet in my more romantic moments, I must admit, I harboured wild dreams of impregnating Luciana and caring for her throughout her pregnancy, as she grew heavy with my child.

It is a vanity on mankind's part to desire progeny, and I know that the reader at this point will judge me harshly. To this, I say that hope is often irrational, and love even more so; it is entirely natural to consider future days with children at the feet of your older self and those of your darling, and in this regard I was like any foolish man in love. For the hope of the moment did make me foolish. Spending each day looking into the pristine face of my sweet bride was enough to convince me that I, too, still had my youth. For these flights of fancy I believe the reader will forgive me.

In truth, I was simply happy.

My girl was recovering her body and her health. Together we had a modest home and a small yard in which to recline. Together we ate, basic but satisfying food, and even took, on odd nights, red wine, when our budget could extend to it; I had never taken to drink, but knowing that my darling enjoyed it, I allowed myself to share in that pleasure. We were making plans for our future; for travel, for children, for spending the rest of our years in happy pursuits. I was able to worship my darling, carrying her around the home, massaging her, feeding her and telling her stories of my youth and my studies. This is the gentle happiness for which everyone surely strives.

In addition, I took professional pleasure in seeing my work achieve results that had never before been recorded. While it is undeniably egotistical to wallow in one's achievements, I ask the reader's mercy for just a moment. Having been frustrated in my professional development because of political upheaval in my youth, I had for most of my adult life felt a sense of lost progress, of wasted potential. I had never regained the heralded position for which I had been primed and trained. My ability to create a home laboratory had been hampered by various challenges; in short, I had never achieved the success that I felt I should have. And yet here was my beautiful young wife, whom I had raised from the dead. Here was living, or almost living, proof that first death is but an obstacle to the continuance of our lives. Here was proof that with the correct care, bodies can be regained, and revitalised; that the soul does indeed exist on another plane and can communicate with the human realm, and can, under the correct circumstances, return to the body it first lived in. Here, with me, was a miracle.

What greater happiness can a scientist have?

As the heat of August gave way to the promising breeze of September, the air pressure began to fall, and that which I should have been cognisant of, but in truth never even considered, became a distinct possibility: that a hurricane would assail Key West.

No serious weather event had ever hit Key West during my residency, and in the previous years I had been so focused on Luciana's care that the goings-on of the outer world were almost completely alien to me; even the passing of the festivities was only alerted to me by the appearance of decorations in the stores to which I was forced to go. While grocery shopping, I read on the front cover of a newspaper that the centre of the storm would come in directly towards Key West in a straight line. A direct line. I purchased a copy of the newspaper, cursing myself for never having bought a television.

On my way back to the house I noticed that everyone else had already been preparing: windows and doors were shuttered, shops were closing and families even evacuating, hoping for the best as they scattered north and west, away from the path of the storm. It was morning; the hurricane was set to hit that very evening.

At first, my plan was to barricade Luciana and myself inside the house, and to that end I began to gather all the wood I could find, to reinforce the doorways and block out the windows. However, my home was not far above the high-water mark, and the newspapers had said that the water level could rise ten metres or more. While I could go as far as to reinforce the house and raise Luciana and all her necessary equipment as high as possible, it struck me that I would not be able to stave off any inquiries from locals, rescuers or law enforcement officers about my well-being. I was known in the area, and my age and solitude, at least as far as they knew, would mark me out as a vulnerable person; it was possible that I would already be on a list to be rounded up and removed from my home for my own safety.

At this, I admit, I panicked. I had long succeeded in keeping neighbours from my home; I did not converse with them, and cultivated the personality of an obtuse and difficult old man who liked his isolation. Carollers did not come to my house; nor did those children at Halloween looking for handouts, and even the travelling Christians kept from my door. The addition of Gorky had assisted in making our home an unwelcoming place for strangers, but the situation in Key West could very quickly become a case of search-and-rescue, and in this instance, I could not rely on prying eyes staying away from my home. As soon as outsiders laid eyes on the medical equipment in our home, or, more horrifyingly, on Luciana's casket or Luciana herself, our fragile contentment would be shattered; they could never understand the important work I was undertaking, nor how much potential benefit it held for them and their loved ones. This much I knew.

The morning gave way to afternoon and it became clear to me that I would have to remove Luciana from her room and enclose her in a more discreet location, ideally one with greater protection than the flimsy construction of our home would afford. To this end, apologising profusely to my darling and talking to her throughout, I placed her inside her original casket and fastened the lid on with screws, being sure not to tighten them too much, lest she needed to be freed quickly. I packed everything we might need for a trip of several days, including the various emollients necessary for the barest minimum of Luciana's daily care. I took several jars of Luciana's puréed food and the scantest of sustenance for myself, and a change of clothing for me and one more layer for my wife, as well as several blankets to wrap around her once she was in a secure location again; it was my fear that if her temperature now dropped, mummification would take place. I took candles, firelighters and a book, along with a few other necessities.

I waited as long as I could, but as the afternoon drew on, the air temperature dropped further, and I could risk it no more.

I still had in my possession the wagon I had used to rescue Luciana from the grave, and with difficulty, and the help of the pulley-lever system which now served essentially as a prosthetic in the absence of my younger, stronger body, I moved her closed casket onto this cart once again. There was much movement out in the streets as people finalised their preparations for the storm, and though my own house was located far enough away from other homes that I should garner no real interest, I was wary of taking Luciana's coffin out in the daylight. Even with the mechanical assistance I employed, the effort of moving Luciana was exhausting and terrifying, and I had to pause several times. I wrapped the bulk of the casket with tarpaulin from the yard, left over from the original construction of the house. Thus covered, I took Luciana out into the driveway and loaded her into my car, having pulled down the seats to make room for the casket's bulk. Leaving Gorky several bowls full of food and water, I locked all the doors, secured the windows with as much wood as I could find, and drove from the house. Luciana was silent. I prayed that her annoyance would not last.

I had read in the newspapers that all but essential wings of the hospital had been closed or evacuated to nearby establishments. Taking my keys with us, we headed for the place I knew so well: my old laboratory, which would be secure, well stocked, and offer us protection from the storm.

28.

Gabriela

It was a warm spring day in nineteen eighty-one when a stranger came to my door. It was my daughter who called me. She was just six then, but already unafraid of the world, bold and unaware of the many things in it that could change her life in an instant. She had never sounded Cuban. She likely never would, and speaking to her, I became less so myself. We had just slipped some baking out of the oven, and she'd taken a handful of the freshly made pie into the front yard, without stopping to consider that she might need a plate. She stood at the front door, grabbing the white frame with berry-stained hands.

'Mamá, there's a man for you.'

'What man, Chabela?'

'I don't know him Mamá. He's on the porch.'

I took up my coffee cup (I now had it white, with sugar, feeling my mother's judgment from beyond the grave) and left my piece of pie on the kitchen table. I went outside; I still did not like having strangers in my house if I could avoid it. He spoke before I could.

'I'm sorry to bother you, Mrs Giro. My name is Mason Miller. I hope I haven't taken you away from something important.'

Mrs Giro. He pronounced it like 'gear-o'.

'Only pie.'

He smiled.

'That always tastes better after a break.'

I decided to like him; he was nice enough, holding his hat in his hands like my father used to and shifting slowly from one foot to another. I asked him to sit on one of the porch seats and he did so.

'Can I get you a slice?'

He thought about it.

'It's cherry.'

He looked down at his feet.

'I better not. It doesn't seem right.'

I sat down then too. Something was wrong, and I felt that shift in my body when you know bad news is coming.

'What did you come for, Mr Miller?'

'Please, call me Mason. And I'm sorry to say, Mrs Giro, but this is about your sister.'

I put the coffee cup down on the floor so he might not see that I had lost all my strength.

'My only sister—' I stopped, thinking of baby Ximena. 'Both my sisters are dead, Mr Miller. I think you might have come to the wrong house.'

He shook his head.

'I've known about your sister—your sick sister—since she was alive, Mrs Giro. I heard that whole story, and I never thought it right. An old man like that, and a foreigner too. You can't trust the Germans.'

'He's Polish,' I said, without thinking. I suppose I had been waiting a long time for a conversation like this.

'So he says, Mrs Giro, so he says.'

I had nothing to say to that, and began to wish I kept my front door locked.

'Well, I never did like that man, Mrs Giro, but the fact of the matter is that we don't have a lot of money, and my wife's very sick, and she's not going to get better. I don't like to admit, but I needed to get my wife some treatment and I heard that man was a doctor, or thereabouts, so I went over to that place of his

248

and knocked on the door and he came out like a shot, like he wanted to get me away from the door. Seems like he isn't doing well either, financially; the whole place was in some state, from the outside, you understand. I didn't go inside but I could smell it, and it smelled part like a hospital, part like an old folk's home. The stench that came out when he did was as if he hadn't let a breeze through in years. I don't know how he can live like that, if I'm honest, Mrs Giro.'

I had lost my ability to talk. I just watched the man's bottom lip, his words coming at me from the end of a long tube, a metal tube, and my skin was cold, and the whole porch was sliding away, everything around me was just shifting away from what I knew—or perhaps towards what I had always known.

'Well, I took a peek into the windows as I left and the whole place was blocked up so you couldn't see inside, and that's just strange isn't it, in a place like Key West? So stuffy and hot and that place holed up like a wooden box? Anyway, that man it seems was in need himself; I heard he no longer works and he almost bit my hand off when I offered him a trade so he might take a look at my wife. I was going to lay some offer on the table but the minute he stepped into our house and saw our pets he said he wanted a dog, a good watchdog, a dog that sounds mean and trains well, that's what he said. So we made an agreement: he'd look at my wife and tell us how we might keep her alive for a good while longer, and I'd give him one of the German shepherds. How's that for a nationalist tendency? He took that dog, Barnie we called him, and, you know, I will say for him that he was professional and gave us some ideas and some medications that have put her out of her pain, and she's still with us. God love her, she's still with us.'

He stopped then and licked his lips. I knew I should offer him a drink but I was stuck to my chair, heavy and cold. The man seemed to have lost his nerve too.

'Maybe I've no business coming here and talking to you

about this, I mean, I have no proof at all. I don't wanna bother you, Mrs Giro, and maybe I'm just paranoid or got to thinking about some bad things—'

'Please,' I said.

'Well, he came and treated my wife, and the whole time there was this smell coming off him, and—well, I guess there's no other way to say it Mrs Giro, but he smelled like the dead.'

Like the dead. Those were his words. *He smelled like the dead.*

'I won't waste any more of your time, but I haven't been sleeping at night for thinking about it, and maybe I'm wrong, or maybe I'm crazy, but I think that man is keeping something secret in that house, and I've got a terrible feeling it's your—'

I stood up. He had been leaning so close that he almost fell off his chair.

'I'm very grateful for your visit, Mr Miller, but my sister has been dead and buried a long time, God rest her soul. It's been a horrible ordeal and I am not interested in hearing any more strange rumours.'

He stood up and started to apologise, but I cut him off.

'I know that there's a lot of interest in my sister, but I think we should all stop putting wild thoughts in each other's heads. Thank you for coming and I'm sorry about your wife.'

He stopped his apologies and his eyes looked right into mine. Then he took a deep breath and put his hat on his head.

'Have a good evening, Mrs Giro, and I hope I haven't ruined your dessert.'

'It's Mrs Herrera Madrigal de Giro,' I said.

He walked off the porch. I went inside and cut myself a second slice of pie. I ate both at once.

After that I had horrible nightmares, dreams where Luci was in my bed at night, in my bathtub, playing with my Chabela on the floor, everywhere but the place she should have been. Every time I saw her she was rotted away, empty in the eyes, all bones and half covered in skin. But it was always the smell that was worst. *He smelled like the dead.* I knew what the man meant, that honey-rotten stench that sticks to your skin. I smelled it when I woke up and then all day afterwards. My husband laughed at me because I started to put cotton wool up my nose before bed but still, every time I saw Luci, it was there. My doctor prescribed pills but I put them in the toilet. I wanted to keep my daytimes clear.

I needed to speak to somebody about what Mr Miller had said, because I couldn't force it out of my head. I knew my husband would not understand; he is a practical man, he would have told me it was ridiculous, and that bad dreams were just bad dreams and nothing more. My brothers had had enough of talking about Luci, and they went about their lives with an adapted happiness that I did not want to upset. I could only talk to God, so I prayed for her, and prayed for me, and God listened to my fears and my nightmares but did not make them go away.

It was in the fall of eighty-two that we had to face the stories. There was a hurricane headed for Key West, the biggest since we had moved to America, and the route they expected it to take ran right over our home. I told my husband that we had survived a hurricane once and it had been after us ever since; he smiled at me indulgently and in that moment, I missed Luci more than ever. We boarded up the house and took our daughter and went north to my husband's distant cousin's farm, where it was nice and big and protected from the storm by the mountains. Andrés and Juan Antonio came too, and brought their loved ones, and as the young cousins played together we reminisced about the island, about grand pianos and hot rains and our mother's evenings with the radio. We wondered what the streets were like in Havana now, at how they might receive us back. At night we drank hot cocoa and in the day, Andrés taught Isabella how to ride the horses, though I could never remember him learning. On the third day she rode alone, and I waved and shouted encouragement and turned away as soon as I could, holding all of my fears in my tense muscles so I might not push them in front of her, so she might not fall over them. My daughter would not be scared like her mother.

Looking in on us then, you would have seen our family just as our father wanted it to be: affluent, happy, together. We were shielded from our cares; we were assimilated perfectly on that little farm. It was a sweet little holiday from the real world, so much so that I barely wanted to leave. When we got back to the house, we found that almost nothing was damaged; our home was uphill and so the flooding had mostly missed us, and everything that had been ruined could be easily replaced. The weathermen had been wrong, but it was the kind of wrong you didn't mind at all.

As soon as we were back the rumours came to find us. Everyone had seen that man moving something heavy into his car and driving away fast. He had left his dog inside the house and as the floodwaters rose the dog barked all morning, so some people kicked the door down to rescue it. The dog was already drowned by the time they got inside—but what they saw in that house was cursed. It disturbed them: lots of medical equipment and a big tank, big enough to hold a person, and bottles and bottles of chemicals. But it was the stench they all talked about. The floodwaters stank, and the mud of course smells in its own way, but these men said it was unmistakable, the stink in that place.

He smelled like the dead.

They left the dog's corpse and got out of there. And then they came to me.

Only the Lord can know why that day was different. My grandmother would have said it was the waters, always the waters. The rains were controlled by a woman in pain, and that day they were sent to wash the sin from Key West. I don't know if I believe all of that, for so much of what Tita said was mere superstition, but that day I opened my doors and made cold tea and listened to everything those people had to say. When they had finished their story, I walked to the kitchen and opened the drawer. I took out a small flashlight. I walked past the men who moved out of my way and I left the front door of the house open and I walked down the street and I wasn't sure if they were following but I turned right and then left and then left and kept turning and walking until I was at the cemetery, the cemetery that contained Luciana's second tomb. At the entrance I started to run and my feet struggled in the mud but I kept going, not thinking of the mess on my skirt and not worrying that I'd lost a shoe and I kept going until I reached her tomb and I fell to my knees and my shoulders were level with the top of the tomb and I fumbled the flashlight and dropped it and wiped the front of it on my blouse and flicked it on and pressed it against the piece of glass that I had always known was there, that small window into her truth, and I shone the light and I looked and I saw once and for all that she was not there. Luci was not there.

29.

Wilhelm

We stayed inside the hospital for three nights, while the storm passed by and afterwards too, for I knew that rescuers and police and neighbours would be in the streets and knocking on doors, checking for anyone trapped or needing help. For the sake of the house, I hoped that Gorky's barking would discourage anyone with a view to stealing any of the valuables within; the liberalisation of certain social norms had brought a lower class of person to Key West, and I feared looting. The hurricane itself felt very removed from our situation; I felt safe within the strong walls of the old hospital and as I kissed, held and spoke to Luciana, the universe shrank until only she and I were within it. I grew hungry, but I had enough food to keep Luciana plumped and full. I pressed my body against hers and covered us both in blankets, hoping to raise her temperature to a level whereby the ill effects of being moved from her home might be negated. I had, thankfully, brought moisturisers, and I worked them into her skin, noting a few appearances of insects and removing them where possible. I did not sleep often, for fear of discovery or something happening to Luciana. Having her outside the home was unsettling in so many ways. If we were found in the hospital, if she were taken from me—I might never live again.

Early on the fourth morning it became clear to me that I would have to move, as there was a notable increase in traffic arriving at the hospital, signalling that life in Key West had resumed, despite the remaining floodwaters. We would have to leave, and, succumbing to panic at the idea that the radiology department might open that very day, I gathered together the small amount of luggage we had and placed Luciana back into her casket. I set up all the mechanics that would be required to move her, and, drawing energy only from the thought that we would be home and safe together again soon, steeled myself for the process. Again I secured the coffin, again I loaded it onto the truck, and before the morning had truly begun we were back inside the station wagon, which I had parked far from the rest of the vehicles, close to the back door through which we had entered the hospital. By noon, we were home.

I left Luciana in the car and went to assess the state of our residence. The damage to the house was minimal; the floodwaters had risen a few metres but by that time had mostly subsided. The result of this was that much of the furniture had been submerged but not destroyed. The front door had been forced open by the weight of the waters, and I was unsettled to find that damage had been sustained to the lock and handle, but I knew this could be replaced; I had spare parts of this type upstairs and could easily do the work in an afternoon once I had regained my strength. Regrettably, Gorky had drowned. I took the body into the backyard so I could bury it at a later date.

I quickly returned Luciana to her room and unscrewed the lid of the casket. Leaving her inside, I apologised for the delay and the necessity of keeping her in repose. After a brief period of respite, I attended to the door and worked until it would close and lock. I removed Luciana from her casket and placed her back into our bed, and spent the rest of the evening attending to her needs and my own. We slept soundly, and I spent the next several days cleaning the home and disposing of the items that were ruined. Thankfully, almost all of my medical equipment had survived the storm and there was little outer damage to the home. I left the windows barricaded; we did not need the light.

We returned then to the schedule of ministrations that had been keeping Luciana so vibrant and so close to returning to her body: the plasma baths, the moisturising, the daily massaging. I was keen to return to our schedule as quickly as possible and perhaps to accelerate the treatments; I felt strongly that Luciana could, within a short period, return to an entirely living state. Of course, she had already survived her first death and was, in a very real sense, alive; her menstrual bleeding was proof beyond all doubt. But having taken samples from Luciana I was disturbed to find less activity under the microscope, and appraising her physicality I had to recognise that some injury had been caused by our sudden and poorly planned trip. If allowed to descend into a second death, I felt sure Luciana would never recover; the state of decay would be too advanced, the soul would depart. After stabilising her as best I could, I worked for an extended period around Luciana's face, taking some of my pencils to fill in her eyebrows, for example, and line her lips, for such things are important to women; the thickness of the silk covering on her skin allowed me to draw there and bring out her delicate features. Then I turned to her body.

I also found that there were rivulets of scarlet running through the gauze in which Luciana's body had originally been wrapped, underneath her clothes. This perplexed me; her plasma baths would have explained the staining, but the gauze had since been covered in silk and wax and sealed in this way, so that no outside contaminants might penetrate her. Inspection with a microscope informed me that insect larvae had succeeded in storming Luciana's barricades by burrowing holes through the protective silk-wax layer and laying eggs therein. They were gnat larvae, the same type that had breached Luciana years before. I was beginning to consider them my nemeses. In order to combat their presence, I was forced to bathe Luciana in a mixture of fungicide and bleach, and had to leave her soaking in this solution for several hours. After I removed Luciana from the bath, I treated the perforations in her epidermis with alcohol and covered them over with yet more silk and wax. Her bodily integrity was preserved once more.

During this time I also conducted a thorough examination of her lower torso—the most extensive I had made to date. I still had not been able to understand her menstrual movements, and I admit to the reader here that the idea of Luciana incubating my child had become my primary goal. With the benefit of hindsight, it could be said that I was operating under extreme stress and was beyond rational thinking, caught between what had been always deemed impossible and what I was seeing and experiencing in real time. The resulting fragmentation of mind may have affected my sense of reason. But by the same token, it is natural to desire a family when in love. I had been pressured into marriage once, with a woman who thankfully failed to conceive, then was forced into a second marriage through circumstance, and had parenthood thrust on me unwillingly. I had never made a family for love, and for the first time, I wanted to. It occurred to me that if there was menstrual activity in Luciana, there was no need to wait for her to fully regain herself; indeed, waiting beyond what was necessary might negatively impact her chances of conceiving. As we know, the viability of a woman's eggs is severely affected by age, and Luciana was no longer the young woman of nineteen that I had first met. If I was able to stabilise her after her unfortunate removal from her treatment schedule, and could find evidence of activity in her reproductive system, then it might be possible to nurse her through a full-term pregnancy even before she had fully returned to her body. In fact, given the vulnerability into which the foetus is placed by the quotidian movements of the mother, it would be a safer pregnancy if the woman were prone throughout. The idea of thus starting a family with Luciana both excited and stimulated me in equal measure; with this possibility in the forefront of my mind I began a manual examination of Luciana. While there was no evidence of further blood leakage (of course, she was at a different point in her cycle) there was some vaginal discharge, and by applying pressure to her lower abdomen I was able to feel a swelling around the area of her uterus. This indicated to me a gradual thickening of the uterus lining; given the trauma of her first death it would only be logical to assume that Luciana's menstrual cycle would have been slowed to half its usual rhythm, and it was impossible to determine when this process had started again. Gynaecology had never been my field of specialisation, and though I considered writing to some known experts in the area, it was unlikely I would receive any useful information without also revealing the nature of my interest to them, thus risking the safety of Luciana and myself.

I instead resolved: I would begin trying to impregnate Luciana. This would be highly irregular in a medical sense, but not in a personal one. It would not be a drain on my own health and would only be a further extension of the love and physical attention I had already been lavishing upon my darling bride. I accepted that it also might induce Luciana to finally return to her body; what could entice a young woman to life more than the prospect of being a mother?

But before I could begin this process, there began a violent and persistent knocking at the door. I went to the window but could not see out, for the barricades were still set against the glass, obscuring my view entirely. I ignored the attention, assuming that it was simply more rescuers looking for trapped individuals, and, highly aroused by the ideas that had presented themselves to me, returned to my work, putting Luciana back into a more modest position and sitting her up in her bed. I fancied that she smiled sadly at me, but put this out of my mind; why would my darling girl be anything but happy?

I heard the male voice, then:

'We know you're in there! Open up! Open up!'

There is a strange sensation when one foresees the permanent changing of their life. It is as if time itself drops you from its stream and all things shift; you are thrown into a realm without gravity, your stomach acid rises, your tongue floats, you have a sensation of falling. The psychology of this moment fascinates me; it is more than dread, it is less than grief, but it is somewhere between the two. I felt all of this in that second.

The second man's voice:

'Don't make us call the cops!'

I could not discern their accents in that moment. I should have.

I began to scrabble around the room, lunging at things that were of no use to me and throwing them onto the floor, grabbing the next thing and dropping it again. This cacophony alerted the intruders to my presence and they began to pound on the front door.

'Open this door right now or we'll kick it down!'

Here I floundered. My first thought was to cover Luciana, to hide her, to shield her from view, and to this end I tried to lift the lid of her empty casket, which I had lifted many times without issue. Yet I could not raise it high enough to place onto the coffin and instead it fell from my hands, cracking from the bottom right corner as it hit the floor. The clattering was loud and alerted my intruders once again.

'I'm serious, von Tore! Let us in!'

Upon hearing my own name, I descended into panic. I started to throw items into my medical bag that lay open by the door, with some vague idea that I could lift Luciana from the bed and run with her from the back door, though having since recovered my rational mind I can recall that there was no gate in the back fence and therefore no safe way out from the back of the building—a security feature I considered essential for keeping Luciana safe. But it also meant there was nowhere to go.

Growing more terrified, I reached for my darling, but violent kicks began pounding at the door; if they knocked it through,

I would have no way to keep them out. I dropped my bag and rushed to the door.

'Please, please! Keep your temper, I am here.'

The blows subsided and no words came. Gathering myself as best I could, worrying about the painful hammering in my chest, I unlocked the door and opened it ever so slightly. Outside, tear-drenched, stood the Cubans.

30

Gabriela

I had run from the cemetery to the house where Andrés lived. His boyfriend met me on their front porch; the gossips must have told him I was coming. I was screaming and my words made little sense. He gave me a drink of warm lemon and honey and held me until Andrés, who had been at the store buying milk, came home. He knew immediately what was wrong. I think deep down we all knew it was not over, but we had pushed it to the back of our minds, hoping that death would be the end of it. But our wounds had healed in the wrong way, and now they were ripped open again, and the pain was deserved.

Andrés called Juan Antonio and an hour later we three were together. In another half an hour, we were at his door.

How can I tell you about my brothers? They are good boys, but they are also strong, and they have my father's temperament. They get happiness from making other people happy. Papá wanted more than this; he wanted what they call notoriety, the pleasure of being known. America had made the boys quiet, but they are passionate and they are sensitive. They will be the first ones to stop a stupid fight outside a bar. But because they hold their tempers all the time, it means that when they finally have a reason to lose them, they lose them entirely. Give them a good reason to let go of their control and they will not be stopped.

We ran over to that small house on the outskirts of town.

Andrés went ahead and banged on the door. The boys shouted; they were shaking, both of them. We could hear him moving around inside and there was a lot of noise; the boys were saying that he was trying to escape, so Andrés kicked the door, trying to get in. All we wanted was to get him out. We never imagined— how could we? No sane person would ever think it; only a devil could. Andrés kicked a couple more times with all his strength. With that, the man shouted out that he would open the door. I felt dizzy. I stepped back.

The door opened a tiny crack. We could not see him well. The smell that rushed out of the room, like it was searching for fresh air, was thick and musty, acrid and dense. I breathed it in and almost fell down. Juan Antonio caught me; Andrés pushed forward.

'Come out here. We want some answers from you.'

The man's voice was much thinner, much older than I remembered. It's funny how you imagine that someone is frozen in time from the last moment you see them to the next.

'I no longer have any business with your family,' he said, but his breathing was short and he sounded afraid. God forgive me, I was enjoying this.

'Where is Luci? What did you do with my sister?' Juan Antonio hit the door with the flat of his hand and the man flinched.

'Your sister is dead. You have seen her grave. I suggest if you ever visited her—'

'I visited. I looked. She is not in that grave,' I said, my voice shaking, my hands too.

'You are mistaken,' the man said. Andrés's foot was in the gap in the door. The man spoke again. 'Darkness tricks the eye easily; assuming that you peered through the glass on the tomb, it was only ever intended as a symbolic addition and does not function well as a viewing window. The shadows of the tomb itself—'

'She is not there!' The force of my shout surprised all of us. 'Where is my sister?' I yelled again.

He shrank back into the house, and that stopped me. Could this sad old man really have done anything to Luci? He lived in squalor, so pathetic and alone. God had not smiled on this man's life. My anger gave way to pity. The boys did not feel the same. Andrés shoved the door and the man stumbled back.

'Andrés, stop—'

But he had already pushed the door open. He walked over the man sprawled on the floor. That man, taking heaving breaths, held his hands up as if to stop Andrés.

'No, no, no…'

'Tonio, the back—'

Andrés was in and Juan Antonio was behind him. I see it all like a film, a very clear view: Andrés went past an open door, looked inside and stopped dead. He put his hands on the door frame and stared into the room. Then Juan Antonio was behind him, their bodies pressed, one front to the other's back, and they were silent and still, like the camera had caught on a single frame. They stared, not speaking, not saying a word, and as the old man tried to get to his feet an ungodly smell came from the house, the open door letting it all out towards me. I gagged and retched and put my hand to my mouth to stop it.

The old man was up onto his knees then, up onto his feet, holding himself up by the wall, back turned to me, reaching out towards the doorway where the boys stood, and he was speaking.

'See, see how beautiful she is? See how well cared for she is?'

No, I thought. *No, no, no.*

'Look at her in her finest clothes and her best jewellery. See her revived. I have saved your sister.'

It was Andrés that turned, his mouth open, his eyes yet dry, and looked at the man. The old man busied past them and the boys moved, both of those big strong men pushed out of the way by the touch of a frail person who had no physical power over them at all. They were suspended. Something stronger than anger held them where they were.

'See how she has been restored. Brought back to the realm of the living. She has lost a little weight, this is true, but she gained much back and we must not worry too much over a little weight loss, after all. Under the circumstances her condition is remarkable.'

I stepped into the house, pulled forward against my will, for I knew what I would see. But then, in so many ways, I could never have known.

'Come closer and see; touch her skin, she is warm. She speaks to me, she tells me she is soon to return completely. She is healthy and her body lives and she is ready to return.'

One step more. Two. The closeness, the smell of it. I retched and caught it with my teeth.

'Oh, holy mother, oh, sweet mother of God—'

It was Juan Antonio, and he brought his hand to his chest.

Another step. So close to the doorway now.

'I've reason to believe she might be able to conceive, with correctly administered medical care, of course.'

Just one more.

'Here she is, your sister. Here is your sister living once again.'

I stepped into the doorway. The boys did not reach out to hold me and I did not reach out for support. My hands fell and my shoulders dropped. My weight was rooted to the floor.

In that room, there was Luci.

Can words really describe what we saw? I look at this writing and the words seem so thin, so incapable of conveying the horror of it all. But words, here, are all I have.

Sitting up in a bed, with blankets and pillows and wilting flowers, some so old their leaves had dropped off, was the corpse of my sister.

It was Luci, but it was not her at all. The body sat stiffly, strangely, its shoulders high, its arms straight down at the sides of its body. The hair sat on her head so strangely I might have laughed; a wig of course, yet the only thing about Luci that was still truly hers. It was long again, like she had never cut it off, and the twisted ends of it hung lightly over her shoulders, curled at the bottom, so different to how she had ever worn it. Her face was nothing more than pencilled features on a wrinkled surface that had been smoothed around her head. There were no ears. No; I looked again. Her ears were pinned down by some material, the material that covered her whole face; I was looking at a mask with her face underneath it. My eyes adjusted and I could see. It was like satin made hard by the secretions of bugs, layers of it on top of her features, her ears pinned to the sides of her head, her eyes nothing but cotton wool, her sockets lined with black pencil, thick, pinned open, fat arches over each eye, too low down at both ends, so she looked surprised. The nose was a pyramid, so different to the nose she'd always had, her poor broken nose, the nose Tita hated. A strange and shoddy construction with layers peeling off. She was white, the colour white, the colour of plaster from her hairline down to her chest, and her mouth was paper, like her lips would disintegrate if touched, but still they were opened, a horrible opening there for—

'Oh, sweet mother,' said Juan Antonio again, and Andrés ran outside to vomit in the street.

It smelled like death, this half-human effigy, and its silk face hung off her cheekbones like a sheet. The body had sunk in parts, and her chest had been plastered too, but you could see the bones through it, see right through to where the death resided. The clothes sat badly on her, clothes that she would have laughed at, middle-aged-woman clothes, and ugly jewellery, far too much, and the brown rotten flesh showed through at her ankles, her feet broken and mashed into a mess. The silk-mask was everywhere above her knees, on all her exposed flesh, everything not covered by the foul-smelling clothes, but from the calves down she was just covered bone. Her dead stare, the expression blank and frozen, as if someone had taken my sister and pushed her and pulled her around into shapes she would never make—emotionless. A child's drawing of a person, but made real, a human doll, and she was so stiff and lay so oddly that I stepped forward, wanting to pick her up, wanting to drop her on the floor so that she might break, like ceramic, and he might see that there was nothing inside, that it was not my sister, that it was just a pottery doll of a girl who looked like a woman we once loved.

I realised he was speaking, that man—he had found his power again, and as God is my witness, he was proud as he talked to us over our sister's mutilated corpse.

'—proved a challenge but Luciana and I have hit upon a process of baths and drying and moisturising that seems to be replenishing the necessary fat and water into her cells, and I've cause to believe, through evidence discharged and through my own experience of the sounds of her body, that there is movement of blood already occurring, and there has been physical movement throughout her recuperation period, though of course I must ask you to trust me in this regard, having little way to prove this to you—'

'How long?' I said. 'How long have you had her?'

He looked down at the body and picked at its sleeve.

'Luciana and I have been living together for seven years as man and wife.'

As man and wife.

'That is not my sister,' I said, looking at the strange mannequin, the shell, the painted corpse. 'That's not Luci. This is some thing you have made.'

At this, he looked offended.

'Put her back.' I said.

I don't know what I was thinking, but it was all I wanted. All I wanted was Luci back where she could rest, where she could be at peace. That man looked straight at me.

'No.'

Stunned, we were silent.

'No, I will not put her back,' he repeated.

Andrés, standing in the doorway and pale from vomiting, began to speak, but the man was excited, he was scared. His voice rose and he began to gesticulate towards the body.

'You've seen where she is, you've seen that she's safe with me, that she's being cared for—that I'm bringing her back to life, for goodness' sake! What is the use of putting her back in the ground, only to rot, to die, to lose all my work? To shatter all the progress we've made? Would you commit your sister to the grave for good?'

We stared at the lifeless thing, the hollow corpse, the sunken features, painted over twice, three times, until she was nothing but the mad dream of an obsessive, made real.

'I would think that you would be grateful for the care I have given to your sister over the past...nine years now! All at my own expense and all through nothing but love. You cast her off the moment she slipped into death and you have been so lackadaisical in your attitude towards her that you did not even realise she wasn't in her tomb. And now you would have me put her back—only for her to be abandoned yet again! Well remember this, Gabriela, and your brutes too. I am her husband, and she is mine. I own that tomb and everything inside of it. If you put her back in the ground she remains mine, and mine alone.'

I turned away and grabbed my brothers, pulling them away, pulling them towards the door. My memory fails at this point, but we left, the three of us. I dragged them—or did they carry me?—away from that house, that house of the never-dead.

31.

Wilhelm

I locked the door after them and quiet descended on the house again. In my heart, too, a strange calmness, though a sense of finality. They would come back and take one of us. They would kill me. They would leave me and take Luciana, putting her into the ground, burning her; they would leave me and I would die. Whichever it was, our time was limited. There was nothing else to do but to enjoy my bride, my beautiful bride, and to entreat her to rise finally and walk into her second life to save herself from death.

I took myself to the backyard and chilled the tightness and violence in my chest. Slowly I returned, chastising myself for a brief lack of decorum on my part, for I had lost my temper at the idiocy of the immigrants, but I also understood that in the context of such a tense confrontation, such outbursts are inevitable.

I returned to the room and held my darling girl. Recognising that she must also be feeling the negativity of the encounter, and being injured as she must have been by the sight of her only living family begging to place her back into the cold dead ground, she would need my tenderness and care more than ever. I brushed Luciana's hair, massaged her skin; I took her in my arms and did whatever I could to make her feel loved. I lied to her that her sister and brothers merely wanted her jewellery. Remembering the promise I had made to keep her safe forever, I whispered to her softly.

'They can take you from me, Luciana, but whatever they do, I will go and get you back again. I am your protector and I will be until I die.'

In this way we passed our last hours together in the happiness of Luciana's resurrection.

Two days later, knocking came again to my door.

I moved a couple of sheets of paper on the dresser, neatening all my files and notes, and dusted myself down. I had changed into a clean shirt and trousers and had dressed Luciana in one of her newest outfits, one that made her look particularly demure. I did not want her to seem frivolous or coquettish in front of the law.

The Cubans brought with them two local sheriffs, a justice of the peace, a lawyer and, worst of all, a hearse. I took a deep breath and allowed them in. They were surprised at my cordiality; I wondered what lies the siblings had told about my conduct and manner. They stepped into the house and remained in the hallway. The smaller of the two sheriffs handed me a piece of paper, a warrant to search the house. I stepped aside.

'The woman you are looking for is in the room on the right.'

The two sheriffs went to the doorway and looked upon Luciana. They were quiet for some time, then turned to me.

'Sir, can you confirm who you are?'

I gave my name, my profession, and listed several of my accomplishments.

'And sir, who is this woman?'

'This is my wife, Luciana Madrigal von Tore.'

At the door Luciana's sister cried out. I did my best to ignore her and carry on the conversation with civility.

'And how long...how long have you had her with you, in this state, that is—how long has this body been in your possession, sir?'

'Luciana has lived in this house with me for seven years,

officer. Here, if you will, I have all her papers.'

I directed them to the dresser, whereupon they rifled through the documents, making a mess.

'As you can see, I have all the necessary documentation.'

They stared at the papers, clearly unsure as to what they were looking at, or why.

'Sir, these are not…'

I lifted the certificate of death.

'This is what you are looking for. As the attending physician I was able to clarify the time and cause of death, and then she was delivered to the undertaker for examination.'

The two sheriffs looked at one another. The taller one made an attempt to speak; I was struck by their incompetence.

'This is not—you can't just have…'

'What are you waiting for?' asked Gabriela, shrill, from the doorway. With her insistence, the smaller sheriff recovered himself slightly. He brought himself up to his full height with his hands on his belt.

'Sir, in order to legally disinter a body, it is necessary to have familial consent and good cause.'

'Luciana was rescued from her grave with the consent of the family.'

'No one could consent to this!' Gabriela was shrill, hysterical. She stepped further into the house; a great imposition when she had not been invited.

The taller sheriff placed his hand gently on Gabriela's shoulder to stop her ravings.

'Sir, I'm afraid you're going to have to come with us.'

He went to take handcuffs from his utility belt.

'Officer, I'm happy to come with you to answer your questions; there is no need for such measures. Simply walk me out to the front and I will lock the house behind me.'

At this, I will admit, my heart was racing, and the pain in my chest had returned. It was a bluff, and I am no gambler.

The sheriffs shared a glance and the smaller one spoke again.

'No, sir, I'm afraid you don't understand. The undertaker will have to take the body from your possession.'

He took me lightly by the arm and led me to the police car. He did not handcuff me, and the Cubans were removed from my path by the other sheriffs and the justice of the peace. They shot angry barbs at me, but I did not listen. I was in shock, perhaps, drawn forward onto a timeline I could not in that moment understand by people who were acting against their own interests; what good would it to do take Luciana away from her treatments? Away from a man who loved her, to place her in the ground where any malicious actor might take advantage of a beautiful young girl like her? The sheriffs led me to the back seat of the car, nodding to the driver as they took their seats on either side of me.

I looked out of the window to see Luciana's casket being carried from the house. They had shoved her inside. She was trapped.

I lunged across the sheriff on my left and felt my arms caught.

'Calm down, sir.'

I felt sick and weak.

'This is a gross invasion of my privacy, a theft of my personal property! Officers, I cannot allow this to occur; this is my private abode and the objects therein belong to me.'

The sheriffs held on to my arms. The driver looked at me in the rear-view mirror. Still, they took my Luciana.

'This is a violation of my rights, and I must protest. I will bring legal proceedings against you if you do not reinstate my property this instant and leave my house in a secure state.'

The smaller sheriff turned his back to the window, blocking my view, and addressed me directly, in lowered tones.

'Look, the body has to be given to the undertaker. It does, that's the law. You don't have the proper documentation for it and the family are livid. But I will leave one of my officers at your door to protect the rest of your belongings, or you can give me the keys and we'll lock up.'

He looked outside at the growing crowd; the street had become something of a parade. The neighbours, who had always harboured a grudge against me due to my European nationality and my inclination to keep to myself, were clearly thrilled by the goings-on.

'There's going to be blowback here, and the public won't like it. But if you just behave yourself and abide by the rules, we'll see what we can do.'

With that the fight was taken from me. I sat back in the seat and both officers let go of my hands. Strangers carried Luciana past the police car and placed her into the hearse, barely caring about the damage they might be causing to the coffin or its delicate contents. I brought my hands to my face so I could smell her on me.

32

Gabriela

We went with Luci's body to the funeral home. They took her into the back. They asked if we wanted to watch them examine her. I said no and told Andrés and Juan Antonio they should not. There is no dignity in being undressed and poked and prodded and watched by so many. They didn't have to see Luci that way and I didn't want them to.

We waited in a different area, but I could see more and more people were going back into that other room. One worker, then the next, then the next. They made noises that even we could hear. I began to feel trapped in there; the air was heavy, and every sound made its way inside my skull. I stepped outside for fresh air and wept for a while.

Finally, the undertaker came to speak to us. The boys called me in. The man sat opposite us. He had his legs crossed and his hands were folded together over his desk.

'First of all, let me offer my apologies that we are here today. I looked after Luciana in the first instance, and I am truly saddened to see that she has not been allowed her deserved rest.'

He spoke gently and with soft words but there was nothing about him that I trusted.

'You have seen the body, is that correct?'

The three of us said that we had.

'And so you're aware of its…condition.'

'We saw what he did to her,' said Andrés.

'What has been done to your sister's body is a travesty, and one not easily undone. Under the circumstances, what are your preferences for…'

He searched for the word. He wanted to say disposal. I saved him from it.

'I want Luci buried.'

'As she is?'

'No, I want her as she was seven years before now, ten years before now. But here we are.'

It was a slap, and he did not deserve it. But I said it anyway.

'Would it be your preference to have Luciana placed into her original grave, or in her tomb?'

At this we had some discussion. After a few moments I realised what I really wanted.

'I want her buried somewhere where that man cannot get to her. I want her buried somewhere that has no marking, so only we, only the three of us, will know where she is. I want her in a normal grave like a normal body, so she can rot into the earth like all of us will. Her soul is already with God. Her body must go to the ground.'

The undertaker nodded.

'Of course, you understand that your sister will have to remain here until the court proceedings are over. There may also be some judgement as to the—as to who will retain possession of your sister's body. In the meantime, we will keep her here until the court informs us of its decision. Is that acceptable?'

It was a stupid question; we couldn't have just picked her up and walked her out of there, even if we had wanted to. But we all nodded, took the man's handshake, and thanked him.

At the courthouse there was a huge fuss—lots of photographers, journalists and other people who wanted to see. We had to struggle through them and into the courtroom. Even then there were men with pens and cameras. We took our seats and did our best to stay calm as that man stood in the dock. Every part of me wanted to stand up and scream.

The sheriff asked him about his relationship—that's how he said it, his relationship—with Luci.

'Luciana came to me in the grip of tuberculosis when she was but nineteen. She was sent to my radiology department at the Key West hospital, and it was immediately clear to me that she was deathly ill. Furthermore, being from a poor immigrant family, there was no money to provide for Luciana's medical care and there was no insurance to cover the costs. It was obvious that if I did not take on this poor young girl's case, she would surely be dead within months, if not weeks.'

Andrés began to protest, but I placed my hand on his arm and he calmed back into his seat.

'So you treated her for free?'

'Indeed, I took pity on the family, and I confess, I had some personal interest in the case, having completed extensive research into possible treatment methods in my native country.'

The sheriff looked through his papers.

'Poland?'

He paused, and then said, 'Yes.'

'So you were able to cure the girl of her illness?'

He looked at his hands.

'No. It is a great tragedy, but tuberculosis is incurable after it has progressed past a certain critical juncture. While I at first believed that Luciana's illness was not so pronounced, my initial treatments of her proved to me that in fact the disease was quite advanced. The family also intervened, with fatal consequences—bringing unvetted medications from overseas—and undermined the progress we had made with her recovery. I believe these medications hastened her death. However, I proceeded with my treatments, having been given some indication that theoretically, there may be a chance for a cure that the medical establishment has not yet discovered.'

'What do you mean, sir?'

It sounded like the sheriff was a curious friend. *We are here about my sister's grave*, I wanted to shout.

'There are many things that we do not yet understand about radiation, its effects on cells, the cryogenic possibilities for stagnation of disease and indeed retardation of its progress. I applied some of these techniques to Luciana while also treating her general declining health and well-being. All of this was made more difficult by the family.'

Andrés slid his hand on top of mine. We were frozen, not by cowardice now, but by a hope that his comments about us might pass. My anger was beset by guilt, just as he intended; he was playing us just as he was playing everyone else.

'And within this context you—you expressed your... admiration for this girl?'

He assumed an embarrassed smile, that snake. He smiled like a blushing child.

'Luciana and I fell in love, officer, like a pair of foolish teens. We had great admiration for each other and during the course of our time together our passion developed. Of course, as her physician I had a duty of care whose importance far exceeded a courtship, and I continued treating her with the utmost professionalism throughout. But it is true that in the evenings, which we increasingly spent together, I would read her poetry, bring her flowers and buy her gifts, even when made to feel unwelcome by her parents and siblings. At times, officer, I felt that my charity in treating Luciana—and much at my own expense, I might add, for her family never contributed to the vast cost of her medications—was little appreciated.'

'But you never married.'

At this, he raised his chin.

'Luciana accepted my proposal, and while she did state that she was too sick to go through a wedding ceremony, she confirmed that we should consider ourselves man and wife from that moment forward. I did.'

'Lies!'

Andrés and Juan Antonio shushed me. The sheriff did too.

'Luciana also indicated that she wished me to look after her even after her illness took its final toll. Of course, I could not stand to see her buried in the ground when I knew that I had within me a method by which she might live again. If I may, officer?'

The sheriff nodded to let him speak.

'It will be impossible for most of you in this room to understand the sensation of watching your dearest loved one be lowered into the ground, trapped in a box, and covered with heavy soil, when you know that they are not yet truly dead. When you have in your heart the knowledge that the soul yearns to return to the body, and that the body might be preserved and regained—can you imagine, then, the pain that I was put through at Luciana's funeral, at her burial, in the months afterward? I visited my darling's grave every night when she was taken from us, and every night she spoke to me. I paid to have a tomb created, so that the natural effects of decay might not affect her too soon, and at my own expense had her moved into it. Still, officer, she spoke to me, appeared to me. Can any of us truly say that if a beautiful young woman came to us nightly and begged to be rescued, we would not do our utmost to facilitate that rescue? I have seen much destruction in my life, and I could not stand to see another beautiful thing be taken from the world needlessly. Beauty and love are both sacred, officer, and here I had the opportunity to save both.'

The justice of the peace leaned forward.

'And were you able to…did any of your methods work to preserve the young woman?'

The man looked up at the justice and all the sound in the room dampened apart from his voice.

'There were significant impediments to my work, your honour. Luciana was buried for twenty-one months before I could remove her into the safety of the laboratory I had constructed, at my own expense, at home. In addition, the undertaker's original processing of the body caused irreparable damage, and of course I was working alone on Luciana, where in truth a team of researchers and additional support would have been necessary. And yet I was able to stop decay and mummification, and tests revealed that Luciana's first death had indeed cured her of her illness, and any others she may have had. This indicates to us that first death is perhaps a resetting of the body, much like Noah's flood.'

'Fascinating.'

My skin reacted to this, all pimples and standing hair, because a revelation was occurring. God granted me vision, and the whole scene sharpened. This *was* a devil, casting his power over other men, yes, but it was so much more. The people in the courtroom were excited by all of this. It was a story for them, a sordid little tale to step into for a while. They were tantalised by what they might see in the shadows, squinting for a glimpse of sharp teeth or pig's feet while we were being devoured right before their eyes. How many people sitting in that room brushed away their cynicism by thinking: *yes, but that's the family with the thieving son—can they be trusted with the truth?* Or: *this man must be mad, but wasn't that girl a whore? It's the best she could have hoped for.* We had tried to ignore false narratives; we had tried to be quiet for the sake of letting lies settle and bury themselves in the ground. But those lies had *become* the ground, the earth on which we all now stood.

Mamá, I thought. *There is no power in silence. You cannot trust others to ignore base lies, when those lies build foundations that would benefit them.*

'I must also report that in recent months Luciana has not only been in a static state of recovery but has in fact exhibited signs of regaining her body. In addition to her constant metaphysical presence, her physical body began to gain weight, she had colour in her cheeks, her skin began to plump. There were signs that blood was beginning to run once more through her veins, and she even appeared to be experiencing a menstrual cycle. I hope that we might—'

'How can you listen to this? This man is crazy! My sister is long dead!'

Andrés took Juan Antonio's hand and tried to pull him back to the bench, but I just stared ahead, seeing what the world was, for the first time.

'You saw her, she is a shell! She is years dead and all this man has done is paint a face on her corpse!'

'Order in the court. Sir, if you cannot hold your temper, you will be removed.'

Andrés finally brought him down to his seat and held his hand against the wood. His outburst at least had had the effect of bringing those men back to their task. The sheriff brushed off his clothes, as if to remind himself that he was wearing a uniform.

'Mr von Tore, is it correct to say that you disinterred this corpse without the proper certification?'

'I removed Luciana from her grave and placed her into a tomb of my construction with the consent of her family and adequate documentation from the town hall clerk.'

'And the second time?'

'I was granted a disinterment; surely there is not a limitation on this document.'

'I'm afraid that there is, sir. You did not have legal consent to disinter this woman's body a second time, nor did you have legal rights over the body, and therefore it was kept in your possession illegally after the disinterment.'

He did not speak. There was high colour in his face.

Reading from a book, the sheriff went on.

'As it stands, sir, you have violated Florida statute 872.02 which states that any individual who wilfully and knowingly excavates, exposes, moves, removes or otherwise disturbs the contents of a grave or tomb has committed a felony of the second degree. You have admitted your actions here.'

That man stayed silent, his chin high. The justice of the peace spoke next, looking down kindly at that dark-hearted man.

'Doctor von Tore, this is a complex case, and one complicated further by your relationship with the girl in question. Regardless, to say that you wantonly destroyed a grave is incorrect; you were, I believe, in good faith, attempting to perform a rescue of love for the woman to whom you were engaged. You have fallen foul of laws that are perhaps outdated or unable to deal with this situation fairly. There is wrong being done to you here. But, sir, I'm afraid that according to the process of the court, you will be retained in the county jail until the court is able to throw this case out; I will set bail at five hundred dollars. Sir, I hope you are able to find some peace again.'

That man was taken down and the members of the court left the room. The press scribbled and chatted and asked us questions. But Andrés, Juan Antonio and I, we could not move. The boys had seen what I had seen. We could not move for some time.

When we finally made it back to the funeral home, there was a line around the building that extended around the whole block.

'Is this for the papers?' asked Andrés, his voice tired.

'It can't be—there are so many. And the papers don't wait in line,' said Juan Antonio.

I did not speak. In my gut I feared the worst.

We got out of the car and pushed through the crowds by the door. As we went by, I could hear the voices of boys, girls, old, young; everyone in Key West was there.

'I hear she's got her original eyes.'

'Eyes don't stay, they sort of melt away.'

'No, you're wrong. I hear she has black eyes.'

'Are we allowed to touch?'

'That's probably extra.'

Surely no, I thought.

Andrés pushed a way through and got us inside. The line went in through the funeral home and out into the garden. There stood a man, a man who worked there, with a small box and a roll of bingo tickets.

'What the hell is this?'

But I knew. Already, I knew.

There she was, out in the backyard. Propped up so the crowds could more easily see. It was our sister, Luciana—Luci, a woman who was once alive and yet in death was a tourist attraction. It was twelve cents to see her. The small boys beside me had paid for their turn twice.

33.

Wilhelm

I was taken directly to the courthouse, where a circus of media was already in attendance. The liberal laws of the United States allow for such intrusions into personal privacy, with the argument that the freedom of the press, a folly in itself, is of greater concern. I did not answer any questions and was taken through to court.

The justice of the peace that had appeared at my door sat in his booth. I was questioned. I complied, and did not lie. I was taken to a cell.

Though I did my best to maintain composure during these proceedings, knowing that my status as a medical professional and my standing in the community must be emphasised in order for me to gain the respect of the court, I nonetheless was wracked with concern for Luciana, knowing as I did that every moment she was out of her own bed and removed from her treatment cycle would constitute another retardation of her recovery. I tried to reason with the officers, stating that I would give them full access to my medical equipment and home laboratory if they would permit me a series of hour-long visitations with Luciana during which I would perform no action not entirely explained to them, but the discussion was not even permitted. I attempted to impart to them the importance of the work I had been undertaking, but their shared glances indicated that this was damaging my case. Ignorance would work against me.

And yet I could not rest. Mummification was most likely occurring, slowly but surely, and none of the attendees had the skills or the emotional cause to work against Luciana's encroaching final death. To be captured when you know that your loved one is dying and only you could save her—that is a torture worse than any physical trauma one could endure. I fell into a deep and enduring melancholy that first evening in the jail cell, one where I prayed, for the first time in many years, and my prayer was a dark one:

Lord, if I am to be torn from my beloved, please take me to that other realm so we might be united finally again.

No sooner had I sent this prayer into the ether than my darling girl appeared before me, more strongly than she had done in years, her hair long, curled and pinned, her jewellery about her neck, and her hands gently stretched out to me. At seeing her, and hearing her entreaties, I brought myself to my feet. She placed her hands around my face; I could almost feel her skin against mine.

'My darling, you have maintained hope for me for all this time. Can you not now hope for yourself?'

I lifted my face, ashamed, and met her gaze.

'To live without you is no life at all, Luciana.'

She held my look.

'I have hope for us both. Not just for you, but for us together. Endure, my love. Endure.'

I closed my eyes to bask in her touch, in her presence, and then she was gone. I had made a promise; in that she was correct. And I was a man of my word.

The next morning, I was awoken with a clatter against the bars. The jailer was opening my cell. I shook myself, expecting to be taken out and wanting at least some clarity of mind to steel me against whatever was to come—but to my surprise, a woman entered the cell. She was a woman in her mid-forties or thereabout, and she carried a flask, some bread and various cheeses in a small cardboard container.

'Five minutes,' said the jailer, not unkindly. He closed the cell door behind us.

'Excuse me, Doctor. You don't know me. I'm Mary Adams. I'm local but we've never spoken.'

I stood and greeted her cordially, being unsure of the nature of her visit and therefore keeping myself relatively closed.

'I've brought you some coffee and a little food. There's milk and sugar in it. The coffee, that is. I hope you like it sweet?'

She held the things out to me and I took them. I stuttered slightly.

'I'm afraid I've no money to pay you with; my things were left in my home when I was taken, but if you can send a bill to my address I can make sure—'

'Oh, honey no, no. I don't want paying. I just heard that you were up here in this cell all alone and I couldn't stand the idea, not with you being an old man an' all. I think it's just awful what they got you in for. It's a crime just to love someone so much you can't accept they're dead? Strike me down if I'll stand for that.'

I motioned for her to take a seat on the bed, the only piece of furniture, and she did so; I moved along so as to not give her cause to worry of any impropriety on my part.

'I'm very glad to have your kindness, Mrs Adams.'

'Oh, you can call me Mary. And honestly, it's my pleasure. You gotta cling to your hospitality in these dark times, Doctor.'

I nodded gently and helped myself to some of the coffee—too milky, too sweet—and made a small sandwich of the bread, which was dry and fairly tasteless. Yet I had been neglecting myself so much that it nourished me greatly, and I let the woman know. I was unsure, however, what she wanted of me, or what I could provide. We sat in silence for some time and then she spoke.

'I just think it's terrible what they're doing to you right now. What harm is it for you to have that girl? She's not gonna get any less dead if you have her.'

I wanted to interject that in fact Luciana was not dead, not in the sense she would understand, but thought better of this.

'You've done nothing bad to that girl. You just wanted to keep her beautiful. I wish I had someone as caring as you, Doctor, to help me keep my looks. We should all be so lucky to have that kind of love.'

I realised, then, that she just wanted to talk; wanted to offer her support and perhaps lament her own romantic affairs. In this way we passed a short period of time before the jailer rapped on the bars again and she left with a wave, promising to come back with sandwiches and coffee if I was kept, immorally, for any length of time. To the jailer, as she left, she said:

'You ought to be ashamed, keeping an old doctor locked up like he's a criminal.' The jailer said nothing.

If I was surprised to receive this visitor, consider the strange situation in which I found myself when all day, from morning to night, I was visited by more strangers, similarly moved by the story of me and Luciana. They brought small cakes, coffee, alcohol (which was quickly removed from me, no doubt going straight into the jailer's pockets, which did not bother me as I did not have much taste for alcohol beyond small celebrations with my wife), home-cooked meals and even books, though many were of a lowbrow nature and of no interest to me. Every single one of my visitors was a woman, and each came to protest my treatment at the hands of the law but also to speak a little of their own love woes, their husbands who did not care for them or their partners who had abandoned them in the twilight of their lives. I accepted their gifts and spoke little, instead giving them space to speak of their traumas and their desire for a love like Luciana and I had. In time I began to feel like a priest receiving confession, or perhaps a patron saint of the under-loved, women placing offerings at my feet and weeping at my hands. The jailers found this situation comedic but were happy with the gifts I shared with them; there was too much coffee for me to consume myself and I ate no food except for nuts and berries, like my grandmother. In this way I bought myself preferential treatment, and was allowed visitors long after the official hours were over. In the end, I had to ask the jailers to refuse any more callers, for I feared I would be kept from sleep.

One morning, my first visitor was the priest from the church that Luciana's family had frequented. Having never attended his church, I was surprised to see him, but did not find his presence objectionable. I gave him a seat on my thin bed and stayed standing.

'I admit, Father, I did not expect a visit from a religious man.'

He crossed his legs and considered this.

'Doctor, I read about your plight, and that of dear Luciana, in the daily papers. I know the family well, and I prayed for Luciana throughout and beyond her illness. It is a tragedy that such a beautiful young thing was taken so young, but God has his plans.'

I was unsure as to whether to correct him; I did not.

'It is rare to hear of a man of science so engaged with matters of the soul. Increasingly the popular narrative is that there is no eternal life at all. So to hear a man so learned as yourself not only accept the existence of the immortal soul but to speak of your own interaction with it—well, quite frankly, Doctor, it moved me. Was Jesus himself not resurrected from a first death? Did he not live again, long after he was buried by those around him?'

He stood up, fingering the cross around his neck, and looked out beyond the bars, ruminating.

'I'm troubled by the thought that we might be sending our loved ones onto the next realm before that realm is ready for them. What you seem to speak of is a type of purgatory—a place where souls linger in wait. If the Lord is trying to show us something, we should take heed. The papers report that you brought Luciana back to a form of living. Is this correct?'

I considered my audience, then replied.

'I can only tell you that Luciana, in the last few months, began to bleed.'

He continued to stare at the outside world.

'Like Christ.'

He fell silent then. I wondered whether science troubled him in other respects, whether he had ever considered the resuscitation of a dying man to be against the will of God. I thought of my youth in Europe and the Church's vocal disdain for the work we did. I said nothing.

'If there is anything I can do to help you, Doctor, in a personal or professional capacity, I would be honoured to do so.'

What could this man do for me? The Church does not supersede the law—at least not in matters individual.

'Father, it is Luciana that needs your help now. I am very concerned that she currently has no one to protect her.'

'She is with the undertaker, is she not? He is a man of good faith.'

I thought of my former arrangements with the man but could not voice my lack of trust.

'Then please pray for her. Please pray for us.'

Later that same day, I was examined by a group of three psychiatrists whose goal, it became obvious, was to clarify my insanity. Their questioning was inane and I was offended by it, but I knew that their presence was by order of the court and, being quite sure that any dissent on my part would be twisted and turned into a declaration that I was not of sound mind, I kept my feelings about their process to myself and answered all of their questions to the best of my abilities. They asked me about my claim to have seen Luciana moving.

'And you say you have witnessed this yourself?'

'Indeed. I have listened to the movement of her blood in her veins. I have felt the twitch of her lips. I have seen her menstruation begin again.'

At this, the quack looked me in the eyes.

'It is the contention of the coroner that the young woman has been partially embalmed.'

'I do not disagree.'

'And yet still you contend that you experienced these things?'

'I do not seek to convince you; I have detailed notes of my findings, and tissue samples where appropriate. You can find these at my home, in the small laboratory I've built there.'

Notes, always notes. They asked me about my history, what day it was. They showed me oil-splat paintings hoping that I would say I saw my mother's genitals or some other coarse thing. Of course, I did not. After several hours the leader of the trio shook my hand.

'I feel it necessary to warn you that we must file a declaration of sanity, Doctor von Tore.'

'I never thought otherwise.'

The leader exchanged a glance with one of the other psychiatrists.

'But you understand what this means, Doctor? That you will be considered *compos mentis*? That everything you have done was done with full knowledge?'

'Your verdict is what I expected and I am vindicated by it,' I replied, indicating towards the cell door, by which they took their leave.

With a visitor later that day, the terrible news of Luciana's fate reached me: to my horror, she had been placed on public display at the mortuary, with hundreds permitted to see her in her vulnerable state. I became incensed at the news that my darling was being so carelessly shown off like a curiosity, an object. To take my property and use it to make money when the property itself was so delicate—was this not an act of wanton destruction? The news was imparted to me by one of my old visitors, and the poor woman was given a message to give to the undertaker: you take my bride and you put her away, as I paid you to do once, away from prying eyes and malicious intent.

It's said that over six thousand residents of Key West had paid to see my darling as she lay in the barren backyard of the undertaker's building. What damage this may have done to her cannot be overstated; I cannot say with certainty whether she was subject to physical violations via touch, or whether the undertaker charged extra for customers to take even further pleasure from her. I will likely never be given this information and I am not sure that I want it. But laying out my beloved in the open air, allowing her to desiccate in the close atmosphere of Key West—I am certain that this began a process of mummification from which she could never be revived. It is this that committed Luciana to her second and final death. With this disgusting display, she was taken from me, and this time, it was to be forever.

34.

Gabriela

It was the boys that kept me going, kept me pushing through the system. I had no faith in it anymore, but they said we must. So we put together our money and paid for a lawyer, a local Cuban who was a friend of a friend of Andrés. He knew the story and did not want anything to do with us. So we offered him more money, money taken from the school funds of all of our children, and he changed his mind. With his help we petitioned the court to remove Luci's body from display. It took five days, during which Luci was seen by many people. They put their faces next to hers and took photographs. A group of artists brought chairs and drew her. People touched her face and held her hand and kissed her dead open mouth. When they finally took her away the crowd chanted: *Keep her out.*

A day after Luci was taken inside, given her privacy, that man was finally up in front of the judge. Our lawyer helped me to testify, because it was I who was bringing the case against him. We arrived early. The papers had written about nothing but Luci since we found her in his house. The journalists had come to our front doors, they had camped outside on the street, and now they were outside the courtroom, inside the courtroom, inside everywhere. You pushed one out of a door and two new ones were there. Like cockroaches.

They said I was 'chief witness'. But why did they need one?

That man told them everything he had done. Everyone in Key West had paid their money and seen his handiwork with their own eyes. His guilt was clear to anyone who wanted to look. The lawyer told me to calm down, to lose my attitude, to just take the stand and say my piece, but I was listless, and grieving, and knew that my words would not be heard.

'You are Mrs Gabriela Maria Herrera Madrigal de Giro, is that correct?'

'Yes.'

'And you are related to the deceased?'

'I am her sister.'

Our lawyer nodded. I was only to speak when spoken to; only to answer questions that were asked.

I was asked everything about what happened to Luci and I told them. Right from the start. I told all of the court and the press people too. I told them because Luci could not speak for herself, and I hoped she could see that I was doing right by her. I told them everything up to finding Luci in that man's house. Then the judge said something crazy:

'And how could you be sure that what you saw there in Doctor von Tore's house was the body of your sister?'

My heart cracked a little; how could they defend him?

'Proverbs 15:3: the eyes of the Lord are in every place, keeping watch on the evil and the good.'

'Please answer the question, Mrs de Giro.'

'You have seen her, your honour. Everyone has seen her.'

He shuffled his papers; he had, then, paid his money like the rest.

'Her body was rotten and hollow and her face was a mask, but it was Luci. Half of Key West could tell you this.'

'And you had not permitted Doctor von Tore to remove your sister's body from the tomb a second time?'

I wanted to say: *why do you not care? Why are you talking*

about Luci like she is something we own, like a piece of furniture?
She was not stolen from our house or car and she is not something
we can buy or sell. She is my dead sister.

Instead, I said:

'No, we did not.'

My face was still dry when I took my seat. I barely heard the
words used when they questioned him again, for all I could
focus on was my pulse in my neck, and all I could see was her
face.

'Doctor von Tore, why did you remove your wife's—this
young woman's body—from the tomb into which you yourself
had placed her?'

'Sir, if you'll permit me a brief romantic intrusion. I had had
my suspicions for a long time that a person's first death was not
the end of their life, but instead was something from which they
could recover, if given the proper treatment and consideration.
But the death of Luciana threw me into self-doubt, and I'll
admit that I failed to hold my conviction here. Instead, I moved
under a black cloud, and Luciana sensed this. So she appeared
to me more often, staying for hours at a time, telling me that I
had to go and save her. If it were not for these interventions, I
may not have rescued her at all.'

You blame my sister? This is what I thought. *You blame Luci*
for this?

'I grew more and more fearful that I had left it too late,
knowing that even the tomb, which I had built specifically to
keep Luci from the degradation of decay, would not be enough
to keep her from falling even deeper into a death from which
I could never save her. But Luciana became adamant, and in
response, I had to act. She made sure I did so. It was Luciana
that forced my hand.'

'Did you have any legal remit to do so, Doctor?'

'I considered her my wife, and felt that under the
circumstances I had every moral right to remove her from the

place to which she had been committed, especially as she herself was instructing me to do so.'

This was his moment. I could see him drawing himself up, ready to give his final manipulation. I reached out to Andrés then, to Juan Antonio, to get up and out of there so I would not have to hear his lies, his fake retelling of my sister's wishes, but it happened too quickly. I was forced to hear.

'Let me be clear, here, sir. Luciana has always been with me. Her spirit came to me and advised me after her death. It was at her bidding that I rescued her from the tomb. Since then, Luciana's soul has spoken to me daily, and thanks to the success of my treatments her physical body has also recovered to the point where it can bleed, and move, and converse. I had a priest visit me this week, and he expressed admiration that I should be bringing together science with an understanding of the soul. For did the Lord himself not die, and was he not buried, and did he not rise from the grave three days later, every bit as alive as he had been before? Any Christian can see that this is a message to us all, that we should not let our loved ones fester in the ground when we might resurrect them with our love. Let me say this again so there is no chance of confusion: my darling girl's soul is returning to her body—and with every moment she is kept from me, she is pushed further away from her second life. By keeping me here, by keeping her in the funeral home, you are killing her, gentleman. You are killing her again.'

I endured the rest of the hearing by the will of God. The judge ordered that Luci's body be buried in an unmarked grave at a site agreeable to us, her family. We nodded; it was all we wanted. I wept with relief. That man argued, but they did not give Luci to him. But he still won a victory, his true victory. They removed him from the court. He was released without charge.

35.

Wilhelm

The judge ordered that my darling bride should be removed from my care. He callously laid down his sentencing; that Luciana should be left in death, indeed to an eternal end, and that I should be cast into a despair from which I would never recover. I believe I protested; I believe I said that it would be the end of me, that I had made a promise to my beloved, that she was my work, my life's work, that my discovery could not be contained. I cannot say with any certainty, however, for with his words a black curtain descended on me. The idea that I should be cleft from the one soul to whom I had not only been promised but had been connected to in a realm beyond that of life or death—how could one accept this? How could I?

They took me back into the jail until I had recovered myself. They gave me hot tea and sweet biscuits, and a newsman came to try to get quotes from me. I may have spoken, I do not know. Everything was both rushing by and static; any action was pointless. I came back into myself later that evening, perhaps I should say that night, for it was long after midnight that I recovered from the shock. I found myself in my house; I cannot say that I was at home, for without Luciana it was nothing more than a shell. I stayed up staring out into the dark yard, sitting in the chair against which she used to recline, speaking out loud and waiting, asking, begging for her soul to return and speak to me, but it did not. Eventually I fell asleep and woke up in the violent light of a new day, the first morning of life without my Luciana.

In the kitchen there was food, sent from those who had visited me in jail: pot roasts and defrosting pies and biscuits and mashed potatoes, every dish with a note from a mournful woman who had lost her love or wished to lose him, those same laments that I had heard in my cell when I still harboured a belief that I might keep Luciana. I could not eat; I placed it all into my small refrigerator, with little chance that I might recover my appetite in time to eat it.

By the door was a pile of letters, some addressed to my home and some with only my name on, which must have been passed on to the jailers who brought me home. A good number of the envelopes were addressed to the justice of the court itself; these letters were opened and had been replaced for me to read. I made a bitter coffee and sat again in Luciana's protected chair in the backyard. I expected hatred. I did not receive it.

To whom it may concern,

We, the undersigned, are writing to implore you in the name of the medical community to allow Doctor von Tore to continue on with his experiments. Though we are not party to the finer details of this fascinating case, we have been led to believe that the doctor not only nursed his young bride though the later stages of tuberculosis but then was able to place her into an incubation chamber which preserved her body until it could be removed from the grave. The doctor then was able to mummify the body in a manner in which it could be kept in his own home; for this alone we consider Doctor von Tore to be of great scientific ability. Sir, if it is true that the doctor then was able to bridge the gap between the physical world of life and the metaphysical world of death, then we beg that this man's noble character and intent be considered in the fullness of the legal system. If you consider him to be a madman holding on to a corpse, what is the harm of allowing him to keep hold of that body? If you consider him to be sane and to have all the faculties of critical thinking about him, it must be worthwhile to allow him to continue his experiments—for if he is right, sir, and as a man of science he must have the ability to assess the situation, then we may be on the brink of one of the greatest discoveries of all the ages.

As to the charges laid against him, the rules of this country do not allow Doctor von Tore to have carried on his essential experiments, leaving him no choice but to break the law. In this instance, it is the law that is wrong, not the accused, and therefore he should be released and given full access to his resources. He should be liberated and indeed given compensation for any distress caused, and any damage to his experiments. In fact, in our roles as physicians we recommend that the state sponsor his research and offer full assistance to the doctor with regard to carrying on his essential work.

We have staunch faith in the motives of this brilliant scientific mind. Please, sir, let him continue.

Signed
Dr V. Alexander
Dr F. T. Gilbert
Dr A. Bayes
Connecticut

Dr v. Tore,

We think that what's being done to you ain't right at all and we would like to send this donation on to help you in your court case or with your lawyers or paying to get your wife back because she is yours and by law it should be that she is yours in death as well as in life. We are sending our addresses if you are ever in the area of Idaho we would surely receive you well, we are just a small group of women who know love when we see it.

Yours, in romance,

Stella, Janine and Anne

Your honour,

I simply could not read about the charge brought before you without writing to express my desire that Doctor von Torr be allowed to carry on with his experiments. As a believer in the Lord I know that there is much beyond death and if there is a small chance of the doctor discovering the link between this life and the next then it is imperative that he be allowed to continue his experiments with that girl to whom he was married. She knew that he would take her body when she died, she asked him to, so it is nonsensical that the law go against the girl's own wishes and have her removed from his home. In these times of war and hatred and killing it is God's work that a man might find a way to defy death via the medium of love; please, sir, I beg of you to restore that girl to the man who

loves her and allow him to carry on his work, for the love
of the Lord.

Best,
Madgelena Salvatore, New York State

It took me several hours to read through the notes of support, of which a small number are represented above. Not a single letter contained a malicious thought, and indeed many were letters to the court to compel the law to work on my side. At the bottom of this pile was a large envelope which at first I thought was padded, but which I soon realised was full of money.

Doctor von Tore,

Please accept these small donations with our warmest
wishes, with hope that you are restored to the beautiful
girl whom we knew so well.

Yours,
Sympathetic residents of Key West

I counted the money; there were several hundreds of dollars. With the amounts taken from other envelopes, there was over a thousand. I was greatly touched.

It is difficult for me to write about this period, and I don't believe there is much in my personal experience that is of historical or scientific significance with regard to my work. Suffice it to say that I fell into a depression, though this word seems inadequate; I don't possess the vocabulary to truly describe the depths of my despair.

My health declined greatly in this short period, as did my

personal finances. I was forced to receive visitors often, some of whom I knew vaguely from acquaintance in the town, and some of whom had travelled great distances to hear my story. I never allowed these visitors into the house, but instead received them in nearby cafés and diners, where they bought me coffee and lunch and asked to hear in my own words the story of Luciana. I partook in these visits in the daytime for the mere reason that I did not have the capacity to turn them away, so far was I from the fullness of my right mind. In the evenings, which were at least my own, I began to make an effigy of my darling. The mannequin head on which I used to keep her wig and jewellery would form her perfect skull; on this I drew her features, hung rings from the ears, draped scarves and necklaces around her neck. I laid an outfit out on our bed and placed the mannequin on top, as if the rest of the body would creep into her clothing and fill out her form. The flatness of the body distressed me; I used rags and coat hangers to give a vague skeleton and some fullness to it, and after many nights' work I had arranged things so as to almost be able to trick myself that a body lay on that bed. But it was not Luciana. It would never be Luciana. I would never have my bride in my arms again.

Yet one day there was a knock at the door, and there was the undertaker.

36.

Gabriela

I suppose now I can give the details. For so long I have kept them secret. The undertaker gave us a cardboard coffin of remains, the size of coffin you'd use for a child, and we got permission, with the help of our lawyer, to place the box beneath a tree. It was not in a graveyard, but in a small patch of green overlooking the sea. We did not use a headstone, no marker, just a small plant of white mariposa that would flower every spring. I found my old jewellery box, though it was scratched and faded and mostly ruined and the inside smelled like age, and inside I placed my little pocket relic, the curled finger of Luci's history, the tiny rubber something that had kept me safe for years. It was worked smooth by my many worryings, but it was there, so I wrapped it up in a new handkerchief and closed the box and buried it right beside Luci. It was all we could afford, but at least we had paid for it. Juan Antonio told me to ask for donations, so that everyone touched by her story might help us bury her properly, but I knew that Mamá would hate to see it, her family begging. Somehow, I don't know how, the idea was spread, and the neighbours came and told me not to ask for money, that it was not right. I didn't realise at the time that they thought us villains; that they had given all their money to someone else. I know it now.

The years between then and now—they were plagued, for me, by distrust, by disgust, by knowing that a devil walked amongst us and could do whatever he wished to do. My girl grew up and I feared for her day and night. If one girl can be destroyed, so can another. I prayed silently, constantly, looking for the knot of gristle that had been my companion and finding only an empty pocket. Felipe could not reach me and Chabela held on tight, stopped me from floating away from the ground entirely, but looking back now, all I can see in my memories is anger, and anxiety, and at the seat of it all a hatred for myself, for not stopping any of it when it was happening, for letting fear make me a witness and nothing more. A waste of a life, a third Madrigal ruined—how disappointed God must be. But with naivety, we paid no mind to Luciana.

37

Wilhelm

In contrast to the first rescue, everything was done for me. The undertaker, being, in his words, 'of a romantic disposition', had with forethought arranged deals with all those in the chain. All I had to do was pay the man, and the public had already given their money to help me. I gave it all for Luci.

But that was not all. The man brought from his car a plain cardboard coffin, the type used for bodies abandoned by all those in the world who might care for them, and into this coffin I placed the remains of Gorky from the backyard. We arranged this with additional weights, some rocks provided by the undertaker himself and some taken from the useless objects I had around the house, including candles and small ornaments, things that I had bought ready for Luciana's resurrection. I would not need them now. Nothing could bring her back to life after such an ordeal.

And yet, my love transcended all. My care for Luciana had never been solely contingent upon her return to life. Our love was one that surpassed the barriers of life and death; our love existed regardless of age, regardless of location, regardless of physical embodiment. Our love was beyond time, beyond the ages, beyond understanding. I would have her in any way she would come to me.

The real Luciana arrived home in a cardboard coffin,

unmarked, unloved. Her family wanted to bury her, like she was a dog. I made her again into a queen.

There was some physical damage to Luciana's body, much like that encountered when I first rescued her from the grave, and some that had been clearly caused by human hands. I fixed Luciana as much as I could, and dressed her once again in new clothes, and her jewellery, and washed her hair. She had become smaller and lighter since she had been taken from me. Unburdened now by the rigours of the scientific process, I completed the full process of mummification, which removed the majority of her remaining weight, no longer labouring under the hope that my darling would return to her body in health again. She would not. But in death, she was still my darling, and in this manner we lived together, as man and wife, from the time of her return to the time of this writing, which I believe to be a short time before my own life expires. As to this last point, I have taken steps to ensure that my soul, when it enters the process of first death, will not be able to return to my body, for, having suffered the greatest injustice of removal from my love for so many of my living days, I do not wish to be kept from her in the afterlife; I wish to remain on the other side with my promised bride for the rest of eternity. This life has nothing left for me.

I have scarcely removed myself from Luciana's presence since she was returned to me, leaving the home only to complete necessary tasks: to buy materials for the home, to donate blood for a small amount of money. In truth, financial assistance from like-minded souls has kept me going, and as this home is mine and I do not care for many things, and neither Luciana nor I eat or drink greatly, my expenses have been few. While neither chanting nor meditation come easily to me, my focus in these periods has been on the presence of Luciana, on the experience of being so close to a being who has already transcended the fickle boundary between life and death, between the eternal and the immediate. I have worked on slowing my breath significantly, on silence and stillness, on meeting my beloved somewhere in between this life and the next. It has been, in many ways, an austere existence, and yet the fact of living out the rest of my life with my promised bride in my arms, and the promise of eternity with our souls entangled—this has made me richer and more fulfilled than any other man alive.

I do not wish for my tale to be considered for sympathy, or indeed to clear my name of any crimes laid against me. The law and its application cannot account for the progress of medicine, and therefore it cannot claim any moral authority. I present this account of my life and my work merely to explain why I did what I did, that it was all for love, and in the hope that another scientific mind might take my experiments and carry them on in the event of my death; that perhaps another man might love enough to save his bride from the unnecessary torture of the first death, of being buried with one foot in this world and one in the next. I have recorded to the best of my ability the details of my work and have included proof as to where and how these things occurred. It is a sad truth that human malice destroyed my beloved city, my laboratory, my life and my career, and prevented a full discovery of something that could have altered and improved the way that all of humanity lives. But I ask for no pity. I had the greatest of loves.

My wish is that the results of my lifelong efforts will transform the American, indeed the entire Western medical understanding of death, and that my experiments can form the basis for the embrace of life post-mortem. My bride, the girl promised to me before I even saw her face, is my everlasting joy, my supreme love. Luciana, my darling girl, survived death once, and into death we go together now that we are ready. In this way love can save us all. Dear reader, I wish this for you too.

38.

Gabriela

I never went to Luci's cardboard box grave. There have been many years between now and then, and I did not go once. Tonio and Andrés thought it too sad to visit, too far removed from how things should have been. But for me, it was different. Luci was part of me, by then, a part I could speak to. A part I could be. I had no need for a hole in the ground. But more than that—I think I knew she was not there.

It was a cold Tuesday morning, the first week of fall. These days I rise early, for it's peaceful in those hours, and peace is something I have come to appreciate. I make a coffee, with milk and sugar too, and I sit on the porch with the previous day's paper. That day I wrapped a blanket around me and sipped my drink. It was on page seven: a man had died, a very old man in a run-down house, and they suspected he had been dead a long time, and they had found on his lap a ludicrous doll, a person-sized doll with the face of a girl. A pyramid nose; a white skin made of wax.

Felipe came down and touched my shoulders, my skin now drier and thin, and I ignored his words. My coffee, milky and half cold, soaked into the newspaper from where I had let it tip. I stared as the day took its light, as the heat gently rose, and not a thing about me felt scared. Not a thing about me felt frozen.

I picked up the phone, and I called my brothers.

*

We dug up the grave in daylight, for there was nothing to hide. To the rest of Key West, it was just a piece of grass beneath a late-blossoming tree, with a view out to sea, and we were just three old Cubans digging up a box. And of course, a box is all it was. Empty but for dog bones, candles and a few rocks wrapped in cloth.

I won't bore you with details of how I made my way into his house. It is simple enough to do, when there is a foreigner dead with no one to claim them. You only need a little help in the end—perhaps from the wife of your brother, who does not share your recognisable face and can keep a secret from her husband. A fake name, a signature, a few simple lies; they are easy to tell, as it turns out. The paper had mentioned there was confusion around his identity; that some of his documentation was fabricated, his name unconnected. They could not bury him until he was claimed and identified. It was Luci who took my hand and opened the door to that rotten old home. It was Luci's spirit that found the book of lies that he'd written, and sat me down in a chair to read it from front to back. It was Luci's burning heart that found the names to give, that held my sister-in-law's hand when she signed the hastily written papers that claimed she was his next of kin, a wife that he had never mentioned. I knew by then what forces dictate justice and injustice. A few dollars to a clerk, a few more to an undertaker to deliver him home, to his home, and there he was.

There was little about him to suggest he'd once lived. He was dry, and rubbery, and his skin was tough. Perhaps it had been years since he'd died; there were so few people left that cared for him. So few people to realise he'd gone.

The newspapers had got it wrong; he wasn't just found with my sister in his lap. He was entwined with her, like a tree entwines with a knife that's been stabbed into its bark. They had not bothered, at the undertaker's, to try to extricate her from him; I suspected they had thought to charge money, to display them as a curiosity once again. The Luci-doll was just bones, wax and rags; anything left of my sister had long since decayed, but she was stiff, unmoving, the solid object around which he'd grown. He was the clinging vines. His arms, emaciated, wrapping around her trunk. His legs twisted amongst her roots. His face pressed to her chest, looking downwards, cowering, I hoped, in something like shame.

My hands were steady when I held them both. They were light; empty of anything. I expected to stop, shaking, heaving, scared. But there was none of that. I had spent so much of my life standing still, holding back just in case I chose the wrong path, in case whatever I chose to do was wrong. And here I was, acting. Doing. Choosing.

He was all gristle and rubber, a person-sized version of my little Luci relic, the one I'd kept in my pocket all those years. He wasn't bloated or swollen; he looked desiccated, as if the dry air of summer had preserved him like meat. I ran my hands over the bones at his chest, over the angles of his face. It was easy to remove him from the grasp of my sister, as if the Luci-doll too was rejecting his advances, but really it was because I cared not what bones I snapped, what joints I dislodged, what broke and tore and ripped in two. He weighed almost nothing when I finally laid him on his own. Claws outstretched, arms emptied, body broken. I stared at him for a single long hour. Then I began.

I took each part of the Luci-doll home. There was not much of her, beneath the wax and the silk and the layers of rags. I tore off her white mask-face and burned it on his cooker. I freed her from her musty old clothes and she fell to pieces in my hands. I lifted her pelvis, which was smashed into bits, and from between her hips dropped a plastic piece of piping, thin and well used. Later that day I fed her bones into the wood stove in our garden—but not before taking a single finger bone and slipping it into my pocket. It lives in a box with a silken inside, unopened on the top of my mantle. The rest of her went into the fire. On breezy nights she will burn with the coals, fierce and bright, and someday I will take her out, grind her down and hold her to the wind. That is how our Luci will go.

And then, it was just us two. I had never before been alone with that man, and I tried to feel what Luci might have felt, alone and vulnerable, sick and abandoned. But I could not, for I was none of those things, and he was just an armful of bones. I thought a long while as I held that man's body. I looked within myself to find my desire, to find an energy that might push me one way or another, and what I found was a certain dark peace: the knowledge that whatever I did, the judgement of Key West, of everyone, would fall upon me. This man in my arms had done so much wrong, yet he had been absolved. Every person who heard it had accepted his story. Now, with a sliver of choice, I would be damned either way. I could hold the concept of vengeance in my hands and let it guide me: I could turn out his eyes, pin open his lids, sew closed his mouth. I could take a knife from his own kitchen and thrust it into his heart. I could take the tip of a blade and draw it down from his chin to the base of his crotch, and once again from armpit to armpit, then tear at him like a wild animal, taking his organs in my hands and filling him with rags. An eye for an eye. But then everything else in my life, in my sister's life, would be erased, and I would be judged by this alone. He would still live as a man with a story, and I would, again, be a criminal. *We lost empathy*, everyone would say, *when she brought herself down to his level. I thought she was better than him, but it turns out she was just as bad.*

Or I could lay his body upon the floor and simply walk home, to my husband who would never ask about the wax beneath my fingernails or the smell on my clothes; the man who would leave that finger-box above our fire for the rest of my life and never once try to open it. People would see me walk from this house, and eventually the abandoned body would be found, and the story would be that I could have taken revenge and chose not to. And then, in whispers, I would be sanctified; the good old woman who had suffered so much, the woman who rose above it all and held her head high. But this would be a lie, for no one is held above the injustice that is done to them; they are dragged down by it, diminished, and everyone who comes after them is diminished too. Everyone who comes later must rise above, rise above, and if they dare to refuse, they are damned twice.

Great freedom comes in strange disguises. Sometimes it is the knowledge that, presented with two choices, either way, you will lose. Sometimes it is choosing not to play a game you cannot win.

I could have destroyed what was left of Wilhelm von Tore. Perhaps I did; you will never know. But whichever I chose, I could not bury his lies, which had become the ground on which we both sat; the foundations of the story within which I would be judged. So I did all I could: I resolved to publish what he'd written, exactly how he'd written it, to show his lies for what they were—deranged and calculating—and show that I lived, and Luci lived, and that we were people with worth and meaning, and that we suffered at his hands. That his was not a story of medical mastery, or love beyond death, but a banal and common evil enabled by so many. There is not a single devil in this story, but many. You must think of that, and look around you, to see where, and who, they are.

And when you think back on this tale, you will think of me, an unwilling character in a terrible story, as neither vengeful harridan nor sainted sufferer. You will think of me only as I sat on that cold stone floor: a sad old woman holding an emaciated corpse, two things that had been of brief interest, and were no more.

Acknowledgments

Effusive thanks: to Kirsty Logan, Camilla Grudova and Heather Palmer for their honest and challenging feedback, and for the constant encouragement to be even more disgusting; to Abubakar Adam Ibrahim and Chris Gribble for the Laxfield Literary Award, and particularly to Olumide Popoola, for her thoughtful response; to Julian Gough, Susie Maguire, Michel Faber, Em Mackie, Cove Park, the Bridge Awards and Moniack Mhor for giving me a creative writing education and encouragement to continue; to Mingthoy Sanjur for being a generous source of Cuban-American societal information; to Eva Schoof for advice around the German aspects of this book; to Josh Anderson and Andy King for keeping me caffeinated and entertained on a trip to freezing Dresden; to Elly and Phil Parberly for getting me halfway to Havana (via Moscow); to Brian Gilbert for having a series of obscure Victorian illnesses and proving quite the inspiration (also Rosemary for the Charmaine); to Jennie Creitzman, Laurence de Clippele, Siobhan Clark, Charley Tassaker, Hayley Cox, Gemma Milne, Julia Armfield, Alice Slater, Esther Clayton and Nyla Ahmad for being inspiring and supportive presences in my life; to Aoife Lyall for the letters and rants; to Maria Whelan for her encouragement, energy and passion for this story; to my agent, Emma Shercliff, who saw something in me and made this book a reality; to Alison Savage, Isabelle Flynn, Gina Rozner, Richard Arcus and Megan Jones for being the dream publishing team; to the many people in the book world who have given me chances, nudged me in the right direction and have become friends; to my cats, Ernesto and Fidel, for waking me up at six to write; to red wine, coffee and bread for their endless support.

To my parents, for never telling me to be quiet, and to my extended family (biological; chosen; in-not-law) for endless and uncompromising love.

And to D. You know.

Author's Note

On 25 October 1931, Elena Milagro de Hoyos, a twenty-two-year-old Cuban-American woman, died of tuberculosis at her parents' home in Key West, Florida. Eighteen months later, a man calling himself Carl Tanzler – or Carl von Cosel, or Count Carl Tanzler von Cosel, depending on where you look – took Elena's body from the mausoleum he'd had built for her, and transferred it under cover of night to his home. He had become obsessed with Elena after she attended the hospital he worked at, declaring he had seen her in visions, that his ancestors had prophesied their relationship. He made claims about his medical knowledge to her family, who allowed him to treat Elena with a series of obscure treatments, including X-ray, none of which worked. He showered her with gifts despite the fact that she was legally married and did not, apparently, reciprocate his affections. He paid for her funeral, and after her death he claimed to have heard voices telling him to rescue her from the grave. Over the next seven years, he rebuilt her decaying body with piano wire and plaster of Paris, stuffing her with rags and dousing her in perfume. He was seen dancing with the body in front of an open window, was challenged finally by her sister Florinda, and when they took Elena's body from his possession, the authorities placed her body on display to almost 7,000 local residents. Carl Tanzler, caught red-handed, was never charged with any crime. He died at his own home in 1952, at the age of seventy-five.

In November 2011, a Russian linguist called Anatoly Moskvin was arrested by police following a number of grave desecrations in his local area. As an academic, Moskvin had cultivated an intense interest in cemeteries and death rituals, to the extent that he described himself as a 'necropolist'. Commissioned by another academic to list the dead in over 700 cemeteries, Moskvin allegedly spent two years travelling between these cemeteries on foot, sleeping in abandoned farms and haystacks, eating and drinking whatever was available to him, and even spending a night in a coffin. When the police entered the apartment that Moskvin shared with his parents, they found the mummified corpses of twenty-six women and girls, placed around the flat like dolls; some sat on shelves, others posed, all visible. Many were clothed and positioned as if they were going about their daily business. His parents believed the bodies to be life-sized ceramic dolls, and considered their son, presumably, to be just a little eccentric; a collector of pottery and nothing more. After his arrest, Moskvin claimed that he believed the women and girls could be brought back to life though science or the occult, and that he chose them through reading obituaries; certain descriptions called to him, and when one did, he would sleep on the deceased's grave to see if the girl inside called to him. If she did, he dug up her body. It was his age, he said, that led him to bringing them home instead of sleeping on their cold, uncomfortable graves. After extensive research around mummification, he dried the bodies with salt and baking soda, then left them around dry places, sometimes in cemeteries again, before bringing them home where he attempted to make them comfortable and attractive; he felt that the girls would not return to physical forms that they considered ugly. Moskvin denied having any sexual attraction to the bodies, instead saying he saw them as his children. Though only twenty-six bodies were found at his home, police believe he may have desecrated as many as 150 graves in this manner.

In March 2013, four men were sentenced to prison in Beijing for digging up the corpses of ten women and selling them. The bodies were stolen to be brides for 'ghost marriages', bought by the families of single men who had died before securing a wife. Traditional custom in parts of Northern China states that the soul of an unmarried man would come back to haunt its family, and so, in a practice that has lasted for around 3,000 years, women's bodies were disinterred and reburied next to the graves of these single men, so they might have a wife in death. Illegal for decades, the practice has seen a relative surge in popularity as China's economy flourishes. Each body can earn thousands of dollars, though the price is higher for the younger, prettier and more recently dead.

In 2015, the body of a twenty-five-year-old woman, Julie Mott, was stolen from her coffin after her funeral service, while her family were preparing for her cremation at a funeral home in San Antonio, Texas. At the time of writing her body has not been recovered.

***

Since *Orpheus Builds a Girl* was first released in October 2022, I have been asked countless times if I found it difficult to write from the perspective of a misogynist, fascist obsessive who saw a woman's body as his inarguable property. My answer to this is always: no. This is not an alien proposition to me; anyone who has inhabited a female body for any length of time will be more than aware of how their physicality is seen, by at least a portion of the population: as something that is there for the taking. Almost every woman I know has been grabbed, manhandled, groped, assaulted; has had a person in a position of authority overstep a line and touch their body. Many suffer worse sexual violence, as children and adults, and though women are not immune from this behaviour the perpetrators are, by and large, men. Politically, women's bodies are seen as existing in service to certain ideals; they are either there to provide babies to bolster nationalist tendencies and protect the idea of the nuclear family, or they are there to service men's sexual desires and not exist outside of this occupation. The level of expected sexual availability differs according to country, region, faith, ideology; what is tolerated in one place may get you killed in another. On the extremes, there are men who imprison their wives, their daughters for decades at a time, impregnating them over and over; there are men who kill their sisters and daughters for bringing the family into disrepute. But these extremes are not untethered from the daily reality of women who cannot walk down the street without being catcalled, without having their breasts grabbed in bars by total strangers; nor from the ones who are challenged for not looking feminine enough, or for being too feminine, or for being a woman in an incorrect way. This is one long line of patriarchal misogyny, and every woman exists along it.

***

As I write this, in the US Roe vs. Wade is nine months repealed. The babies conceived in one of the twenty-four abortion-hostile US states in June 2022 – the month that the US Supreme Court revoked a woman's right to abortion on a federal level – are now being born. Or perhaps some of them are not being born; perhaps some of these women managed to receive abortion care in those uncertain few months after the law was repealed, when it was unclear what the rules were and healthcare providers continued to do their jobs until they absolutely couldn't. Perhaps some of them were able to travel to friendlier states or even countries to receive the care they needed, to end the pregnancy, to carry on with their lives – to care for the children they already have, or to remain without them. Access to this most vital care now depends more than ever on where you sit on the social ladder; the wealthier, more privileged might have choice, but marginalised women increasingly do not. Many in the US and similar countries considered this an issue that had been put to bed; women of my age grew up with the understanding that, at least theoretically, their right to abortion was sacrosanct, and that if anything, other countries would begin to catch up. We thought that the issues of unequal access across racial, gender, nationality and class lines would be slowly improved upon. We thought that the main fight had been won. Of course, when it comes to women's bodies, such an assumption is always naïve.

The question at the centre of this book is this: *who owns a woman's body?* In truth, I do not know how to answer that question. Right now, there are laws that both enforce and ban the covering of women's bodies, in Iran and France respectively. Across the US and the UK, new laws segregate access to vital women's services, depending on what 'type' of woman you are. In the Mediterranean, women risk their lives on boats to make it to a safe harbour, only to be demonised, impoverished, punished. At any point, on any day, our bodies are sites of political debate, our bodily freedoms subjected to the whims of religious or ideological fervour. Our images are used to further fascistic or imperialist ideals. Our physical autonomy is fleeting and changeable; one woman may access abortion care while another woman only miles away is denied it. The outcomes of our healthcare vary vastly if we are black, disabled, immigrant, trans. Our femininity is conditional, depending on what others believe about our race, our gender presentation, our sexuality, our disabilities, our age. Words are placed into our mouths even after we're dead; we're said to have consented, vocally, to the desecration of our graves, to the removal of our rights. We're said to have contributed to the causes of our own murders, to have

317

seeded reasons for violence against us. The faces of dead women become banners under which political or social movements are pushed. Millions across the world are subjected to forced marriage, genital mutilation, forced sterilisation, a lack of access to education, gender-based violence, forced pregnancy, lack of healthcare, workplace assault, domestic violence, and poverty. The marginalised, the racialised, the disabled, the sick, the poor, the queer, the gender nonconforming – it is these women who most often suffer.

But I know that change does come. There are shelves and shelves of feminist thought from across the glove on the walls of any bookshop. There are people improving the lives of women on a grassroots basis everywhere you look, if you can induce yourself to be hopeful. When I think of the women struggling to access abortion, I think of the women of Jane, and others like them across the world, who defied and continue to defy laws to provide healthcare to other women no matter what the risks; of women who, when their offices were raided, chewed and swallowed the health records of vulnerable women to save them being prosecuted. I think of women shaving their heads in defiance of laws requiring that they cover their hair. I think of the many women across the world refusing to give up their autonomy no matter what laws say. Perhaps change comes in the form of a brave and hopeful answer to a question we have already posed. Who owns a woman's body? *She does.*

Book Club Questions

- In what ways do the characters in this novel engage with the idea of the relic – thinking of Gabriela, her mother and von Tore himself?

- There is undeniably an unreliable narrator in this book. But are there two?

- What role does nationality/ethnicity play in the events of this book?

- Would this story have played out differently if the main events occurred in a different country? Can you imagine what difference this would make?

- Can you imagine this story playing out similarly if the central gender roles were switched? If not, how do you think it would play out?

- What classical or gothic literary references did you notice in the book, and what is the intent of their inclusion?

- If you had to identify what belief systems each character had, what would they be?

- What role does science play in this book?

- What role does mysticism play?

- Who do you most identify with most in this story, and why?